The Lord will grant you abundant prosperity-in the fruit of your womb, the young of your livestock and the crops of your ground-in the land he swore to your forefathers to give you. The Lord will open the heavens, the storehouse of his bounty, to send rain on your land in season and to bless all the work of your hands. You will lend to many nations but will borrow from none. The Lord will make you the head, not the tail. If you pay attention to the commands of the Lord your God that I give you this day and carefully follow them, you will always be at the top, never at the bottom.

Deuteronomy 28:11-13

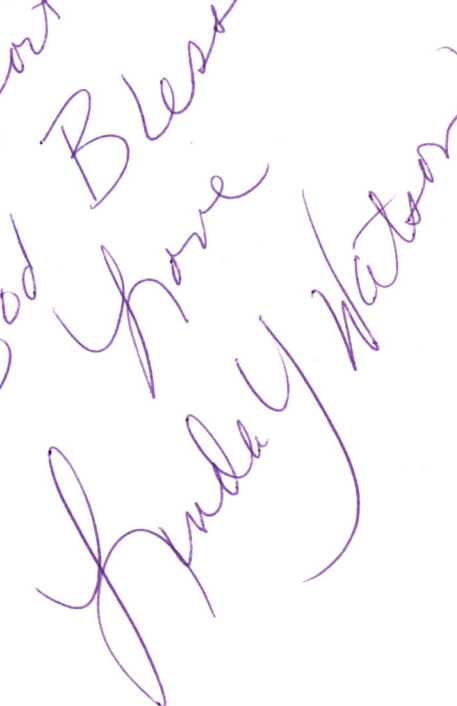

Necessary Measures

LINDA Y. WATSON

1000 Lakes Publishing, LLC

This book is a work of fiction. Names, characters, places and incidents are products of the author's imagination or are used fictitiously. Any resemblance to actual events or locales or persons, living or dead, is entirely coincidental.

Copyright © 2010 by Linda Y. Watson

Published by 1000 Lakes Publishing LLC

All rights reserved, including the right to reproduce this book or portions thereof in any form whatsoever.

LCCN: 2010904767

ISBN: 978-0-9826444-0-9

Printed in the United States of America

Dedication

This book is dedicated in loving memory to my father, Willie P. Lake Sr., a loving, caring, and hard working man who always provided for his family. My father stressed the importance of education. He often told stories about our ancestors and how they educated themselves and became one of the first African American families to purchase land in Tennessee. He encouraged his children to follow their dreams and when I was a little girl he would sit and listen to my dreams. He told me that one day I would achieve them. Unfortunately, he's not here to celebrate one of my accomplished dreams which is publishing my first novel but I know he's smiling saying, I knew it. I love you dad.

In loving memory to my mother-in-law and father-in-law who I never got the opportunity to meet, but from the stories that my husband told me they were strong people who raised five successful black men.

In loving memory to my grandmother Tula who lived with me and my siblings and to my grandmother Millie who we visited often in Tennessee. Thanks to their strictness and southern roots we grew up to be respectable women. I love you both.

Acknowledgement

First and foremost, God I thank you for allowing me to understand that we are all flawed, damaged and fall short of your glory. Thank You for your guidance and using me as a vessel to deliver your message.

To my husband Elliott, thank you for believing in me and supporting me in every way whether it was emotionally, financially, or just being a sounding board for me to bounce my ideas off of. I can go on and on. Thank you.

To my mom Lee Anna Lake, thank you for instilling great values in your children where we were all able to grow up productively realizing that life is about giving back and helping others.

To my children, KeShanna, Ronald (Djaliba, Koba, Ahlonko, Elia), Elliott Jr., Ory and Sade and grandchildren Jamail, Elijah and Lilly, thank you for your encouraging words and prayers.

To my siblings, Christine (Ed), Caryn (Greg), Sheila (Michael), Sharon (Floyd), Rochelle, Jesselynne, Willie (Shawn) and Wendy, and my In-Laws Van (Glinda), Steven, Ernest (Andrea) and Bruce (Amber) I love you and thank you for your support and prayers.

To all of my nieces, nephews, cousins, aunts, uncles, too many to name, thank you for always encouraging me to dream.

People come into your life for a reason, season or a lifetime. For all of those gone and still here who have impacted my life, I thank you. To name a few of my specials friends, Chris, Jewell, Cynthia, Deborah, Karen, LaTanya, Eva, Rachel, Joyce, Renee, Erika, Caroline, Mamietta, Gail & Mike, Arvis, Felicia, Kristy, Millicent, Donna, Bridgett, Nina & Chris, Joseph & Vickie, thank you for your support and prayers. I love you.

To my IT team, Serrell, Donna and Robert who came to my rescue when my computer crashed thank you.

To my Book Cover Designer, Barron, you are amazing, God blessed you with a phenomenal talent and I am humbled and thankful that God sent you to me. Thank you for putting my vision into print.

To my Editorial Consultant Erica and Proofreaders, Debra and Anna, thank you for reading my work and making it flow. I will forever be indebted to you. God bless you.

To my web designer, Jeremy, thank you for designing a professional site that captures the element of my book and highlights my best personal attributes. God bless you.

To my Story Development Consultant and Publishing Consultant, Lissa Woodson, I am humbled and truly blessed for God to send me you. Being a new author, it is a privilege and I am truly thankful to have taken this journey with someone who is so knowledgeable and passionate about writing and doesn't expect anything but the best. I thank God for you. You have started a fire inside of me that makes me want to learn and explore more and desire to become a great writer.

Thanks to my dogs Goldie and Gizmo who hung out with me late nights and early into the morning lying right there by my side while I read and typed until I couldn't see straight.

To the readers, I pray that there is a message, word, or scene that inspires you. I hope you enjoy my story and learn what measures you should take vs. those you should avoid . . .

THE BEST IS YET TO COME!

Chapter 1

Karyn James had a dangerous decision to make: kill or be killed. She knew if she didn't make the first move, her husband could make her disappear without a trace. Any one of the policemen in Mark's back pocket would take his wife out in a split second. He had bragged about this simple fact on so many occasions, that these days, she knew he wasn't just trying to frighten her anymore. It was only a matter of time before he followed through with the act.

She threw on a t-shirt, jeans, sneakers and a baseball cap and slipped into the black Yukon Denali, gripping her sweaty palms around the steering wheel with a strength she didn't realize she still had. Screeching up the block, Karyn quickly covered the ground that would land her on I-94 North leading to downtown Chicago.

Finally, after sixteen years of conversations with her family and three best friends, she had reached her breaking point. Karyn had no intention of dying young. Unfortunately, leaving Mark outright was out of the question. Just as he had before, he would find her again. But this time, she was going to make sure that no one could find *him*. Could she count on her best friends to help?

Sherry Lakeside, Veronica Smith, Yvette Moss, and Karyn James had met as children over twenty years ago when they attended gatherings with their parents. Karyn could remember them playing together on the block in their Country Club Hills community, going to school functions and church events. Then it went on to supporting each other through college, with family and through life's challenges. They had stayed tight ever since. Well, until Mark James came into the picture. But were they close enough for the women to kill to protect one of their own?

The three women were sitting at a window booth at the Atwood Cafe, enjoying American cuisine and pleasant conversation that stumbled to a halt. Karyn's unannounced appearance, coupled with the frantic look on her face, surprised them all. Picking up Sherry's glass of whiskey, Karyn took a long swallow, hoping the eighty-proof liquor would give her the courage to say what needed to be said. As if the vision of her son aiming a gun while his father laid down the rules on how to take someone out wasn't enough. The memory constantly played in her mind, her son standing in that dark basement, nearly lifeless eyes locking a gaze on her, as if to say, "Really mom? Is this what life is all about?" Even more than that, the thought of the possibility that Mark would have her son kill her was more than she could bear.

Veronica and Yvette, dressed in designer Italian suits, and Sherry in a powder blue nurse's uniform had just come from work. They tried, and failed, to mask their shock, at Karyn's sudden arrival, and at her overall appearance, a far cry from a woman who had once held the world in her hand. The bruises and welts on her caramel complexion were common signs that Mark no longer bothered to hide the physical repercussions of his anger. The vacant look in Karyn's dark brown eyes, however, frightened them more than anything else. There was complete silence at the table, enough to cause a stab of fear to cross her heart.

They hadn't been expecting her this time—or any of the other times for that matter. After their roles in her previous escape attempts, Mark forbid her to have anything to do with them or her parents. She risked a severe beating just by being here. Beatings she could handle. Death? Not so much.

Karyn took another swallow of Sherry's drink then signaled the waiter over to get one of her own. The three women watched her warily. The fact that she had come at all meant something–or someone–had driven her to disobey a direct order. And from the look of things, it had not happened a moment too soon.

Karyn shifted in the booth, turning over a few scenarios in her mind, trying to come up with the best way to broach such a sensitive and dangerous subject. Veronica, the bronze–skinned diplomat of the group, gestured for the waiter to come back. "Please bring a Greek salad and grilled chicken, too." She didn't make eye contact with Karyn as she murmured, "It looks like you haven't eaten in days."

Veronica didn't know how close she was to the truth. Karyn glanced at her watch realizing that she could probably stay long enough to eat, but she would have to leave soon. If she wasn't back by the time Mark stepped through the front door of their five–bedroom Victorian house, he would definitely suspect something. She had never been able to hide anything from him, which was why he found her so easily when she actually managed to get away. Repercussions were more severe than the last. Now, the only threat that remained was to end her life altogether.

While she choked down a few bites of salad, she opened up, expressing the fact that she was living with a lunatic, something that wasn't news to the group of women. But with her next statement, they knew he had taken things to a whole new level. "Last night he said, 'I will beat you until you stop breathing. Then I'll cut your body up into small pieces and make you disappear. The police will cover my back and my tracks. And no one will believe it when your family or your girlfriends tell them that a businessman like myself, would sacrifice his status by killing a prostitute like you...'

The three friends sat in stunned silence. They had heard a lot from Karyn over the years, but it had never been so sinister, so ominous. What came next out of Karyn's mouth would change each of their lives forever. "I have to kill him before he kills me, and I need your help."

Veronica's big brown eyes widened in alarm. "Are you serious? Kill Mark?" she yelped, ignoring Yvette's signal to lower her voice. "What do we know about killing someone?" She shook off Yvette's attempt to shush her.

"What if we get caught?" Veronica grimaced and shook her head. "I'm not built for jail. I'm not doing it."

"What about Karyn?" Yvette shot back, glaring at the unsympathetic woman, whose high cheekbones were now flushed with angry color. "What about the pain and hurt she's endured at the hands of that monster?" She looked at each woman, not bothering to mention the number of times Karyn and her two children had hidden in her apartment, trying, once again, to unsuccessfully escape her husband for good. "Do you remember when he forced her to sell her body on the streets? Did you forget that *he's* the reason she has a record for prostitution? Do you remember all the times he put her in the hospital? The fractured ribs and bones?" She settled back into the plush velvet seat, grimacing. "Personally, I think she's waited too long."

"He deserves whatever the hell he gets," Sherry said through clenched teeth, her dark brown skin peppered with perspiration.

"And if we do it, who would suspect us?" She looked at them, took in the range of serious expressions. "We're three professional women who haven't considered doing anything criminal."

"Until now," Veronica added dryly, running a trembling hand through dark, silken tresses, trying to come up with another argument against this plan. And she noticed that Sherry had said three, not four, professional women, since Mark had successfully put an end to Karyn's aspirations the moment they had surfaced. Veronica sighed and let her gaze wander toward the Washington Street traffic since she could tell by the direction of their conversation that the voice of reason had been out voted.

And though deep down inside she understood Karyn's pain, she also realized that it had been Karyn's choice to marry Mark when they had warned her against it. It was her choice to stay with him, even after the first sign of abuse. Veronica felt, and had voiced, that she should have been long gone after the first time she laid on her back, servicing whoever would pay Mark's fees. She'd bought passports for Karyn and the children, along with first class flight tickets, and even though it taxed her salary from the fashion house, she even had a nice apartment waiting for their arrival to Paris. Veronica was sorely disappointed as she waited outside of Karyn's home, waiting for them to show. Even a knock on the door, at first received no answer, then a disheveled Karyn cracked the door, and whispered, "I can't leave. I can't leave him. He's the father of my children." What woman in her right mind would stay with a man like that? And now she expected her friends to fix her mistakes? She expected them to get blood on their hands?

God only knew that none of the four women were natural born killers, but after looking at Karyn's near lifeless form, Veronica understood that this was finally the point that there was no other way.

Karyn was no longer the vibrant and vivacious woman she once had been. Gone were the days of Karyn's "motivational pep talks" to keep her friends moving toward their dreams and goals. Now, all that sat before them was the shell of a woman that once was.

Yvette also recognized the signs of a woman who was at the place where she would do anything to protect herself and her children, and by God, if something happened to the pitiful woman, her daughter would definitely be in trouble at the hands of that man. If the man could pimp the woman he had sworn before God to love, honor, and protect, then he would have no boundaries when it came to his daughter if she defied him.

Though neither Yvette nor Sherry needed any further argument, Veronica still did. Karyn began describing what had happened with her son and it didn't take long for these new sordid pieces of information to seal the deal for the whole group, including the more reluctant Veronica.

Mark James had to die—and soon.

Chapter 2

Four weeks later, Yvette and Sherry had charted Mark's every move. Veronica had even managed to find out who his enemies were, and there were plenty. He did business with some of the most ruthless people known to man. José Romero, for example, was a Columbian drug lord whose territory spanned the Midwest and was rumored to have connections with the mafia as well. Mark had been one of his biggest clients until a "miscommunication" occurred during a transaction. Mark had gone to meet José with the incorrect amount of money in hand and found himself surrounded by José's men, with their guns pointed directly at his head. They were about to take him out when one of Mark's employees showed up with the rest of the money. Although Mark had since ended his involvement with José and found another supplier from the East coast, word on the street was that José was merely biding his time before he taught Mark a hard lesson.

Then there was Little Macy, one of Mark's bitter rivals. Just a few months ago, he had killed a few of Mark's men when they showed up on the west side near his turf. Little Macy was always on the alert, but since the shootout that followed, the area had been very tense. Based on Mark's ruthless reputation, he expected him to retaliate at any given moment. All attempts to stay on the breathing side of the game and extinguish Mark's life before he could get to Little Macy had been unsuccessful. Though all had been quiet because the area was crawling with police, Little Macy, whose hefty size belied his small name, had not been fooled into thinking that Mark had forgotten his error and was prepared to protect himself through taking any and all necessary measures.

José and Macy were among the many who could take the fall for Mark's death if the women handled things correctly. The trail would be so far from them that they certainly would not be considered suspects.

On an evening just like any other, the group met one last time to finalize things. For an easy-going, thick-bodied woman, Sherry was certainly shaping up to be the mastermind of the group. Her profession as an emergency room nurse gave her an edge, providing her with a wealth of knowledge on death in its many forms that the rest of the women lacked. She also had access to the tools critical to pull this off successfully—surgical gloves and scalpels, along with a body bag—the back-up plan in case the original one fell through.

The details necessary to confirm the day, time, and place of the murder had fallen on Veronica. Her discovery of Mark's warehouse, along with the meticulous report of his daily routine, had been the foundation to their plans. Although none of the women had any street connections, somehow Yvette had managed to secure a gun. No one in the group dared asked how.

Karyn, meanwhile, was trying to maintain the illusion of the loyal wife, folding to Mark's every whim. The bruises had faded to only a slight discoloration, but she knew the scars on her heart, all too present and painful, would never vanish completely. Karyn's submissiveness had lulled Mark into a false security, making him calmer with each passing day. He no longer spoke of killing her, believing that finally, his once stubborn wife had finally succumbed to his will.

The purpose of this last meeting was to discuss the execution of their plan. Based on the research, Veronica and Sherry agreed that a single gunshot to the head would do the trick, putting suspicion on anyone but them. Though she had done her part to solidify the plan, Veronica let it be known that her assistance, which had been the least of all of them, had finally come to an end. "There's no fuckin' way I'm going to pull that trigger."

An eerie silence followed that declaration. Somehow that major detail hadn't been broached. Seeing the somber looks on her friends' faces, Veronica added, "I might freak out and shoot something, or *someone*, I shouldn't." She gave each of them a level look.

"It's her problem," she said just above a whisper. "We could get him in a position where he can't move and then she can do the deadly deed. I'm all for covering up if we need to, pass the shovel and all that, but we shouldn't do it, because it didn't have to come to this." They all sat, stunned by Veronica's statements. "I even tried to get her and the children out of the country. She didn't even come out of the house. So, hell no, I'm not killing anybody." Then mumbled, "Not after I bought passports, airline tickets, and got her an apartment, too. *Shoooooot.*"

Sherry leaned against the counter in Yvette's Asian inspired one–bedroom apartment and shook her head. "Karyn would be considered a prime suspect. She'll have to stay home and follow her normal routine." Then her gaze fell to Veronica and Yvette, both sitting in stony silence. "We should pull the name at random to decide who'll actually kill him."

At that, the temperature in the apartment seemed to fall a few degrees. Yvette looked at Karyn. "You don't need to know anymore than you know right now. From this point on we'll take care of everything. Go on home."

"Why am I being left out? Like Veronica said, it's my problem."

Sherry could only nod. "It's best that you're home to receive the call or visit from the police."

The women looked at Karyn, then at each other, collectively wondering, *Are we really going to do this? Are we going to take a man's life? Are we really sitting here talking about this as though we were planning a Sunday meal?*

Veronica placed a reassuring hand over Karyn's. "I agree with Sherry. You can't know any of the details in case they question you."

Karyn gripped her friend's hand, then stood to hug each one of them. "I don't know what to say. 'Thank you' just doesn't seem enough." Wiping away the last of her tears, she trudged to the front door, looking back once more at her lifesavers, her friends, her sisters, and then opened the door to wait in the lobby for the taxi to deliver her to her prison.

After Karyn left, Yvette turned to the remaining two women. She had range shooting experience, and was known as the "rough and fearless" one in the group. Yet Sherry and Veronica still felt a bit of surprise when she said, "We won't have to pull names. I'll do it."

Chapter 3

A thick fog blanketed the streets and sidewalks, making it impossible to see the night sky. The ghostly weather matched the ominous mood of the night. It had been one week since that final meeting at Yvette's place, and Karyn was struggling to keep her hands steady and her head clear.

"Where's Mary and Mark Jr.?" Mark demanded.

Karyn didn't try to make eye contact as she whispered, "They had a play date with one of the children from school. I wanted it to just be me and you tonight."

Mark peered closely at her, waiting.

"They begged to spend the night. They'll be home in the morning," she added as an afterthought.

Actually, they wouldn't be. Earlier that afternoon, Veronica had come by the house to pick them up and take them to her grandmother's home in Country Club Hills. Ma Bertha often babysat the kids, sometimes for days at a time after an especially bad beating from Mark. Karyn knew they would be happy and safe there until this all blew over.

Mark's keen gaze took in the romantic setting, appreciating the classical music playing in the background, the candle lit dinner on the table, and the sexy black satin gown draping his wife's body. He nodded slowly, gaze flickering over her before he took a seat at the dining room table. "Next time, check with me first."

"All right," she answered softly and lowered her gaze.

In no time at all, Mark had devoured the hearty meal Karyn had prepared for him.

"That was delicious," he said, wiping his napkin across his thick lips.

Mark looked at Karyn, noticing she had barely touched the food on her plate. "I wish you had told me about tonight."

"I wanted it to be a surprise."

"I've got plans," he replied, before walking over to her side of the table, pulling her to him. "But I'll be back." He kissed her, then went upstairs to shower and dress for work as Karyn cleared the table. A spotless house always made him happy.

Thirty minutes later, Mark strolled back into the dining room wearing a gray Kenneth Cole suit, the scent of Dolce and Gabbana cologne swirling around him. He took one look at Karyn in her skimpy gown, one of his requirements, and before she realized what was happening, he grabbed her around the waist and planted a passionate kiss on her lips, leaving her breathless.

"I love you so much," he whispered against her ear, stroking her buttocks with the same heavy hands that had landed blows causing one or more of her God–given senses to shut down. "I don't know what I'd do without you." His voice, husky with need, washed over her and filled her with fear.

He couldn't want to do that right now. It will make him late! Karyn thought, trying to force herself not to make any movement or sound. Panic was fast overtaking her fear. Everything could go wrong if Mark wasn't in the right place at the right time.

"I'm sorry for all the things I've done to you," he said. "Please forgive me, baby."

He kissed her forehead as she stood silently, letting her tears stream down her face. "If I could change things, I would. I just hope one day we can go back to the way we were in the beginning."

"The way we were?"

"When you were happy staying at home, raising the kids, and having dinner prepared for me when I walked through the door."

Mark was sorely mistaken. Karyn had never been happy with just that—but she wasn't about to correct him. She couldn't risk his anger. He was almost out the door. *Please God, let him leave, let him leave now!*

"Or when we used to take romantic get-away trips to Jamaica and Mexico," he brushed a deceptively gentle hand along her cheek. "The moment you decided you needed more than your family, trying to do outside shit like that event planning business, things changed. Having you away from home all the time, and having me come home to an empty house, made *me* unhappy."

Karyn stared at him, wondering if he suspected—or even worse— *knew* something was going on. He didn't allow her very much time to linger on her thoughts, though. Mark pulled her into his arms and began undressing her. Right there, he made love to her on the dining room floor. Unlike so many other times, this time was tender and loving–better than it had ever been before. He penetrated her with sure, smooth strokes, reaching her very core with a practiced ease that was all too familiar to her. She closed her eyes, timing what she knew would be a short–lived venture, against the schedule that the girls had so carefully planned. Hands that she had come to fear had suddenly, unexpectedly, tried to turn into the most pleasant touch she had ever experienced. He watched her expression, which she immediately tried to form into one that would signal pleasure of some sort. She thought he had long forgotten how to be affectionate, yet his caresses proved that he clearly remembered all the places that had been neglected for far too long. So, why, on this night of all nights, did Mark want her to feel something when it had never mattered before now.

For a moment, she opened her heart and mind to the hope and possibility that just maybe, this time, he meant it when he said he loved her. Catching a glimpse of a photo on the mantle, the thought vanished as quickly as it had come. The image she had seen haunted her every day—it was the empty look in her daughter's beautiful brown eyes. Her beautiful little Mary hadn't even tried to smile for this year's classroom picture, or even the ones before. Karyn knew if she and her children had any hope at leading a normal, healthy life, it would not be at 4599 Oakwood Lane.

When their spontaneous love-making session had come to an end, Mark strolled into the half bath to clean himself up and straighten out his suit and tie. Once he looked presentable, he walked back into the dining room, stopping to kiss Karyn once more, before scooping up his black leather briefcase and leaving the house while whistling a happy tune.

Back in the kitchen, emotions of fear and confusion battled within. Karyn rested her back against the refrigerator, debating whether or not she should call Sherry, or any one of the women, to talk some sense into her. Instead, she went upstairs to the bathroom and cleaned up the mess Mark had left behind. The plan strictly stated, "You are not to speak to any one of us today. Wait for the officers to call you."

She was going to be strong, for once, and stick to the plan. After all, freedom was only a gunshot away.

Chapter 4

Just down the block from Karyn's house, Sherry, Veronica and Yvette sat in a rented black Toyota Camry. They watched through the rear view mirror as Mark strolled confidently from the house, walking the brick–lined path toward his truck and tossing a briefcase on the back seat. As he pulled out of the driveway, Sherry started the car and began to follow him at a safe distance, keeping at least three car lengths in between them, even on the expressway. After traveling for fifty minutes, their journey ended at what appeared to be an abandoned building.

Yvette, dressed in dark denim slacks and a black jacket, with the hood pulled over freshly corn–rowed hair, got out of the car and hid in the shadows of the alley just a few feet away from the building that served as Mark's warehouse. Even though the area was practically deserted, her senses were heightened with fear and anticipation, making her extra sensitive to any slight sound or movement. Not only was she thinking about what was about to happen, but she also knew from the news reports that multiple murders and rapes had happened on this very block. The violence and danger lurking in this area didn't exactly welcome folks. People avoided it whenever possible.

After what felt like hours, but was actually only forty-five minutes, Yvette slipped out of her hiding spot, still staying within the shadows of the alley. Tightening the black gloves around her delicate hands, she reached into her pocket and securely grasped the gun. The other two women watched from the car as Mark left the building heading toward his truck—right on time according to their plan.

Yvette waited for the signal—flashing lights from Veronica's rental car—which meant the coast was clear, with no one within view from their range. They flashed the headlights, once, twice, and then a final time. With her heart hammering against her chest, she emerged from her spot in the alley and approached Mark from behind. Sensing her presence, he froze and swung around to face her. He immediately braced to deflect an attack, but relaxed the moment he recognized Yvette's petite frame. His furrowed brow reflected his confusion at her presence outside of his warehouse so late at night.

"What are you doing here?" he demanded, moving closer to take a good look at her.

Yvette parted trembling pink lips to answer, but before she had the chance, a husky man swept down the stairs. Instinctively, she lowered her gaze then swiftly turned her back toward the person approaching them.

Inside the car, Sherry saw the move. "Wow! She's really good at this."

"No, she's just smart," Veronica replied softly, shifting uncomfortably in the passenger seat. "We don't want anyone to be able to recognize or identify her later. I thought those corn rows were a nice touch. I wouldn't know who she was."

Back in the alley, Yvette was desperately trying to control her erratic breathing. She stole a quick glance toward the parked car, as though asking for assistance. But what could the other two women do at that point? Sherry might come charging in, but it was heads or tails on whether Veronica would make a move. Now she wished she hadn't been so eager to be the trigger woman. What if she had to shoot both men?

"This isn't going as planned," Veronica whispered, her heartbeat nearly matching the fear–filled pace of Yvette's. "We need to call the whole thing off and get her away from Mark *right now.*"

Sherry gripped her friend's hand, halting her move to open the car door. "Calm down. She's all right." Glancing toward the alley, they saw that their friend had regained her composure and they chorused a sigh of relief.

"I need to talk to you about my boyfriend," Yvette whispered to Mark. "I've been having some problems and Karyn suggested I speak to you." Keeping her head low, her gaze swept toward the building, making sure no one else had followed the other man outside.

On Mark's signal, the dark–skinned bruiser stopped in his tracks. Yvette could tell he was trying to get a better look at her, but decided to keep moving the moment his boss gave him an impatient look. Peering at the shadowy–looking female one last time, he turned on his heels and went back through the graffiti–covered doors.

Veronica exhaled slowly, finally releasing her grip on the car door handle as she settled back in the seat. "That was a really close call."

Sherry could only nod.

"Can we talk for a second? Maybe take a ride somewhere?" Yvette asked in a voice that was somewhere between vulnerable and vixen.

"Sure…" Mark's sharp gaze covered the length of her body, then finally came up again landing on her flushed cheeks. "Why are you dressed like that? I thought you were some thug."

She gazed over her shoulder. "I think he's following me." Hoping Mark would attribute her twitchy behavior to simply being paranoid of a stalker boyfriend, but in reality, she was letting her friends know she was following everything to the letter.

Mark led Yvette to the Chevy Tahoe parked directly across from the warehouse. After driving around the block and past a neighborhood bank which had closed decades ago, other equally as dilapidated warehouses, and the last hold–out–a liquor store; she placed a hand over his. "Want to pull into that alley way right up ahead? He won't be able to find us in there, and we'll be able to talk."

Once Mark had turned off the engine, Yvette stepped out of the vehicle, taking several deep breaths in an attempt to steady her hands that were shaking uncontrollably. She chanced a look over her shoulder and almost dropped the gun. When he got out, Mark flexed and cracked his neck as though preparing for battle. She steadied herself enough to unzip the hoodie, exposing a lace camisole and a length of cleavage that would immobilize any living, breathing man.

The diversion was a success. With his gaze roaming over her curves, Mark didn't notice the car inching toward the back end of the alley or catch Yvette's sigh of relief.

Yvette inched further into the shadows past a barricaded door, then leaned against the brick wall, praying she wouldn't pass out. Mark followed, never taking his eyes off her exposed breasts. "What's going on Yvette?"

In theory, killing someone, especially a person like Mark who had done the things he had to Karyn, could be understood, even validated, for the right reasons. But going through with the act was a completely different ballgame. This was someone else's *life*. If she killed him, there was no undoing what was done. No taking it back. No "do overs."

He reached out and placed a hand on her face, trailing it down her cheek, neck, and shoulder, resting along the smooth curve of her breasts, causing Yvette to catch her breath. Mistaking her reaction for pleasure, he pressed his body against her. She could feel his erection growing as he tried to slip a hand into her denim pants. The stench from the overflowing dumpster, mingled with the scent of his cologne, nauseated her to the point that she worried her dinner might make an untimely comeback.

"Whatever you need, I can help you, Yvette," he whispered huskily. "But what are you going to do for me?"

"I'm sorry I have to do this," she whispered, tears blurring her vision as she pushed him away. An image of her friend's bloody and battered face flashed before her eyes, giving her the strength and courage she so desperately needed in order to continue. "But Karyn's my girl and I love her so much."

Mark looked up, peering at her as though he hadn't heard her right.

"You've destroyed her! You've done so many evil things—"

"What?" Mark pulled back just a little. "I thought this was about you." His beady eyes searched hers. "What the fuck's going on?" He looked around and finally noticed the two women creeping his way. They, too, looked vaguely familiar. He started to reach into his vest, but Yvette was a few seconds faster.

"Toss the gun over here." Yvette's heart was hammering in her chest. "Now Mark! Or I'll blow your ass away."

Mark turned back to face her and the thirty–eight caliber that Yvette held securely in her trembling hands. With the threat of a gun pointed at his head, he glared his displeasure. He slowly opened his jacket, pulled the gun from its holster, tossing it to a point just behind her. It hit the wall and came to a stop at the edge of the dumpster.

"I don't believe this shit!" he growled, eyes flashing with anger.

"Well you should." She backed away, leaving only a foot between her extended arms and his chest. "Turn around. Walk toward the other end of the alley."

Mark glared at Yvette, but didn't move. "You don't have it in you," he shot back, lips arched into a snarl. "You've never killed anyone. That's where we're different."

For a moment, fear held Yvette prisoner. *Was she actually going through with this?*

That pregnant pause was all Mark needed to press the advantage. "And you've insulted me with this pathetic attempt at what? Hurting me? Teaching me a lesson?" He laughed, a bitter vengeful sound that chilled her blood. "You know what I'm going to do, Yvette? I'm gonna fuck you like the whore you are. Then I'm going to take you back into my building and have my men take real good care of you. Just like they took care of Karyn's stupid ass. There's about twenty of 'em. You'll love what they do to you." His lips curled into a sneer. "When they've all had a turn, then I'll watch you die the slow, agonizing death you deserve for this shit."

Before Yvette could blink a solid time, Mark lunged toward her, reaching for her gun, but instead, knocked it out of her hand and sent it flying down the alley. Abandoning any attempt to regain possession of her weapon, she dove for his gun on the ground behind her. Yvette rolled onto her back and pointed the gun at him. And he froze.

Veronica and Sherry had broken into a sprint, but they were still too far away to make a difference.

"You don't have it in you," he spat. "I'm going to enjoy what I do to you."

Yvette closed her eyes and pulled the trigger.

Chapter 5

Eleven years later...

"Why couldn't y'all just let me stay home? I have work to do!" Yvette Glover whined as she followed Sherry, Veronica and Karyn along the path that flanked the traffic-filled intersections of Wacker Drive.

Her excuses and fruitless attempts to stay home that evening didn't faze the other women as they continued walking toward their desired destination. First it was that her husband, Derrick, had demanded that she stay home so that they could talk. Then it was that she just wanted to stay curled up in bed with a good book and a glass of wine. Then it was a horrible headache brought on by an argument with Derrick. Now it was work. The other women wouldn't hear of it. Argument with Derrick? Please!! They had the perfect marriage, the perfect life—what did they have to argue about?

Whether it was the full moon, or just the fact that it had been eleven years to the day since that fateful incident, Yvette had a bad feeling that something was bound to test the bonds of their friendship, sooner rather than later. Her ivory skin, which often caused her to be mistaken for a White woman, was flushed with color, visibly displaying her uneasiness. Her normal arrogance was nowhere in sight, having been replaced by a sudden onset of anxiety and fear she couldn't quite get under control.

All of the women, except for Yvette, were dressed in a chic black wardrobe of varied styles, ranging from conservative to flashy. Yvette, dressed in a dark purple suit, felt like the other three women's attire looked more fitting for a funeral instead of heading to the LiBay nightclub for a night of dancing and fun.

The group strolled into the upscale spot located in the heart of downtown Chicago with an air of cool confidence swirling around them. The place was where the crème de le crème came to enjoy themselves, to mix and mingle, network if possible, and pick up a little overnight fun if it worked out that way. It was one of those places to see and be seen, and the women were proud to finally be able to fit right in with the elite movers and shakers of the Windy City.

Since their early years, they had always stuck by one another. Together, they'd survived the challenges of growing up in a suburban neighborhood; supported each other through their college years which took them to different states; and now they encouraged each other throughout all their professional endeavors, past and present. Their fashions reflected not only their personal tastes, but also spoke to the strides they had taken to distance themselves from their small town upbringing. The choice to wear all black tonight was normally their unique way of expressing their unity, having adopted the code after attending an All White Stepper's Party in Chicago a few years ago. But for some reason, Yvette refused to wear black tonight, which had brought a range of curious comments from her friends.

The foursome easily passed through security as they entered the foyer and were greeted with the sounds of competing rhythms, beautiful abstract artwork, and the aroma of cuisine that ranged from American, Japanese, to Italian. Heading toward the plush, carpeted stairs, the group ignored Sherry's pleas to explore the first level with its blaring Hip–hop music and noticeably barely legal crowd.

"But the youngsters love full–figured women like me," she protested, poking out her bottom lip.

"Is that right?" Veronica shot back, hooking an arm under the fleshy woman and moving her forward. "Well, you'll just have to take your *full–figured* chances with men your own age tonight."

Karyn and Yvette roared with laughter at Sherry's stricken expression, as they were the ones who were a little concerned when the establishment had relaxed their standards and allowed the 21–and up set to get into the club but only in the Hip–Hop level. Sherry had no such qualms and had often dipped into that area to select some eager young man to hook up with at a later time. Karyn was certainly against it, noting that she never wanted to party with people close to her children's age, and also noting that security was a little lax on the more "adult" floors when someone slipped a few dollars in their hands.

At the third floor, the group stopped short before entering the Blues club. The music and live performers from all over the world made the top level a nice place for older folks to socialize, but these four beautiful women didn't fit that description by a long shot. While they could appreciate Blues and jazz, they preferred a blend of R&B and old school music—something with a rhythm they could Step to.

They headed back down to the second level, entering a room with artfully placed dim lights and brass casings on rose colored walls, giving the Stepper's Level a more romantic, intimate setting. The moment they strolled past the threshold, the group elicited appreciative stares of men near the entrance—a direct contrast to the envious glares of women scattered about the outlying areas. Sherry motioned for her friends to follow her toward the reserved table near the Steppers working their grooves on the dance floor.

Once seated, the women couldn't help but notice one particularly bold admirer gazing longingly at Sherry with her sienna complexion, naturally curly fro, and backless mini–dress hugging generous curves. In keeping with her outgoing personality, Sherry gave the tall, handsome man a slow, easy smile, which encouraged him to approach her—something that had been happening regularly since she changed her hair style from a long, silky weave to a style that mirrored Jill Scott's. Although her complexion was a darker hue, Sherry was often mistaken for the sultry singer. But the women's similarities ended with their looks. While Jill constantly wrote about love, female power, and having a dynamic soul mate, Sherry had yet to experience any of these first hand.

Veronica leaned over to Sherry, whose gaze was still locked on her admirer, nudging her in the side. "Stop drooling, woman."

"I'm not the one drooling."

The man acknowledged the laughing women with the lift of his brow while smoothly slipping a business card into Sherry's hand. He leaned in, a black muscle shirt outlining his rippling abs and whispered something in her ear before sauntering back to the end of the bar where his three friends were perched. Veronica followed his movements, winking at Sherry who had also noticed his nice round butt and gave an appreciative smile.

Sherry placed the card in a place between her breast and the smooth silk fabric of her bra. "This night's starting out on a good note."

Karyn shrugged. "Well, at least he's of legal age."

"Barely," Yvette shot back.

Sherry's hand rode up on her hip as she glared. "Honey, he's a man and he's breathing, that's all that counts."

"Yes," Yvette gave her a long look. "but you still need to check identification along with a pulse."

Veronica roared with laughter. "I'll bet she's even tackled some of those barely alive patients of hers."

"Oh come on, I do have some morals."

"Shoot, I'm surprised you can even say that word."

Sherry glowered angrily at Yvette. "It begins with MO, the same as the thing you love more than men–M–O–N–E–Y. So don't talk to me about morals. Have money in one hand and a man in another and old boy's going to be left high and dry."

"Fuck you!"

"Behave ladies," Karyn said as another man came up to acknowledge Sherry.

Veronica's smile faltered slightly at her displeasure at being passed over for the curvy woman of the group. She was the very definition of chic with her shoulder–length bob framing a heart–shaped face, expressive dark brown eyes with lashes to die for, and svelte figure. Normally, she or Yvette would be on the receiving end of such attention, but the tides were changing, and more men were appreciating curvy women, as well as those who opted to go natural instead of the model type. Veronica had dressed to impress, wearing a black form–fitting jumper with her pant legs tucked into silver designer boots which complimented the bag she had on her lap. Her job in the fashion industry meant that she was always dressed on the cutting edge, guaranteeing she always stood out. Evidently, it wasn't working for her tonight.

The women surveyed the area while taking in the sounds of Luther Vandross', "Take You Out" and basking in the seductive mood of the room. Exotic, colorful fish swam under the plexi–glass squares of the dance floor, moving seemingly in time with the rhythm of the music while the women took turns pointing out the ills and successes of the dancers working classic Stepper's moves.

As if out of thin air, a handsome waiter appeared in the space beside Karyn. "I want you to know that I was hired specifically to service you four beautiful ladies," he said, giving each of them a pointed look. "My name is Jerome, and your wish is my command."

The women's reaction to his statement was more like something from a bunch of teenage girls, not successful, mature women out on the town.

Sherry placed a manicured hand over her breasts. "Oh, sweetheart, you have no idea what I would wish."

"How many wishes do we get," Veronica purred with a suggestive lift of her eyebrow.

Silently, Yvette wished the night was over.

Jerome gave them a wide grin. "What are you ladies drinking tonight?"

Sherry reached out and trailed her hand over his rippled abs. "We would love to be drinking you, baby, because you're as fine as aged wine."

With a roll of her eyes, Yvette plucked Sherry's fingers from the man's rib cage. "I'll have a gin and tonic, please."

Veronica, trying to stifle a nervous laugh, ordered a peach bellini, and not a moment too soon. The poor waiter almost lost his balance as Sherry slipped a single hand down his thigh. "Give me a *dirty* martini," she purred, giving him a wicked smile as her hand moved a little closer toward the bulge in his pants.

Karyn shook her head as Jerome adjusted himself and put some distance between his precious gems and Sherry's wandering hands. Wanting to help the poor guy out, the "mother" of the group grabbed Sherry's hand and held it securely in her lap as she ordered her drink.

"Grey Goose and Cranberry with a twist of lime, please."

Jerome recited their orders before heading back to the bar, but not without taking one last look at Sherry. As one man was leaving the women, another was making his way toward them. Stopping next to Veronica, but making eye contact with Karyn, he asked, "Do you Step?"

He didn't have to ask twice. Karyn loved dancing and believed she had perfected the art of Stepping—a Chicago dance style based on the Walk and the Chicago Bop dances from the '60s and '70s. If done right, couples looked like they were gliding on air. If done incorrectly, they looked like perfect idiots.

Karyn stood, smoothed a hand over the knit material of her form-fitting dress, and strolled toward the dance floor. Weaving through the moving bodies, the couple found themselves a spot not too far from the table, giving her friends a prime view to watch what category they would fall into.

Yvette grimaced as she watched Karyn and the sharply dressed mystery man. "Look at her. She's not even counting her moves. They look like two White people trying to blend in."

Sherry and Veronica chuckled at the fitting description. "As if you can talk," Veronica said with a laugh. "Last time you didn't do so hot yourself, sister."

"She needs to be home with her fine ass husband before I make a move on him."

The laughter died instantly as Veronica gasped at Yvette's boldness. "You know you're wrong for that. It's *Girls'* Night Out. Sometimes we need a break from men." Returning her watchful gaze to Karyn and her dance partner she commented, "But maybe break time is over. He sure is fine, though."

Yvette cocked her head checking out the man's rear view before murmuring an agreement.

As the night continued, Yvette mentally withdrew from the group, tuning out the music and the conversation between Sherry and Veronica. Immersed with her own thoughts, she wondered how Karyn, of all people, could be so carefree on this night. Had she really forgotten that at this very hour, eleven years ago, she was being questioned by the police?

Looking up, Yvette saw that Sherry and Veronica were sharing a good-hearted laugh about something—knowing them, probably some inane story about one of their co-workers or another diatribe about men according to the world of Sherry of the "open your legs now, ask questions later" clan. She still couldn't grasp how they could sleep at night, let alone laugh. How could they have scheduled a girls' night out on tonight of all nights? Obviously, Yvette would never verbalize why she hadn't wanted to go. They had vowed never to speak about what had happened, but that didn't mean the awful memory didn't nag at her when she was awake or haunt her dreams when she laid down to rest. She could never escape the nightmare she had created. And now she needed to create a nightmare of another kind.

This time, Karyn would have to do the deadly honors.

Chapter 6

Karyn, winded but still flashing a happy smile, returned to the table, frowning as her gaze swept the table. "He's not back with our drinks yet?"

"Girl, you know you were jamming!" Sherry replied, with a knowing look at Veronica.

"Yes you were," Veronica added, before they broke into a fit of giggles.

Karyn didn't miss their teasing tone. "Yeah? I love the both of you too!" She adjusted her heels, so she could rub her aching feet. "If that man stepped on my toes one more time…"

"Yeah, we saw that, too." Yvette said, finally focusing her attention on the group. "No rhythm on the dance floor means, no rhythm in the bedroom."

Sherry shook her head. "Weeeeeell, you can't always say that. If they have the right size equipment, and you're willing to do the work, it's all good."

As if on cue, Jerome appeared with their drinks in tow. He handed each woman their glass—two for Sherry—and then slipped back into the crowd as quickly as he had come.

"So much for our genie," Karyn said dryly. "What happened to your wish is my command?"

As Sherry tossed back her first drink, she scooped up the napkin displaying Jerome's number, folded it, and placed it in her bra next to the business card she had collected earlier.

"Looks like he already got what he wanted," Yvette quipped in a dry tone.

Sherry shrugged and gave them a sly wink. "Can't help it if I got it like that."

"What you have is I'm–easy–itis and men can tell," Yvette countered, crossing one leg over the other. "Notice you're not attracting the best of the lot."

"What I notice is that you're not attracting anything at all," Sherry shot back. "Not even your own husband."

"Sherry!" Karyn admonished, giving her a hard look.

"It's the truth! When was the last time Derrick came to any of our parties?"

Veronica placed a hand over Yvette's mouth and said, "Hey, let's toast to success and rekindled relationships for those that have them and hoping for a wonderful *new* relationship for those who don't."

"Here, here," Karyn said with a lift of her glass.

Yvette plucked Veronica's hand from her mouth, tore her angry glare from Sherry and lifted her own glass, saying, "Yes, *some* of us need it more than others. And it's not those of us who actually *have* a husband."

"Watch it," Veronica snapped with a quick look at Yvette. "I'm not married."

Yvette never took her gaze off Sherry as she answered with, "And it's through no fault of your own, either. Some can't even land a husband if they tried."

"Oh, please, Veronica doesn't get off that easy," Sherry responded with a dismissing wave of her hand. "She hasn't had any man the first, second or third. Maybe she's into women. If I didn't know better, I'd think the same of you, since despite what you say about me, word on the street is you don't seem to discriminate either."

At that statement Veronica's skin colored to an angry red. She glowered angrily at Sherry, turned her back to all three women and gripped the edge of the table, and tried to hold it together before she said something equally as nasty.

"Ladies, what is wrong with you?" Karyn asked, looking from Sherry then to Yvette as she rubbed a calming hand on Veronica's back. "I'd swear you were enemies with the way you're acting tonight."

"If she can't take it, then she shouldn't serve it up," Sherry countered still locked into a glaring standoff with Yvette.

"Oh, I can take it," Yvette said, lips curled in a sly smile as she set her drink on the table. "Especially since I've been with *one* man for all these years and you've been with," Yvette flashed her hands to signal ten, twenty, thirty, forty, fifty…

"Oh so, it's like that, huh?" Sherry shot back, squaring her shoulders as she moved in to stand toe–to–toe with Yvette, who had stood the exact moment that Sherry got up. "You haven't been with your husband all this time, you've been married to his money. Get it straight, girlfriend. It ain't the brown of the man, it's the green of his cash."

"What's gotten into you two?" Karyn shrieked, placing a hand on Yvette's chest to keep her still. She reached down, lifted her glass so that it was in the center of the group. "Let's just toast to success and leave it at that."

Reluctantly Veronica turned to face the group, eyes moist with unshed tears.

Sherry sighed as she reached for Veronica's hand. "I apologize. I shouldn't have said that to you. I shouldn't have brought you into it like that."

Veronica didn't look the fleshy woman in the eyes, but nodded before she locked gazes with Karyn. The women all lifted their glasses to toast, but before they had a chance to start, the music for the latest slide came through the speakers, a beat none of them could resist. Quickly draining their glasses, they jetted onto the dance floor, barely managing to get a spot to work their hips to the line dance. Half way through their routine, Sherry looked up to see a fine young brother across the room checking her out. A wink and a wide smile from him was all the encouragement she needed to leave her friends behind and head in his direction.

Several minutes later, three of the friends returned to the table. "Wonder where Sherry went to," Veronica said, as she skimmed the dance floor and surrounding areas without finding the full figured woman.

"I'll give you three guesses," Yvette said with a wry twist of her cupid bow lips. "It starts with M and ends with AN."

Karyn shook her head at the truth behind those words, though she kept any smart comment to herself.

As the girls chatted about their latest misadventures with the men in their lives, Sherry returned with a new drink in hand. Finishing it in one swallow, she placed the empty glass onto the table, then grabbed her black wrap, and tossed it over her shoulder. "Well ladies, I'm done for the night. I met this great brother and he seems really nice." She reached into her purse, pulled out the plum gloss, gave her lips a quick touch–up. "He invited me out for breakfast, so I'll talk to you pretty ladies tomorrow. Ciao!"

Her declaration was met with an uneasy silence. Veronica, Yvette and Karyn looked at each other, then at Sherry. Karyn, jumped to her feet and spoke for all of them. "Sorry, Sherry, but you're not going with that brother, or any other brother tonight, nice or not. You came with us, and you'll be leaving with us." She looked up to see a tall, chocolate-skinned man walking toward them. "So tell that nice *young* man good night."

Veronica polished off the last of her cocktail, casting a quick glance at Sherry over the rim of the glass. "But don't forget to get his number, girl."

Yvette just shrugged, but Karyn didn't bother to mask her anger at Veronica's words, encouraging the baby of the group to pick up yet another total stranger.

The man in question, now standing behind Sherry, nuzzled his head into the smooth curve of her neck and whispered something into her ear as he wrapped his muscular arms around her. Sherry swayed into him, nearly melting from his touch.

"Tell him good night, Sherry," Karyn said through clenched teeth, locking gazes with the intruder who hadn't bothered to loosen his firm grip on her ample hips. "Don't act like a whore."

"Hold up!" Sherry shot back, squaring her shoulders and forcing her new 'whatever' to back up a few inches. "Who the hell do you think you are?"

Karyn maneuvered herself between her feisty friend and the frowning man. "Someone who knows better than to let her friend go home with a perfect stranger." Facing him, Karyn gave him a curt nod and a short, "Good night." She grabbed her purse and turned back to Sherry. "Let's go, Ms. Lakeside."

When Sherry didn't move, Karyn looked to the other two women. Veronica and Yvette got up and flanked Sherry on both sides, lacing an arm under hers. They unsuccessfully tried to move the stubborn woman toward the exit and away from their table, causing a scene that others were now beginning to notice.

Sherry angrily shook them off, glaring openly at Karyn who had turned from her in disgust. "You've got a lot of nerve telling me what's right and wrong after what you asked us to do."

Everyone froze.

Karyn pivoted so she could look Sherry directly in the eye. "What the hell did you just say?"

"I said exactly what you thought I said," Sherry quipped, moving forward so she was standing toe–to–toe with Karyn. "Always so damn judgmental! You want to be Ms. High and Mighty and tell *me* how to live *my* life? Then let's bring everything out in the open—and I do mean *everything*. Let's see what you have to say then."

With tears welling in her eyes, Veronica dropped into the nearest seat, knocking over Karyn's glass of Grey Goose and Cranberry. Mr. Right Now backed away with a curt, dismissing nod in Sherry's direction as the three women followed Veronica's lead.

If you looked at them from a distance, you saw four glamorous women sitting together at a table. But while they were physically present, each one of them was now locked in their own world of memories, completely oblivious to the bright red liquid spilling onto their designer outfits.

Chapter 7

Yvette was jolted from a deep sleep by a loud–BANG! Sitting up, she looked around to discover that her husband was the cause for the commotion. She peered at Derrick, trying to comprehend the situation unfolding before her very eyes. Frantically pacing from the closet to the bed, where his overnight bag was open, he was stuffing clothes inside with no care whether they ended up wrinkled or not. Pounding footsteps, matched with whatever other noise he could create, made it clear to Yvette that he wanted her awake and very much aware of his untimely departure.

"Honey, where are you going?" Yvette asked softly, trying hard to maintain peace in her home by not adding fuel to the fire by exposing her growing anger of Derrick's constant weekend disappearances. She was way past being sick and tired of making excuses for him when their twin daughters would ask about their dad's whereabouts. And even they were giving her "the look" when she would say that Derrick was working.

"That's really not your concern," he snapped, tossing the last of his clothing into the overnight bag. "You lost the right to know what I'm doing, where I'm going, and who I'm going with when you decided to play games with my life."

Yvette jumped up from the bed, quickly crossing the span of the room until she was standing face to face with her angry husband as she reached for him. "Baby, I don't know what you're talking about! But whatever you think I did, please forgive me. I love you!"

Derrick took a couple of steps backward, distancing himself from her clutches. "How can you say you love me? You don't even know what love is!" He moved away, snatched another jacket from the closet. "I guess it was love when you were sleeping with all those men at my company, fucking your way to the top? You *loooooooooved* them too, right?" Flickering his eyes over her scantily clad form, his thick lips twisted into a frown. "You've made me look like a fool in front of my colleagues. You disgust me!"

Yvette didn't know how to respond, so she did the only thing she knew how. She allowed the chemise to fall to the floor. She looked up at him then moved slowly toward him, in measured steps that covered the distance between them, but also gave him a full view of the body he swore up and down was the best he'd ever seen. "You don't understand what I've gone through," she said in a voice just above a whisper. "I've always been afraid to trust someone." She gazed deep into his dark brown eyes, hoping he would believe that she was sincere this time. "Now I realize I can trust someone—I can trust you. Your love has helped me become a better person. I've changed."

"Changed?" he spat with a harsh laugh as he pushed her away. "Since when? Last night? Look at you! Thinking you can still get what you want with your body. Well, guess what? I'm so over that." He fanned her away. "And I'm so over you."

"No, that's not true," Yvette shrieked, a sense of panic causing an increase in her heart rate. "I don't do the things I used to because I love you." She gripped the edges of his jacket. "I would never do anything to jeopardize our family and the life that we've built together."

"Too late!" Picking up her gown from the floor, he tossed it in her face. "You should've thought about that before you created this mess. Or better yet, instead of going out with your girls last night, you should've stayed home to talk about our marriage that you claim," he crooked his fingers as quotes, "you so desperately want to save."

With that last dig, Derrick grabbed his keys and the fully stuffed overnight bag and stormed out of the house.

Yvette almost ran after him to get in the last word, but thought better of it. Slamming the door, she made her way back to her bedroom and fell across the bed, letting tears of frustration finally have their way. "I hate him!" she screamed to the empty room. But really she loved him. Well, as much as Yvette Moss–Glover could love anyway.

"I won't take this bullshit too much longer."

Lying on their bed, she remembered some of their happiest memories. Derrick had always been a wonderful husband and a loving, caring, and compassionate father. In all their years of marriage, under the circumstances of how it began, he had doted on her, providing her anything she wanted or desired. From the outside, they looked like the perfect family.

Their careers and sound investments had allowed them the lavish lifestyle many envied. They lived in an upscale neighborhood in Oak Park that had some of the most coveted pieces of real estate Chicago had to offer. There, they owned a ten–bedroom, seven bath, Frank Lloyd Wright home with a live–in cook, housekeeper, and nanny who resided in coach homes which were also situated on the property. Without Derrick, though, none of the material things mattered. She had fought to get him, and she would do everything in her power to keep him.

How could she win him back? What would she do without him? Who would she be without him in her life? All the charity balls, the fundraising galas, spreads in magazines who touted them as the successful power couple would go away. And most importantly, how would she be able to maintain her lifestyle without his money?

Derrick was serious this time—accusing her of sleeping her way to the top. Who would have given him that information? Had all this made him angry enough to change his will? What if he threatened to take her daughters, spoiled little brats that they were? She would benefit more if he outright died. The insurance money alone would carry her a lifetime. She really should have stayed her ass home last night. Maybe he wouldn't be so angry this morning.

But the truth of the matter was, she had everything—and nothing. Nothing made her feel right anymore—not her husband or the daughters she had never felt a connection to, which is why she insisted on having nannies for them, and it would be boarding school the moment they reached twelve, earlier if she could manage. Ever since that night she shot Mark, her world had never quite come together—it was as if life's puzzle had been given to her but a valuable piece of her soul was missing.

She snatched the phone from the cradle, hoping to reach Karyn. She had beef with her after how last night went down, then to follow it by an equally bad morning with her marriage completely unraveling before her very eyes. Oh, yes, she had a few choice words for Karyn Johnson.

After several rings, Karyn didn't bother to mask her heavy sigh as she said, "Yeah, Yvette, what's up?"

Yvette bristled at her weary tone, too furious to call Karyn out on the fact that she sounded like she couldn't be bothered with her. "Why did you force me to go out last night?"

"What?"

Yvette made every attempt to keep calm, but failed as she growled, "You, of all people, should have known it wasn't going to be a good night."

"Calm down Yvette," Karyn replied evenly as something cluttered in the background. "What the hell are you talking about?"

"You mean to tell me you didn't know what night it was?"

Silence on the other end signaled that she was at least trying to think it over. Finally, Karyn cleared her throat. "No, actually, I didn't. Well, at least not until Sherry opened her big mouth."

"Well, I knew *exactly* what night it was," Yvette countered, smoothly noticing that the noise on Karyn's end, signaled she was preparing breakfast for her husband. The husband she wouldn't have if it wasn't for Yvette's sacrifice. "How can you act as though everything's fine, as though you don't have a worry in the world? For the life of me, I can't understand how you can laugh and dance and make toasts. It pissed me off watching you last night."

There was a brief pause on Karyn's end before she finally said, "It pissed you off because I was having a good time. Why?"

Yvette moved the phone away from her ear and looked into it for a moment. She couldn't believe what she was hearing. "Because we killed someone and you're acting as if nothing ever happened. How can you forget so easily?"

Dishes clanged into the kitchen signaling the woman's irritation. "For God's sake, that was eleven years ago, Yvette!" she shrieked. "We all should have forgotten by now. Why are you bringing it up? First, Sherry's bullshit, now you."

Yvette had passed the point of being angry and had reached the level of livid. Hopping out of bed, she stood in front of the widescreen television, trying her damndest to keep a composure she hadn't felt all week. "I've had to live with it more than you know. But I guess it wouldn't affect you, though. You weren't there to watch him take his last breath. You didn't have to see or hear him beg for his life."

"No, I wasn't there," Karyn whispered as though afraid to say the words out loud. "But that was only because we all agreed that it was best."

"Yeah, and now all of *your* problems are behind you. You walk around like you haven't got a care in the world." Yvette snatched some tissues from off her bedside table, dabbed at the tears. "You finally have your perfect little life. You're married to a good man who would never dream of knocking you upside the head. Of course *you* have nothing to worry about. You're enjoying the benefits of my dirty work. If it weren't for me, you wouldn't be living the perfect little lifestyle you are. Hell, you might not even be living!"

"Hold up Yvette," Karyn shot back, slamming a pot so hard the vibration echoed through the phone. "I've heard enough from you! Listen to how you sound. He was a selfish, abusive, mean bastard who got what he deserved, and you know it. It was eleven years ago. Get over it already!"

Yvette couldn't hold back the malicious laugh that escaped her mouth. "You always were naïve. Who are you trying to fool? It doesn't matter how much time passes. When you kill someone, you *never* forget. It gnaws at your insides, each and every day."

Yvette thought maybe Karyn had hung up, the silence went on for just that long.

"I'm sorry for what you're going through," she said finally. "I didn't even know it was you who…until. I know what you did wasn't easy, and I thank God every day for your act of courage. But you did it so that I could finally be free and happy. You helped me because you wanted me to live and live well. I feel it would be more of a slap in your face and a complete disregard for the sacrifice you, and the others made for me, to walk around feeling sorry for myself and waste away. Mark would win if I did that."

Yvette had no response because everything Karyn said was true. At the same time, though, she didn't think it was fair that Karyn's life had become so perfect when her own life was falling to pieces.

"Are you jealous of me for some reason?"

"Jealous? Of you?" Yvette laughed. "I don't think so."

"I thought the reason you girls helped me was because you're my friends. I thought you wanted me to get out of that situation, alive. I guess I was wrong."

After a pregnant pause where Yvette didn't respond one way on another, Karyn sighed deeply. "Listen Yvette, I'm not going to try and make excuses. I'm not sorry he's dead. I don't feel guilty about what happened to him. He got what he deserved. He tortured me for years, and finally my friends put a stop to it. I'm happier today than I ever imagined, and I'm grateful to have the friends who helped me achieve that. I'll forever be indebted to you all for giving me, and my children, our lives back."

Yvette fell back on her bed, yawning as she listened to Karyn's Academy Award acceptance speech as she then went on and on about how "grateful she was." Which would have been the perfect opportunity for Yvette to usher in her request and the real reason she had called, but unlike Karyn, she was too afraid to say it out loud.

Karyn's next words snapped her back to the present. "But if you think after everything you all have done for me that I wouldn't try to have a good life, then that's too fucking bad!"

A sob escaped Karyn's mouth before she could stop it. She muffled the phone for a moment. "You know, I think you're just ashamed to admit it, but for you to come at me this way, it has to be something, if you're not jealous what is it?"

"No one's jealous of you," Yvette retorted, gripping the Lalique figurine in her hands, nearly snapping it in two. "I have no reason to be jealous of you, or anyone else for that matter. I'm just saying that you've forgotten that you're not the only person who had to deal with things since that night. We all knew Mark was a disgusting, evil man that had no respect for you or any woman. He didn't deserve to live." Yvette locked gazes on the portrait taken on her wedding day, then remember Derrick's threat. "And he's not the only evil man in this world."

Karyn lowered her voice to ask, "What do you mean?"

Yvette swallowed hard, still nervous despite the fact that she had finally managed to turn the conversation around and bring it to the point where she had wanted all along.

"The man in my life doesn't deserve to live."

Karyn gasped, but she recovered quickly, saying, "Yvette, that's a mighty strong statement to make. What's going on over there? Is Derrick beating you?"

"No, it's not like that," she replied evenly, tossing the sheer pink gown into the hamper. "But while I'm home making a good life for him and our children, he's out sleeping around."

"What?" Karyn responded, shocked at this revelation and sounding a bit relieved at the same time. Infidelity wasn't a killing matter. Certainly not in her book. "Derrick's cheating on you? I never thought he was the type. I thought he loved your dirty drawers."

"He did at one time," Yvette said and left it at that. She was not ready to reveal that she was actually the cause of her failing marriage. That there was some truth to the allegations that Derrick had made. This new guy she hooked up with was totally off his radar. If Derrick was handling his business then there would be no need for her to get the loving she desperately craved from somewhere else. She had made sure the men she slept with were married and wouldn't dare talk. All Derrick had were the words of someone who might be suspicious, but no actual proof. She couldn't share this with Karyn, she wouldn't understand and would be judgmental—as if she had a right.

"We used to be so happy," she whispered. "I don't know when it started going wrong or why. Now he hates to be in the same room with me. We're like two airplanes sharing the same airspace, but trying to avoid a major collision. He's been staying somewhere else at least two or three nights a week."

"I'm sorry Yvette," Karyn said softly, her nurturing nature coming through in her tone even though she was still miffed at the previous turn of the conversation. "What happened to make him change?"

"I wish I knew," Yvette lied smoothly. "I've tried to talk to him about it so many times, but he's completely shut me out." Yvette slammed her hand down on her night stand. "I've been a good wife and a good mother to our kids. How dare he treat me like this!"

Karyn took a moment to weigh her next words carefully. "The four of us need to get together. We can talk about what's been going on with you and Derrick and everything you've been thinking about as far as that whole situation with me."

Though the last thing she wanted to do was bring the other women into this, Yvette didn't bother to argue with her.

"We all thought we could go back to living normal lives, but evidently if you and Sherry are feeling some kind of way, that's not the case," Karyn said, her tone laced with sadness. "I truly don't understand why you would be upset with me, and we need to find a way to get you through the pain."

Yvette released a long, sad sigh. Talking was the last thing she wanted to do–she wanted *action.* Real action. And soon! Derrick could change his will in a matter of hours.

"We'll work it all out, and make things right, okay?"

"Sure, we'll talk soon," Yvette said in a deceptively cheery voice, then placed the phone back on the bedroom nightstand, tears welling up in her eyes, more out of frustration than sadness. If Karyn thought she had given Yvette what she wanted by suggesting the girls get together to *talk through her pain,* little did she know that was only the tip of the iceberg.

What she had done for Karyn went way beyond friendship. Now the happy woman could finally make up for all the nightmares Yvette had endured for all of these years. This time, she would have to do the dirty work. This time, Karyn–and only Karyn–would have blood on her hands.

Derrick Glover's blood.

Chapter 8

Sherry fumbled her way into the bathroom, reached into the medicine cabinet and grabbed three Ibuprofens, hoping they would stop the pounding in her head. She lay down in the sleigh bed, looking up at the mirrored ceiling before closing her eyes to shield against the bright sunlight filtering through the blinds. She tried to close out the blaring sounds coming from the cars which seemed to trail each other back to back, with music vibrating from her Southside Chicago apartment on a rotating basis; Ms. Marchert arguing with Ms. Zook about who had left the front gate open, sirens far off signaling that some other crime had been committed or hopefully that the boys in blue would arrive before one could be committed.

The girls still hadn't made it home yet. For the first time Sherry wasn't worried and considered it a much needed break from all their teenage drama that seemed to mirror the adult dramas in her life. She was ready to strangle her youngest daughter Jaynene, who refused to tell Sherry which one of those no-count thugs had the gall to stick his dick into her without wearing a condom. How could she allow that kind of thing to happen? It wasn't like Sherry hadn't drilled it into their heads to protect themselves. Sherry wouldn't lie to herself and believe that KeAnna, her oldest, wasn't sleeping with somebody. But at least she hadn't had the presence of mind to stroll into the house and present Sherry with any evidence.

When Sherry had finished her internship at Cook County Hospital, she had bought a house out in Country Club Hills, not too far from her parents' home because she believed the area would be safer than the crime–riddled area where she'd resided at the time. Then because her daughters weren't doing well in public school, she'd had to spring to put them into a private school which took a substantial chunk of the modest paycheck she held. This drastic change, combined with a series of unforeseen financial setbacks had forced Sherry to file bankruptcy, which cost her the house, and forced her to move back into the city. She barely gave her friends the real reason why. She was too embarrassed to ask for more help. They already had done so much. Her French Provincial furniture looked out of place in the three bedroom apartment along with the other classy furnishings she still had in her possession. Especially since her daughters didn't appreciate what they had when they were living good out in the 'burbs and it was obvious that the friends they snuck in when Sherry wasn't home, didn't have respect for themselves, her daughters, and certainly not her belongings.

The pills finally worked, easing her headache, but also allowing the events of last night to come rushing back with startling clarity.

Oh my God! Poor Karyn. What have I done?

Sherry scrambled through the messy house, tossed a week's worth of laundry off the sofa, trying to find her cordless. She took several deep breaths, trying to calm her nerves, before dialing Karyn's number.

After it rang for what felt like forever before she received a muffled answer of, "Hello?"

Sherry closed her eyes and said a silent prayer that Karyn could forgive her. "Karyn, I think I owe you an apology," she said slowly, carefully.

"You *think*?"

"I had no right to say the things I did."

"You're right about that!" Karyn snapped back, voice suddenly clearer than at first. "Your comments last night have put everyone on edge. How could you do that to *us*? How could you do that to me?"

"I'm sorry I didn't mean to—"

"Yes, I'm sure you are," Karyn spat, not bothering to temper her sarcasm. "How am I supposed to trust you after last night?" She paused, pretending she actually wanted to hear an answer before continuing. "You were drunk last night, and whenever you get more than a single drink in you, your lips get loose and so do your legs! How can I know that you haven't already told one of the brothers you've slept with?"

"No, I promise I haven't said a word to anyone!" Sherry protested, stunned by the insult, and shocked that Karyn, of all people, would be so cruel to her. She knew that she should let it go, especially after what she had said the night before, but she couldn't help adding, "And that's low, Karyn, even for you."

"If you can't handle your liquor, maybe you should think before you start throwing them back. Your carelessness could land us all in jail."

Sherry stumbled over the stacks of magazines and dirty dishes as she navigated her way to the kitchen, grabbed an empty glass, then headed toward her favorite cabinet. She paused in mid–reach, suddenly found the self discipline, at least this time, not to give in to temptation. Lately, it seemed like whenever she needed to calm her nerves, she went straight to the liquor cabinet.

This time though, she took a seat at the kitchen table with an empty glass in her hand. She slid it forward out of her way as though it already held that damning liquid which had done more damage in her life than good. Dropping her head into her hands, disappointment filled her heart at the pain she had caused Karyn, followed by fear of Karyn finding out the secret that she knew nothing about.

"I truly regret asking for your help," Karyn snarled. "I should've done it myself without involving anyone—especially my *friends*. First, your madness now Yvette's bull–"

"Please don't feel that way," Sherry pleaded while silently wondering what the hell Yvette had done. Had she been so out of it that she had missed something else last night?

"How should I feel? Eleven years after the fact and you bring it up the way you did?"

Despite the pills' earlier effectiveness, Sherry's head was beginning to pound all over again, making her consider tossing back two more. Instead, her gaze landed on the open cabinet with every range of spirits a woman could need. Vodka to take the edge off, Zinfandel for entertaining a lover, whiskey for the harder moments in life–like finding out your seventeen–year–old daughter had gotten knocked up by some thug and now there would be three ungrateful mouths to feed instead of the normal two. "I know it wasn't the smartest or nicest thing for me to do. It just gets to me when you act all high and mighty. Sometimes, I can't believe you're the same woman who talked us into killing your husband."

"Excuse me? I did what?" Karyn shrieked. Sherry pulled the phone away, letting the ringing in her ear stop before she put the receiver back. "I know you didn't just say I talked you into killing my husband. That's a bald–faced lie! You volunteered!"

Sherry remembered things more clearly than her denial–stricken friend. *I have to kill him before he kills me. I need you to help me.*

"I didn't mean for you to think I was pointing the finger at you," Sherry said in the most soothing tone she could manage. "I'm dealing with some really tough issues right now."

"Then don't call me until you get them all worked out."

The phone disconnected with a resounding click. Sherry slumped down on the kitchen floor, thinking about the mess she'd created for herself. Every aspect of her life, except for her job, was in shambles. She was sleeping with all the wrong men, and one in particular could bring the world as she knew it to an end. Now she'd just had a fight with her best friend. She couldn't afford to lose a single one of them. Her girlfriends had always been there for her especially when she had been abandoned by her family and the one man she had ever loved.

There were days when life seemed to kick her ass from all directions when she wondered what happened to Raynard Cosey. And she also wondered what would have happened if he hadn't disappeared at such a crucial point in her life. Maybe she would be the doctor she had always wanted to be, instead of the emergency room nurse she had settled on because it made more sense to take care of her family than rack up more debt in student loans. The sacrifices her three friends had made was the only thing that made it possible for her to get this far.

Now she feared that she was on the brink of losing not one, but two people that mattered most to her in life.

* * *

Sherry met Raynard in her junior year of Rich Central High School when they were assigned to work together on a science project for honors Chemistry class. Because they were equally bright, they challenged each other, making everything a competition during the three months of the project. Sometimes, they had heated discussions that ended with neither of them speaking to each other for days. One afternoon, while working on their project in Raynard's bedroom, one such debate flared. Fed up, Sherry grabbed her books and headed toward the door.

Raynard ran past her, blocking her flight down the stairs. "Sherry, please don't leave. I didn't mean to say that." He reached out, surprising her when he wrapped his arms around her.

"You make me so angry I could scream!" she said, trying to remove herself from his embrace, but feeling a slight bit of warmth at his touch. "Everything is always about you and how you're better than me. You're not better than me, you just think diff–"

He placed his lips on hers, ending the debate civilly, sparking the attraction that they had long denied, and paved the way for them to become a much talked about item at school. Through his friendship, she finally had a reprieve from her overbearing parents and their negative drivel of how lazy she was, how fat she was, how ugly she was.

The following year, Sherry and Raynard were still going strong, making plans to attend their senior prom and going off to college. They had planned to marry right after completing college. Since they were already experiencing the major highlights of the last year of school–the luncheon, the class party, the class picnic and school dances, Sherry made the decision that she wanted to experience one more thing with Raynard. She planned on losing her virginity on the most romantic night of the year.

His parents were proud of both of them for excelling in their classes, landing them a spot in the top ten percentile of their class. As a reward for their hard work, his parents rented a limousine, and for the first time in Lakeside history, her parents had allowed her to stay out past their curfew so that they could attend some of the after-parties.

Sherry sought Karyn's advice since she was married at the time, and should have been the most experienced of the four friends. Since she was older than Sherry, she just knew that a married woman would have the art of love making down to a science. Karyn schooled her on what she knew as the ins and outs of having sex, telling her what to expect for her first time, as well as what special things could be added to the night to make it memorable. With Karyn's help, Sherry bought a sexy red and black lingerie that complimented her dark brown skin. She purchased chocolate covered strawberries, and somehow a bottle of champagne found its way into Sherry's bag of goodies. Raynard was responsible for bringing the condoms and getting them a hotel room.

On prom night, the white stretch limousine pulled up to Sherry's house and even the neighbors came out to see the couple dressed in a lilac satin gown and black tuxedo with white shirt and a lilac cummerbund. Even though they were still in high school, all dressed up they looked more like a stunning adult couple attending a gala event. Even Sherry's father, cantankerous old cuss that he was, muttered the first compliment Sherry had ever heard from him.

When they were finally alone in the limo, Raynard turned to Sherry. "Baby, my friend was us able to get a room at the Palmer House Hotel. It's going to be a special night."

"I know! I'm so excited to share this night with you."

And she was. From that special kiss after their biggest argument, they had become real friends, sharing their dreams, their goals and sometimes their fears; helping each other through tough times with their parents—mostly Sherry's. Money from Raynard's job found its way to Sherry in the form of beautiful clothes, jewelry, and other memorable items. They even attended church functions together on Sundays where their belief in God would bring them closer. They could argue for hours about the movies they watched—mostly sci-fi flicks—debating the plot and characters. Trips to the bookstore could turn into half-day journeys. But studying is what really did it for them, the debates still continued, but they had found a way not to allow them to tear them apart. She loved him with all of her being, and how he treated her had not gone unnoticed by other girls at school, and other guys, too—who had wanted to sample what they felt Raynard was getting.

When the moment came for them to make love, both of them were understandably nervous since neither one of them knew what they were doing. The champagne helped them to relax, and together, they fumbled their way through the beautiful, yet comical, experience. Neither one of them would forget it.

Especially nine months later.

When Sherry informed Raynard of the news, she was surprised to learn that unlike some of the other girls who had found themselves in the same situation, he was at first concerned, then happy about this unplanned situation. They had used condoms, so what had happened? She was downright stunned when he suggested they marry right away. Even though they were accepted at different colleges, he promised to take on another job while in school so that he could send her money to help.

She was grateful for all of Raynard's support and encouraging words, but that didn't lessen the fear that consumed her every time she thought about confronting her parents. She waited until she'd been at college for a month before calling. She dialed their phone number at least a dozen times, hanging up before it even got a chance to ring. Finally, she dialed, let it ring, all while chanting, "*I think I can, I know I can, I think I can I know I can,"* in a fruitless attempt to bolster her courage.

When that familiar soft voice answered the other line, Sherry took a deep breath. "Hi Mom. I need to talk to you."

"Baby, is everything okay? What's going on? Is everything all right with your classes?"

"Mom, everything's fine with school, I wasn't calling about school."

"Then what is it, Sherry?"

Taking a deep breath, Sherry forced herself to open her mouth and allow the words to form so she could verbalize the very thing they had warned her against. "Mom, I'm pregnant."

Holding her breath, Sherry waited for her mother to respond. After several moments of silence, Sherry thought the woman might have passed out from shock, but she was quickly proven wrong by a screeching, "What!" followed by the sound of the phone hitting the floor and the echo of her mother screaming, "Henry! Henry come here! This girl's saying she's pregnant."

Footsteps thundered loud enough to reach Sherry's ears, which matched the pounding in her heart.

"Pregnant!" Her dad roared when he came on the line. "No, no, no, no! I know damn well you're not pregnant."

Tears rolled down Sherry's face as she heard her mother trying unsuccessfully to calm the man down. Threats of shooting the bastard and ripping his dick off came between statements of 'no daughter of mine would whore herself,' and her mother's impassioned pleas.

Finally, her mother came back on the line. "Sherry, are you sure? Maybe you just missed this month because you're very stressed about your new living situation and classes, and this just might be your body's way of coping."

"Mom, I took a test. Actually, I've taken five. I'm four months pregnant. It happened the night of prom."

Her mother was crying so hard it took several moments for her to regain her composure before being able to continue. "We've worked so hard to give you everything you need in order to be successful, and this is how you repay us? You go and get pregnant? How stupid can you be? This is the biggest mistake you've ever made. Your life is through! How will you finish school with a baby?"

"Mom, I'll finish school. They have programs for single moms."

With that, there were more gut-wrenching sobs coming through the line.

"We only asked two things of you, and that was to finish college and no babies until you were married. You broke our rules, and we're not going to support your mistakes. You knew what we expected and you knew the consequences of your actions from the start. From this point forward, you're on your own."

This is what Sherry had feared all along. In the following days, true to their word, her parents cut off all financial support, mailed the last of her personal items, sealing the fact that they wanted nothing to do with their only daughter.

With her family no longer there to support her, emotionally or financially, Sherry turned to Raynard for reassurance and love. After several days and attempts of trying to reach him, she discovered his phone service had been disconnected. His parents called her every name in the book and of course, wouldn't give her any information. Then she tried to reach him at the school he was supposed to be attending and found that he had been transferred to another university–but they wouldn't say where. Sherry was hit with the sad truth that the lovable, "responsible" Raynard she knew in high school was long gone.

Alone, depressed, and nearing a breakdown, Sherry called her girls for help, and they, unlike her parents and Raynard, did not let her down. Veronica and Yvette took on work study jobs, sending her the cash they made, while Karyn sent funds from the stash her husband had made available for emergencies. With the grace of God and the kindness of her friends, she was able to stay in school, graduate, and support her daughter, KeAnna. She had overcome the hardest hurdle she'd ever encountered because of the emotional, physical and financial support of her sisters.

All her life, Sherry had been unlucky on the man scale. Raynard had abandoned her when she needed him most and nineteen years later, he still hadn't seen his daughter, nor had Sherry heard from him. And a brief tryst years later, saddled her with another unwanted kid. The man she should've been able to count on at all times—her father—had left her high and dry.

She couldn't remember a time when she'd had good luck with men, and the predicament she found herself in now only solidified the fact that she always picked the wrong ones. She had no idea how to get out of this latest jam without ruining her friendship with the girls. She stared at her reflection in the mirror, hating what she had become. The dark brown eyes were filled with worry. Bags were forming underneath her eyes. She'd dropped a few pounds, and it wasn't because she was trying either.

How could I have stooped so low to allow myself to sleep with Derrick?

She hoped and prayed that Yvette didn't find out. Infidelity was unforgivable, but it was taken to a whole other level when it involved a best friend or sister.

Sherry strolled over to the liquor cabinet, pulling out what remained of the fifth of Crown Royal. She poured herself three fingers worth, when a startling realization hit her—Karyn wasn't far from being wrong when she accused her of having a big mouth. Sherry couldn't remember if she had, or hadn't, let her guard down while sleeping with Derrick.

The glass slipped from her fingers, crashing to the floor. Sherry slumped over and wept.

Chapter 9

Dinner time had come and gone. Derrick still wasn't home. Yvette had been fuming all day, and the mess in her house showed the wake of negligence. Unfortunately, in her frustration, she had sent the maids and her cook away and had tired herself out trying to pick up the slack. She regretted such a hasty act as she was now left to clean the entire place herself—well, at least the areas that mattered to Derrick. He was a stickler for cleanliness, having come from a home where the mother had run a tight ship, and his father had strict rules that kept everyone in line.

She now lay in bed, on Derrick's side, inhaling his scent while wetting his pillow with her silent tears. The anger had passed and the grief had set in, followed by sadness and loneliness. Laying there by herself in their empty home, Yvette started running through the happier memories of her time with Derrick. They came in no particular order, seeming to all bleed together, but soon she stilled her mind and started at the beginning—when she was the one in control.

* * *

Eleven years earlier, Yvette Moss sat patiently in Corpus National Bank's huge boardroom preparing to meet her new co-workers. Two walls of floor to ceiling windows, offered a breath–taking view of the city. Sitting in a luxurious black leather chair at the cherry wood table that extended the length of the expansive room, Yvette took in the Chicago skyline with a range of towering colors and historical architecture. She was impressed with the set–up and knew at that moment she had made the right decision to stay in Chicago instead of taking the leasing agent position in Atlanta.

Glancing down at the Movado watch which had taken nearly an entire paycheck to procure, she noted that she was twenty minutes early which gave her a chance to relax and shake off some of the nervousness.

Derrick Glover, the vice president of Corpus National Bank, along with the rest of his team, walked in just before the clock struck twelve. Yvette had heard plenty about him from the news and from every major magazine, but this was the first time she'd be meeting him in the flesh. Her gaze flickered over his six foot frame that was draped in a black Michael Kors suit, white shirt, and blue paisley tie. Mr. Glover stood at the podium as the others took their seats. Yvette, who was practically falling out of her seat at the handsome sight of him, attempted to look composed in front of her new colleagues.

"Good afternoon."

A range of warm answering replies responded to his deep, commanding voice.

"I've asked you here today to welcome Yvette Moss to the real estate team." His gaze went first to her, then to the group of people gathered in the board room.

"She just completed the two year training program here at CNB and has decided to accept a permanent position within our department as we're expanding to include financing vehicles as well." His gaze lingered on her a moment before asking, "Yvette, would you like to tell us a little bit about yourself?"

She stood, adjusted her clothes, and strolled to the front of the room to stand next to him. "Thank you, Mr. Glover. I'd be happy to." Trying not to look as nervous as she felt, Yvette turned on her most charming smile and faced everyone. "Thank you for having me here today. After obtaining a Master's Degree in finance, I interned with CNB. The training program allowed me the opportunity to learn the products offered by CNB and how each department figures in the profitability of the company." She took a small, calming breath while making eye contact with some of the men in the group who smiled their encouragement. "After completing the training program, I thought I'd be a good fit in this department because you are on the cutting edge of all successful real estate ventures here in Chicago. I, like Mr. Glover," she gestured to him. "Am excited that we're going to take the modules created here to a national level. Again, I would like to thank Mr. Glover for this opportunity."

Mr. Glover stepped toward her, manicured hand extended as he said, "Welcome, Yvette, and please call me Derrick."

"Thank you…Derrick, I'm honored to be here." She let her hand linger just a tad bit longer than deemed workplace appropriate. She noted that he hadn't let go of her hand, either.

As the introduction commenced, the other team members came around, some with a welcoming hand shake and a smile, others with advice and more questions.

"Hi, I'm Jackie, Mr. Glover's assistant. Welcome."

Yvette smiled at the professionally dressed redhead, noting that as Derrick's personal assistant the woman would know a lot about the man himself. Yvette inclined her head and gave a simple, "Thank you," before she continued to introduce herself to the rest of the team, which were from a wide range of ethnic backgrounds. She did note that she was the only African American female. As the introduction moved into a meeting which covered the new direction of the department, reinforcement of current policies, and discussions of items which needed to be addressed, Yvette still hadn't been able to take her mind or eyes off Derrick. Whenever she could, without being caught by anyone, she'd steal a glance in his direction, taking in the total package. His ivory skin mirrored her own. She could tell that under his suit, he was physically fit with a muscular frame. His position as vice president, along with the fact that he was constantly being recognized for innovative, creative financial ideas and programs made it obvious to her that he was highly intelligent. He was just her type of man, and she wanted him – no matter what it would take.

That first meeting in the boardroom took place only days and several sleepless nights after Mark's murder. Focusing her energy on winning Derrick over would be the perfect antidote to taking her mind off that dreadful night. She still couldn't believe she had actually gone through with it, or that none of them had been suspects. All that mattered was that Karyn and her children were alive and safe.

Yvette formulated another game plan, this time with far less deadly consequences and a more pleasing outcome. She set out to learn everything there was to know about Derrick Glover, things that weren't mentioned in Forbes, GQ, Newsweek and the local magazines.

During her break one afternoon, Yvette noticed Jackie sitting in the employee's lounge. She did a quick sweep of the area and found that they were alone, at least for the moment. Pasting on another one of her winning smiles, Yvette approached the woman whose wrinkled face was set in an intense expression. "Hi Jackie, how are you today?"

Jackie looked up from the book she was reading. "I'm fine, how are you?"

Yvette crossed the room, making herself comfortable in the lounger next to Jackie. "I'm doing well. It's the first week, so I'm still trying to keep track of names and faces. I never realized this place was so huge."

Jackie grinned, then focused her attention to the book she held. Yvette tapped the hardcover and said, "I love Stephen King. I've read all of his work."

"Me too!" Jackie said in an excited rush, before putting the book aside and launching into a diatribe about all of her favorite works by their mutually adored author. From there, Yvette learned that Jackie Shoemocker was nearing her late fifties, was twice divorced, childless, loved to read, knit and sew and made handmade baby design quilts as a hobby. She was tall and slender and as the week had shown, always dressed in professional attire. Her silky, curly red hair was pinned up in a bun, accenting blue eyes that were as clear as a sunny day in Chicago. She was a beautiful woman and if she removed the owl–rimmed glasses and let her hair down, she would look much younger than she actually was.

"So, Jackie," Yvette said, leaning back a little, "How long have you been working for Derrick?"

"Five years," she replied beaming as though the man was a saint. "When he first started here at the company, he was about twenty–five or so, he was so passionate about this business. He spent countless hours working to prove how valuable he was and in that short five year span, his career has skyrocketed!" Then she leaned forward as though someone else was listening in. "And so did my salary."

"No doubt," Yvette said with a sly smile.

"He's extremely dedicated, and pleasant to work for, unlike some of the other arrogant assholes around here." She smiled, then took a sip from a tumbler which read, *What Happens in Vegas Stays in Vegas.* "He is the best boss ever. You'll love working with him."

"I bet I will," Yvette said, while thinking, especially if you help me land the man I want.

"He recently became engaged to Lisa Pickett, an administrative assistant who works in the corporate banking department. You'll be working close to him. You two should meet each other. Come on, I'll introduce you," she said, standing and moving toward the elevator.

On their elevator ride to the fourth floor, Yvette learned that at the age of thirty, Derrick had made quite a name for himself. He drove a Jaguar, owned several buildings and was very much into buying property that had historical significance. His peers at CNB called him "The Professor" because of his accomplishments and the way he had excelled all through life. Jackie told Yvette that Derrick's parents had pushed him to excel to the highest, and he had exceeded their expectations by completing the high school he attended in Memphis, Tennessee at the young age of sixteen, going on to attend Yale University where he received his undergraduate degree and his Master's degree in Economics, graduating magna cum laude.

By the end of the elevator ride and the walk to the far northeast corner of the building, it was clear to Yvette that, just as she thought, the man had a lot going for him. There was only one obstacle standing in her way: his fiancée.

Jackie swiped the key card to get past the security doors and led Yvette to the semi–circle maze of cubicles that connected to Lisa's desk. "Lisa, this is Yvette, the newest member of the real estate team. She'll be working closely with Derrick over the next six months."

Lisa, an ivory skinned beauty, with hazel eyes, greeted Yvette with a hand shake and simple smile which brightened her cute, round face and cupid bow lips that were very much like Yvette's. Though ethnic backgrounds and eye colors differed, their looks and build were so similar that they could actually be sisters! Only Yvette had a bit of an edge with more curves in all the right places, where Lisa was a little lacking on that score. "Hello Yvette," she said, giving the newcomer a thorough once over. "Welcome to CNB. It's a pleasure to meet you."

"Thank you for such a warm welcome," Yvette replied, trying to keep her tone light and friendly, noting the edge in the woman's voice and the fact that Lisa was checking her out so thoroughly Yvette had to wonder if the petite woman was sizing her up for something more than competition. "Hopefully we can do lunch sometime."

"I would love that."

Lisa's mild–mannered spirit matched her physical attributes perfectly. After only few minutes of short conversation with the woman, Yvette realized she had no backbone. At any other time, Yvette might have liked Lisa–hell, she might have even wanted to be her friend. But she wanted something Lisa already had and that trumped any desire for a friendship.

That night, long after everyone had left, Yvette knocked at Derrick's door and waited for him to invite her in. Moments passed before he finally looked up from the papers scattered all over his desk. "Oh, hello Yvette. I thought I was the only one still here" He gestured her to move forward. "Please, come in."

"Thank you," she replied, sweeping into the office before perching on a leather chair across from his desk. "I know I'm new to your department, but I'm eager to be challenged. I wanted you to know that I'm available to take on special projects."

"That's wonderful to hear, but special projects normally are done in what's considered spare time and require many late nights." His eyebrow lifted. "Won't your *husband* be expecting you for dinners?"

Yvette smiled, knowing that he already knew she wasn't married. "The only one who'll be expecting me for dinner is Tucker." At his furrowed brow, she added, "my cat."

His grin faltered a little as he focused on the papers in front of him, then peered at her. "Well, I love when people take the initiative." He leaned back in the sliver mesh chair, his gaze narrowed on her as though sizing her up for a good meal. "Matter of fact, I'm working on something right now. Maybe you'd like to be involved?"

"Thank you, Mr. Glover. I'd be honored," she said, giving him the sexiest smile she could manage as she crossed one leg over the other, exposing a nice little length of thigh.

"There's a catch, though," he replied with a quick flash at her thighs then back to her face. "You'll definitely need to work late hours until it's completed. We're on a deadline."

"That's not a problem. Just tell me what you need me to do." The thought of spending more time with him filled her with anticipation.

After that night, Yvette began the gradual transformation from conservative business suits to those that were more provocative. Within a week, skirts were tightly fitted around her hips and round, shapely butt. Perfume went from innocent florals to musky jasmines and sandalwoods. Her hair went from love knots and buns, to layering around her shoulders.

From time to time, she would catch him checking her out through her peripheral vision. A few months after she began working on that special project, one that, under her suggestion, included courting a new range of homeowners, winning them over from aggressive second rate lenders; then moving them into a program that would provide debt management classes with realistic timelines. This allowed CNB to refinance them with a lower interest rate than they had currently, while at the same time encouraging them to save the additional income for emergency and household repairs—which are the main reasons many people default on their mortgages; Derrick came to her saying, "Yvette, I'm amazed at your dedication and work ethic.

You are a Godsend and will definitely go far in this company. With your intelligence, I don't worry about you doing well. There aren't too many Black women who make it as vice presidents in this industry. I want you to make it. I'll teach you everything I know."

* * *

Yvette had become so obsessed with getting Derrick that it had become like a second job. Lisa and Yvette had become extremely close over the next several months, eating lunch together when their schedules would permit. Yvette confided in Lisa, telling her intimate details about a fake love life which made Lisa feel comfortable sharing information about Derrick.

She would call Sherry, sometimes giving her the latest details on the "Derrick case" as they had come to call it. She couldn't share any of what was going on with Veronica who was now in Paris working for Christian Lacroix on their haute courture line, or Miss Righteous, also known as Karyn, who would surely have some not–so–nice words for Yvette on her current plans to land a man. After one particularly juicy lunch, she couldn't wait to get home and relay everything to the one girlfriend who wasn't too busy and didn't have a right to judge.

"Hello?" Sherry answered in a haggard voice.

"Wake up girl. It's Yvette. I found out some pretty interesting things about Derrick today."

Sherry didn't bother to hide her weary sigh. "Girl, I'm tired. I worked a double yesterday."

"Oh, you don't want to miss this juicy update. You'll *never* believe what Lisa told me today."

Sherry sighed again. "Okay, let me splash some water on my face. I'll be right back." She dropped the phone with a loud thunk, and Yvette almost believed the woman had hung up on her. Yvette thrummed her fingers across her bare stomach as she lay back on her bed, waiting for Sherry to return.

"All right. I want to hear everything."

"Well, I know he's highly sexed and can go for hours," she said with a giddy laugh. "Thanks to his loose-lipped girlfriend, I now know what he likes in bed, and how he likes it, and I can't wait to get my chance to lay it on him."

"You know, as much as I love these stories," Sherry began in a voice that made Yvette bristle. "I think you might be taking this too far. You said she's a nice girl and she trusts you enough to tell you these things, and all you're going to do is use it against her." Silence came over the phone again and Yvette could have scorned she heard a male voice in the background. "Yvette, you better think twice about what you're doing. You're going to blow a great career over a man. I'm telling you from experience, it's not worth it. Focus on the money, woman, then land your own man."

"I want *this* man."

"There are plenty of men out there. Ask me how I know. Somebody out there is right for you.

"You don't know what he does to me." Yvette hopped up from the bed and began scrambling through the dresser for a night gown. "I won't be happy until I have him. He's rich, he's successful and he's—"

"About to marry somebody else," Sherry supplied in a dry tone.

"Not if I can help it."

* * *

Several weeks later, Yvette was packing her things to go home after another late night at the office, when Derrick walked into her office. "Only six months, and as I predicted, you've proven yourself to be a major asset. You're ready to put your own team in place to help you with all of the new accounts we're bringing in." He handed her a stack of folders. "I've set–up appointments for you to accompany me to the East coast so you can present the program to our executives out there. You'll launch our campaign in New York and oversee the project from Chicago."

"Really?" She clasped her hands together as excitement rushed through her. "Thank you so much Derrick! I'm grateful for this opportunity."

"It'll mean more work, and definitely more travel, but I think you've proven that you don't mind that at all." He turned to walk out, saying. "We'll leave early Wednesday morning for New York."

After a day full of back to back meetings in New York, Derrick and Yvette celebrated with dinner at Maxwell's Bar & Restaurant, followed by a few drinks in the hotel's private lounge. As the night went on, the conversation shifted from business to personal.

"So Yvette," Derrick said over the rim of his glass, "Tell me what makes you tick."

She looked over at him and smiled, responding only with a questioning lift of her eyebrow.

"You're a beautiful woman, and so well put together, but I haven't seen you with a man. I'm sure men gravitate to you."

"Well of course, I'm irresistible, don't you know?" she said, displaying an air of arrogance, as she placed a hand over her slightly exposed cleavage.

To her statement he let out a little laugh, but his gaze traveled the length of her body, lingering on the creamy thighs that always seemed to gain his attention. Definitely a leg man.

"I have yet to meet Mister Right."

"Maybe you have, but you just haven't given him the time of day," he answered in a voice that was filled with husky promise.

"Derrick, trust me, I would *know* if Mr. Right came along." She shifted in her chair, crossing one leg over the other. "And if he did, I certainly wouldn't let him get away."

"Yvette, be honest. You're a workaholic," he said, gesturing to the barmaid for another gin and tonic. "You've dedicated your whole life to your career. Nothing else matters to you."

She couldn't very well correct him and say that *he* mattered to her; that would give everything away. And the fact that he was even asking about her status and her personal life said plenty. "I'm only twenty-six years old. I have plenty of time to find my soul mate." Yvette gestured the length of his suit to his polished shoes, an outward sign of his success. "And look who's talking, vice president of a major national bank at thirty."

He laughed at her verbal and physical jab. "That's why I know what I'm talking about. But even with all the work and late nights, I still managed to carve out a little time to find my soul mate."

"Yes, Lisa Pickett," she said with a giggle, then watched him over the rim of her glass as she took a sip of her cosmo. "She is a *sweet* girl."

"Why the laughter?"

Yvette shrugged, pursed her lips a little as she looked at him. "If you don't mind me saying..."

He leaned forward, giving her his complete attention.

"Personally, I think Lisa's too meek for a *strong* man like you," she said, gauging his puzzled expression. "Please don't take this the wrong way, but she has no fire, no depth, and even though she handles the *wife, the eye candy* role pretty well, you will eventually grow tired of that." Yvette's voice went to a sultry level that made his eyes flash with desire. "You need a woman who can challenge you, not only in the bedroom, but in the boardroom as well. A woman who can come up with the Plan B and C, to your Plan A to Z. Who can match you strength for strength, who can share your vision and can actually help bring it to light."

"What do you mean?" Derrick replied gripping his glass tightly before releasing it to set it on the table between them. "Lisa's a great woman. I love her, and we can leave it at that." He took a deep, cleansing breath, but his eyes flashed with anger. "Once you find your strong man, then you can holla back at me."

Yvette smiled at him, lifting her glass in a mock salute. *Am I hearing clearly? Did the vice president of CNB really say holla back?* Under all that polished exterior the brother might actually have some street, too? Now that was one hell of a sexy thought.

"I apologize. I didn't realize that answering your question as honestly as I could would offend you." She placed her empty martini glass on the table in front of her, then stood. "Let's call it a night."

He reached out, grabbed her arm. "You didn't offend me."

Yvette looked down at where their skin connected, then focused her gaze on him. Derrick instantly removed his hand, and watched as she walked away and didn't look back.

"Yvette, wait!" He paid the tab and caught up to her, trailing her to her suite.

Despite her protests that a regular room would suit her just fine, he insisted on her having a suite like his. He threw her off guard by pulling her into a hug, causing her panties to moisten. "Goodnight Yvette," he whispered. "It's been great getting to know you a little better."

"Goodnight, Derrick," she answered, lowering her lashes to cover the desire that was sure to present itself now that he was mere inches from her. "I promise I'll do my best to make you proud."

Once inside the privacy of her room, Yvette went to the bar and poured a glass of chardonnay. She then perched to sit on the edge of her bed, contemplating if she should make her move. Like Sherry had said, it could be the end to a promising career, or it could be the last opportunity to tell him how she felt before they got back to Chicago and he was under the influence of his sweet little girlfriend. She would be kicking herself if things turned disastrous. She could also be cursing herself if she didn't try. Their wedding was only ten months away.

Three glasses of chardonnay, which trailed the two cosmos she'd had after dinner was all the liquid courage she needed. Yvette slipped into a sexy red gown, covered it with a white cotton hotel robe, and made her way to his room.

She was still knocking on his door when it opened quickly, as if he had been waiting for her. Before he could say a word, she dropped the robe to the ground, watched the flicker of need flash within his dark brown eyes before she planted a passionate kiss on his thick lips. Pulling away, his face was flushed with a mixture of emotions – shock, pleasure, then guilt. His lips set in a thin, hard line, but his tongue moistened his lips as though ready for dessert.

Yvette pulled herself close, molding to his body and felt his erection spring to life which caused her own desire to break loose, untamed and undeniable. The full extent of his hardened member pressed toward the apex of her thighs. He moved back into the room, taking her with him. Yvette leaned up on her toes and covered his lips with her own using her tongue to find every sensitive spot in his mouth.

Inching him away from the door, she used her bare foot to close it all the way, then pressed him backward until he stood at the foot of the bed. Her fingernails became claws as she ripped away his shirt. "Damn you look good," he whispered, then lowered to take a nipple between his lips. He groaned and then groaned again. She pulled away, unzipped his pants, slipped them off in one fluid motion. He could only stare down at her as she went to work, making her way down to take the full length of him in her mouth, sucking him as if her very life depended on it. She had taken total control and he couldn't resist as his body thrust upward into her mouth, straining for release. She straddled him, positioning the hard length of him at her moist center. She rode him, teased him, tortured him, until he gripped her hips and screamed her name, thrusting into her until that much needed release ended with jets of semen spilling into her womb.

She looked down at him, holding him inside, keeping every ounce of his seed within her.

He hardened again, and this time he flipped her under him, and thrust into her heat until she cried out with pleasure. This time she was the one screaming as the hard length of him demanded entrance into the answering sheath of heat to welcome him. Their kisses were almost punishing in their intensity.

Spent and sated, they slept in each other's arms as if it was the right thing to do.

The feeling of triumph rushed through her as she knew then that her mission had been more than accomplished. Derrick would be hers whether he wanted to be or not.

* * *

The next morning, Yvette freshened up, called room service, and had breakfast waiting for him when he woke. From the silence that enveloped the room the moment he opened his eyes and the horror-stricken expression that followed, she knew she had to take control of the situation. She went to him, placed the most delicate kiss on his lips, reassuring him that, "Derrick, this will be our little secret. I promise I'll never tell anyone."

Derrick sat up in the bed, pulled the covers off his naked body and tried to focus his vision. "You know I'm engaged." He ran a hand over his mussed, short–cropped hair. "I didn't intend for this to happen. I love Lisa very much, and I should never…" He shook his head, a sad movement which matched his serious tone. "This was a mistake and I apologize, but we can't see each other like this, ever again."

Yvette summoned the tears that wasn't as hard of a stretch as she had imagined. His words had hurt a little, but they didn't matter. She caressed Derrick's hand. "I tried to ignore the feelings I have for you but I just couldn't. Please forgive me. It's not your fault. I'd never want to come between you and Lisa. But I had to do this for me." She looked away from him, taking in the contrast of bright sunlight filtering through the draperies, which was not at all like what was happening on this side of the room. "I see the way you look at me sometimes and I just … I thought you wanted me, too."

Derrick pulled Yvette to him and gave her an apologetic hug. "I'm so sorry, Yvette."

She gazed in his eyes, "Yes, I'm sure you are."

Yvette strolled to the door, looking back at him one last time, wondering at the gaze fixated on his face. Was he pained by what he had done, or was he regretting watching her walk out that door?

He was sorry? Derrick Glover had no fucking idea!

Chapter 10

Karyn Johnson opened her eyes, biting back a string of curses. Instead, she tried, and failed, to calm herself down so that she could reign in the thoughts racing through her mind. Sherry and Yvette could destroy her life!!

Now that she had finally found happiness in all aspects of her life, especially her children who were doing well, she wasn't going to allow anything to interfere with that. They were now enjoying adulthood and living normal healthy lives. Thanks to church and counseling the traumatic experiences they encountered by their father was behind them. Mary was able to overcome being withdrawn and was able to finish College, becoming a school teacher and now happily married with one child. Mark Jr. had finally out grown his behavioral problems he experienced during high school and is now working on his doctorate.

She cupped her hands over her eyes, gaze narrowed, trying to shield them from the sunlight beaming through the bedroom window. A quick glance at the clock on the nightstand confirmed that cleaning the house before meeting her husband, Carl, at the gym was out of the question. With the few pounds she had packed on recently, she couldn't afford to miss her workout, but she also couldn't move a muscle, even if she wanted.

Their forty-five minute aerobic workout, fifteen minute sauna, and thirty minute swim wasn't going to be enough to rid her mind of last night's events. Carl was a stickler when it came to their health, with fitness at the top of his list, right above diet, and routine check-ups with their doctor. He kept Karyn focused on being her best, looking her best, and reaching her full potential – a far cry from Mark who had wanted nothing more than for her to cater to his every need. Unlike Carl, who always wanted her input before making decisions that affected their lives, Mark never allowed Karyn to make a single decision regarding her life, let alone their family life. The man even controlled things as mundane as making out the grocery list. Why did it have to come down to taking his life in order for her to live? Why hadn't she seen his cruel, controlling nature before it was too late?

* * *

Karyn was only seventeen, close to finishing high school, when Mark James came into the picture. She was leaving the library, carrying an armful of books that would help her prepare for college entry exams and following that, the life of a business woman, when the books came spilling out of her arms. She didn't know where he had come from, but all of a sudden he was beside her, reaching down and gathering the textbooks. She looked up from a kneeling position, and all she could see was pearly white teeth and the most inviting eyes ever. In a deep, husky voice Mark said with a light laugh, "Hello Ms. Lady, I couldn't help but notice you coming out of the library looking so beautiful and studious."

To this she said nothing, but she could feel the flush of heat traveling up her face as she stood, collecting the last of her things.

"Those big brown eyes of yours caught my attention. Would you like to go and have a bite to eat with me?"

Karyn looked at the handsome man in his gray business suit with a burgundy leather briefcase in his hand, and a professional demeanor and thought, *Wow! He wants to go out with me? He is gorgeous! And so different from those stupid old high school boys.* They were no match for her – a straight A student, class president, and captain of the debate team—a young lady who was called most likely to succeed. She didn't even bother to waste her time with dating any of her classmates. Looking at the tall, handsome stranger she knew he was from a totally different world than her God-fearing, church-going, middle class parents. He didn't look much older than her, but she knew he had to be, dressed like that and acting so polite.

"A bite to eat?" She shook her head. "Thank you, but my parents have taught me to be leery of strangers."

Even if he had wanted to persist, Mark was too smooth for that. "Well, can I call you sometime? There shouldn't be anything wrong with that, right? It's just talk."

Karyn hesitated a moment before writing her number on a sheet of paper and placing it in his hand before walking away.

After that day, her life changed forever. She had a handsome businessman calling her every day, wanting to know everything about her while giving her one compliment after another. They talked about anything and everything.

"Karyn, you are the most beautiful woman I've ever met," he said. "And you're so mature for your age. I know you have boys chasing you."

She blushed at the compliment and felt empowered that he had called her a woman.

"I must say, you're a bright woman, and a woman like you deserves the world, and I'd like to give you the world."

"Mark, you know I'll be leaving for college in a year," she answered. "A relationship would be useless. Let's just be friends."

"Darling, we'll always be friends first, but I want more than a friendship. I want you to be my woman. If you decide to go to college, I'll visit whenever I can. I can even help you with the cost. Didn't you say your parents were a little strapped?"

She was thrilled at his offer. Her parents, who were struggling under the weight of family obligations which included nursing home and hospital bills for her grandmother, liked the sound of him too. Only her father was concerned because of the ten year age difference.

"You are so understanding and supportive," Karyn told Mark.

"Like I said baby, I want to give you the world. Let me *show* you. Accept my invitation to dinner."

She thought about it for a moment. He had showered her with gifts – jewelry that he'd surprise her with before she arrived at school and flowers left on the car for her to find after she got out of her last class. He called her all the time and seemed genuinely interested in her.

"How can I say no to you, Mr. James."

"How many times do I have to keep saying, it's just Mark. No more of that Mister James crap."

"All right, Mark it is."

Mark was compassionate and attentive to her every word. What she didn't know was that he stored everything he learned about her for future use. He seemed to admire her strong will and ambitions for life, and he loved the fact that she knew exactly what she wanted.

"I was just like you," he said, one day when they were at the local ice cream store down the street from her school. "I was planning to go to college, but then my mom died and I had to go to work to support my brothers and sisters."

"Where was your dad?"

Mark shrugged, sampling a little of the chocolate milk shake. "I never knew my father."

"What type of work do you do?" She asked, letting her gaze travel to the black leather briefcase he carried that day. "You look like some big time executive from the city."

Mark took a moment, taking in the white blouse tucked into a black A–line skirt, modest heels that gave her a little height; the light sprinkling of make–up over her pretty face. "You're just about right, I'm a sales representative for a marketing firm. I make a pretty good buck for myself."

Karyn questioned him about the women he had been with and soon realized, although he didn't say it outright, that Mark James was used to a woman instantly melting in his arms and falling for his charm. But there was no way she was going to let him, or any man get into her pants right away. Her mom and her mom's girlfriends had taught her well. She couldn't let some man, and a handsome, obviously wealthy one, come into her life and veer her off course from achieving the college education that was a stepping stone to any career she would choose.

Mark knew he was on to what she liked and what she desired so he stepped up his game, coming to her house with gifts for her parents. He made promises to her and to her father that if she married him he would take care of her and she would go to college and they wouldn't have to pay a dime. Her parent's objections were waning. He pursued her for months until, finally, they were married, and soon after that all her dreams and aspirations for college and a career were nothing more than a distant memory. Her aunts may have taught her well, but evidently, with everything Mark James had promised, she didn't learn the lesson.

* * *

Karyn shook off the memories of Mark James a lot easier than she had shaken off current fear. Sherry and Yvette were on some bullshit!

Carl hadn't tried to call yet and by now it was late enough for him to worry if she'd decided to slack off. She closed her eyes, envisioning placing one foot, then the other on the floor. Unfortunately, after ten minutes, it had only happened in her mind.

Her earlier heated conversations with Sherry and Yvette had forced her to remain in bed as a massive migraine flared. She refused to believe that after all these years, the memories of her former husband were back to haunt her.

The shrill ring of the phone forced her head to turn too quickly, causing the room to swim in and out of focus. Now she was regretting that she hadn't pulled the phone off the hook. She checked the display. What in the world did Veronica have to talk about?

Karyn whispered, "Hello?"

Veronica, highly agitated since her first attempts had been left unanswered, barked into the phone, "Why aren't you answering your phone? I've called you five times this morning."

Karyn managed to slip out of bed and make her way to the kitchen in search of some caffeine. "I've heard enough already. I spoke to the other girls and I'm pissed off. Frankly, I don't want to talk to you or anybody else right now."

"Well you have to understand how everyone is feeling."

Karyn fumbled through the kitchen cabinet to find something to use as a coffee pot since Carl refused to have one in the house. Caffeine was a no–no. "If they are feeling so bad, why hasn't anyone brought it up before?" She walked to the sink, shoved the boiler under the running water, then placed it on the stove to boil. She reached under the bags of green tea and pulled out the private stash of coffee pods hidden at the bottom. "Eleven years have gone by and they've been able to cope all this time, and then all of a sudden, it's difficult for them. Isn't that strange? That's why I'm having a hard time wrapping my head around this."

"I see your point," Veronica said smoothly. "I guess it's a little strange from your point of view. But are you thinking about how it's been for them?"

As Karyn waited for the water to come to a boil, she relayed her conversations with Sherry and Yvette to Veronica. "And now I'm worried that Sherry, with her big mouth, might've said something to someone else. She can't hold her liquor to save her life!"

"Yes, she has been drinking a lot more lately," Veronica agreed. "But do you really think she would just blurt something out like that in front of just anyone?"

"At this point, I'm not sure what she would do." Karyn poured the water into the cup. "She did last night in front of a total stranger."

"Why would she do such a thing? I just don't get it."

"When you talked to her, did she say anything to you about why she did it?"

"All she could say was that she was 'going through some issues right now'."

"Issues?"

"Yes, issues!" Karyn took a deep breath and rolled her eyes heavenward, almost burning her tongue on the forbidden sip of coffee. "And because she's going through *issues*, apparently she's going to take it out on me. How is that a true friend?"

"Do you know what she's dealing with?"

"I didn't give her a chance." Karyn took a quick peek at the clock near the kitchen entrance.

"You know, Yvette's been uptight for a while, too," Veronica added. "And for some reason she's angry with you, too. She even made a comment about making a move on Carl last night. That was so not cool."

"What?" Karyn shrieked, nearly spilling the hot brew on her hand. Then she let out a bitter laugh as she grabbed up a paper towel to clean up the mess on the table. "It's probably because her husband's cheating on her."

"Are you serious?" Veronica whispered, as though someone were listening in on the conversation. "Derrick's cheating on Yvette?"

"She told me today."

"That bastard!" Veronica said. "To be honest, I'm really worried about the twins. If I didn't know her, I'd swear that she didn't have any children at all. She never says anything about them. And they're always gone. Always at someone else's house. We need to get to the bottom of this."

"I need to cool off first. I'm hurt that they would do this to me. They should think more about how this could affect my life!"

"Karyn, do you hear yourself? How it affects *your* life? We don't have time for you to get over your hurt and pain. This could affect *all* of us," Veronica snapped, then added, "*We* have a situation on *our* hands. So if you need to cool off, do it quick, or we *all* may end up in jail. And I've got too much going on for me to end up serving time for getting caught up in your mess. I told you not to marry him—that something was off about him. You married him anyway."

"Hold up Veronica." Karyn said, lowering her voice to a more soothing tone. "We're *not* going to jail. What we need is to support each other."

"Right." Veronica hung up without saying anything more.

Karyn trudged up the stairs and fell back into bed. Focusing on this new development and Veronica's contention that it was about we, not just Karyn alone, she pulled the pillow over her head, but sleep still eluded her. So did peace of mind. Sherry's stupidity, in her drunken stupor, had caused that uncontrollable outburst, which had, in one night, unearthed all of the pain they had carried around from the secret they had tried so hard to protect.

Karyn looked at the clock again. If she didn't get moving soon, she wouldn't make it to the gym at all. Then she'd have something else to answer for.

Chapter 11

Karyn ignored the second set of calls from Sherry and then one from Yvette, grabbed her bag and rushed out of the door. She hopped in her pearl colored Lexus, a gift that Carl surprised her with for her last birthday, and headed down the block. Luckily, the gym was close to their home and it only took her a few minutes to get there. It was a beautiful day for March and people were certainly taking advantage of it. Children were playing in the park. Everywhere she looked people were riding their bikes, chatting with their neighbors or walking their dogs. She pulled into the parking lot, lucking out with a spot near the door, and ran through the entrance.

As soon as their eyes met, Carl's stride broke and he hurried toward Karyn. "Honey, there you are! I was about to send a search party out for you." He planted a kiss on her lips, eliciting the cheers of his friends working out on the machines nearby.

"Get a life," Carl shot back, which only elicited more jeers, as someone shot back, "Get a room!" He took Karyn's hand and lead her away from the area.

"Sorry I'm late, baby. The phone kept ringing. First Yvette, then Sherry and then Veronica. I ended one conversation, and the phone would ring again."

Carl rolled his eyes heavenward but smiled.

She loved the fact that she could be honest with her husband about everything. Well mostly everything. Eleven years ago, Mark would've knocked her into next week for being late, especially because of her "trifling" girlfriends.

"You had to catch up with them?" Carl asked, his dark brown gaze focused on her. "But weren't you with them last night? What were you doing, if that wasn't 'catching up?'"

Karyn's breath hitched a little.

Carl, observant as always, pulled back to look at her. "Is everything okay? You're not your usual self."

"Just my girlfriends and their drama," she replied, waving him off as she pulled out of his arms and hurried to the treadmill, hoping Carl wouldn't press the issue. "You know how it is."

He trailed her across the moss green carpeting, but didn't say anything more. Mark could always tell when she was lying. Carl didn't have that particular gift. He didn't have to, though. Karyn was always, well, almost always, honest with him. Except about the one thing she could never talk about with anyone.

Carl stepped onto the machine next to her.

"I'm ready to get my work out on!" she said in a falsely cheery voice. "I really need it today."

Next to him was a slim, athletic blonde, whose pace was almost impossible to match. The woman's features were stern, determined, and perspiration covered her face. The area smelled as if a room full of football players had just finished a four quarter game.

"Wow, is it safe?" he whispered to Karyn, despite the woman's obvious inability to hear them over the headphones firmly placed in her ears.

"Looks like she's preparing for the Olympics."

Carl grimaced, switching to the machine on Karyn's opposite side. "Smells like she should be making a mad dash to the showers."

They fell into a comfortable pace. In the mirror in front of her, Karyn gazed at her husband's toned physique and she couldn't help but thank God that she had been blessed with someone as wonderful as Carl. Not only was he concerned with her physical well–being, but he cared about her mentally, emotionally, and spiritually. And she had to straighten out her friends so they couldn't mess up her good thing. She never wanted to lose him.

After completing a thirty minute cardio workout on the treadmill, they headed to the aerobic class which was already in progress. The instructor had just finished the warm–up, and the music switched to a fast–paced number that got the blood pumping. The room was nearly full, but the couple managed to squeeze their way into a spot in the corner.

"One, two, three, four, five, six!" The male instructor yelled to the room. "Eight sets of jumping jacks for an eight count! Let's go class!"

The class groaned in protest.

"I can't hear you!"

With a quick glance in the mirror, Karyn could see that Carl kept the pace, but he also kept glancing at her. Karyn pretended to be totally focused on the workout.

"Let's go, people!"

The response to the instructor's command was immediate in the shift of bodies that ranged from overweight to physically fit.

She could no longer avoid the inevitable, and was forced to look in Carl's direction. Their gazes locked in the mirrors. The worried furrow of his brow, the grim set of his sensually curved lips, spoke volumes on the fact that he knew something was wrong. He mouthed the words, "I love you," between movements and her heart sank with guilt.

Lately, whenever they talked, he had told her that he couldn't put his finger on it, but he felt as if she was holding something back. Even though they were blissfully happy and madly in love, he felt like no matter what he did, it was never enough. She tried to reassure him, but it didn't ease his doubts. All he could do was tell her that he loved her and prayed that she would one day feel comfortable and safe enough to open up to him completely. But until that day, he'd have to come to grips with the fact that she still hadn't let her guard down.

That certainly didn't bode well with her. She knew he was right. How much longer could she keep it together? Especially if loose lips kept running her damn mouth and Ms. Moneybags felt that Karyn owed her something, and fashion queen thought that she was being selfish.

"Baby, that was the best workout ever," she managed to say when the instructor finished the cool down period. "I think I lost about twenty pounds today."

"I think the lady exaggerates," he said with a smile and kiss to her temple. "Let's meet in the sauna in ten."

"Last one in does the laundry."

He dashed off, his laughter trailing in his wake.

Eight minutes later, Carl strolled into the sauna to find Karyn already stretched out with a towel draped over her face. Conversation with him would prove to be impossible as she couldn't get the conversations she'd had earlier with her girlfriends out of her head.

Silently, she prayed that Carl would leave her to her own thoughts to mull things over. *God, you know I've begged and pleaded for forgiveness for what I've done. Why am I still being haunted by this? I didn't have a choice! What do you want from me? After all these years, my girlfriends are breaking down. I can see it in their eyes. Hear it in their voice. They resent the life I've created. Please, God, don't let all this be taken from me. I'm finally happy. Don't I deserve to be happy? Especially after all those horrible things he did to me?*

Lord, I realize now that regardless of how bad a situation may be it's never good to take matters into my own hands or to involve friends in my mess. I was wrong to ask such a thing of my friends. But to have people who love you so much they will kill to protect your safety is truly a blessing and unheard of. I thought you hadn't heard my prayers. I thought you had forgotten about me.

* * *

Two months after her marriage to Mark, Karyn learned she was pregnant. That, coupled with his seeming forgetfulness in regards to his promises, ended any ideas of her going off to college, or even attending one near home. If she hadn't known any better, she would have thought that Mark had diligently worked to ensure that she got knocked up–fast. The birth control hadn't kicked in all the way. Though she loved him, she was weary of how much sex he demanded of her on a daily basis.

Once he learned that she was carrying his child, he became so overprotective, it was frightening. He didn't want her lifting a finger or anything else, and immediately demanded that all of her efforts were to rest and prepare for the baby. No friends, no visits to her parents. That bit of news did not sit well with her, but he was her husband. She could always go back to school once the baby was walking. Although, he didn't say much about that fact when she brought it up. Actually he never said anything at all.

Daily conversations shifted from what she wanted and began to center only on the baby.

"Karyn, I'll be home early from work and was calling to see if you need me to pick up anything at the store?"

"I'm fine," she would reply, trying to mask her boredom and frustration. "I was just about to start dinner."

"No!" he said in a voice loud enough to startle her. "I don't want you lifting any heavy pots or pans. I'll prepare dinner when I get home. We need to be careful so that nothing harms the baby."

"I'm only eight weeks pregnant!" she shot back, then remembered how angry he could get when she used that tone with him and lowered her voice. "I appreciate your concern, but I'm okay. The doctor said it's perfectly acceptable for me to continue my normal routine."

"Well that's all well and fine," he retorted in a stern tone, "But as your husband, I don't want you doing anything." Then his voice softened as he said, "It's my time to cater to you. I picked up your vitamin and iron pills. I spoke to the doctor and he gave me a list of foods I can prepare for you so our child will be healthy and strong."

At the time, Karyn felt like the luckiest woman in the world to have such a loving and caring husband. But it soon became obvious that he was only happy when she submitted to him. He wanted control even over her simplest thoughts. She had thought of leaving so many times, but she didn't want to hear her parent's or her friend's words of "I told you so." She was a grown woman. She could deal with it.

"Baby you are the best," she would tell him, but felt more than a tinge of doubt regarding his overbearing and controlling attitude.

Toward the end of the pregnancy, Karyn's mother had come to stay with her until the baby was born. The "official" emergency bag had been packed and the "flight plan" was in place. Karyn was only a month away from her nineteenth birthday and didn't know anything about having a baby, let alone raising one. All she knew was it had to come out the small end, and from the looks of her huge stomach, it wouldn't be fun.

When she went into labor, her mother called Mark. Then she called her girlfriends who practically beat her to the hospital.

In the delivery room, where Mark was noticeably absent, Karyn's mother spoke soothing, encouraging words. "You're a woman now, and you're going to raise this baby to be an amazing person. I know I've prepared you for this moment, and you're going to be just fine. Just remember to breathe, darling."

Karyn gripped the older woman's hand even tighter as pain tore through her body. Everything was going through her mind at once, but nothing to do with her being a good mom. *What have I done?* Karyn wondered. *Oh, how I wish I could reverse this moment and go back to being a child again.*

The pain was worse than she had imagined, but having her mom and her girlfriends there helped her through the delivery. They were able to keep her somewhat at ease and her mind off the pain by telling funny stories, including the tale about Karyn being a celebrity in her home town as a baby. "You were the first baby to be delivered in a taxi in our town. It ran in the local newspaper. Even made the front page."

"Mom, you can't be serious," Karyn whispered through her pain. "You're making this whole story up."

"No, I'm not," she protested amidst the peals of laughter from her friends. "I still have the newspaper to prove it!"

While others shared their stories, Karen conjured up some laughs and a few smiles in between hard contractions. "What was I thinking, having a baby so soon?" she said to no one in particular. Actually, when she thought about it for a minute, she realized it was Mark who had wanted a baby, and when she thought for a minute longer, his motivation for wanting her pregnant became crystal clear. Despite his promises, he was totally against her going to college, or being outside the home for any reason except grocery shopping, to pick up clothes from the cleaners, or visiting her parents—and that was only on sparing occasions.

Karyn wished she could blink her eyes and undo that moment of conception, undo the moment she had married him. Maybe then she'd be at some college pursing her dreams.

Twenty-five hours later, Karyn still had not dilated and all the begging, pleading and screaming had finally gotten on everyone's nerves, including the doctor who agreed to perform a caesarean. Mary Elizabeth James came screaming into the world the evening of March 27th. And for all his actions leading up to the birth of how he would be the perfect, doting father, Mark James was still nowhere to be found.

When the nurse wheeled in a healthy, eight pound, nine ounce, baby girl, Karyn accepted the bundle placed in her arms, whispering, "This is my daughter."

Her mother, who stood beside the bed with tears glistening in her eyes, nodded her head. "She's beautiful."

The little girl had a head full of black curly hair, big eyes like her mother, and reddish brown skin. At that moment, all the pain was forgotten, all anger at Mark for missing this moment, all doubts swept aside and only the little bundle of joy mattered to her.

A year later, Karyn was pregnant again, and Mark Jr. was born February 25th in a winter most people would never forget. The bitter cold had closed down schools, as well as federal, state and city offices, and even private companies. Karyn had fallen in love with the beauty of being a mother, but was severely disappointed by her life as a housewife. She was living a lavish lifestyle, constantly being showered with gifts and love by her adoring husband—but she felt empty and unfulfilled.

For the next five years, Karyn stayed home to raise the children. She recognized that there were many women who weren't as fortunate, who had to put their children in the hands of total strangers while she had the opportunity to be with them for every milestone, and she was grateful. She became part of a "sisterhood," a group of stay–at–home mothers who shared their parenting wisdom that they had gathered from trial and error, past experiences, and of course, mistakes. They would go to lunch together, children in tow and have play dates at the park and at each other's houses. The women taught Karyn how to balance motherhood while still being a good wife and housekeeper. As grateful as she was for everything, there were times when she was shocked to hear some of the things that came out of their mouths, especially when they would talk about the ways they pleased their men.

At about the same time Mary and Mark Jr. entered the second and third grades, spending full days at school followed by after school activities, Mark began spending more and more time at work. With her days free of the children, the sisterhood no longer had the same appeal and neither did the idea of being home alone with nothing to do.

Karyn wanted to finally pursue her dream of becoming a wedding planner. Using the money Mark left for her, she registered for a class. She saw no problem in attending one class. And wedding planning certainly wouldn't be a full–time job. She could think of no reason for Mark to have a problem with something that would fill her days with something more than cleaning the house, keeping the kids, cooking his dinner, and fulfilling his unusually demanding sex drive.

She thought wrong. A few nights later, she approached the subject once the kids were in bed. Mark lay in bed with his head in her lap. As she gently stroked his head, oblivious to the television show which held his rapt attention, she took a breath and told him, "I decided to take a class at the local community college to learn the ins and outs of being a successful wedding planner."

Mark slowly sat up, a baffled expression marring his handsome features. "Sweetheart, why do you want to work? You have everything you need. *I* work hard so that you don't have to."

"Honey, becoming a wedding planner has been a dream of mine since I was a little girl. I went to the most beautiful fairy tale wedding and I knew I wanted to be involved with planning wonderful weddings for couples who are in love."

"What about the children?" he asked as an angry glint had formed in his eye. "They might need you while you are away…" he crooked his fingers. "*in class.*" What about me? I thought *this* was your dream." It should have been a question, but the way he said it sounded more like a definitive statement.

Karen placed a passionate kiss on Mark's lips, hoping to calm him down a little. "Baby, you *are* my dream, nothing comes before you and the kids. But I get lonely when you're all away, doing your own thing." She gathered his hand into hers. "This will keep me occupied and with technology today, I can take the class online. There won't be a need for me to be away from home. If you or the kids need me, I'll still be right here for you. You won't have to worry."

She had successfully appeased Mark, if only slightly. "Wow, school has changed." He thought it over for a moment, then laid his head back onto Karyn's lap. "Okay. If that makes you happy, I'm happy. If you'll still be at home, I don't see a problem with it."

Now that the children were old enough to handle quite a few things on their own, Karyn had the flexibility and freedom to focus on her class for the next several months. Implementing the tools and techniques she had learned from the "sisterhood," she was able to manage being a mom and a student, working on her class at her own pace and scheduling the children's activities around her study times. All was well.

One night, while sitting at the computer working on an assignment, Mark tiptoed up behind Karyn, wrapped his strong arms around her small frame, and kissed her on the neck.

"Baby, you look so sexy sitting there at the computer. How are things going with your class?"

It touched her to see that he cared, especially with how resistant he was in the beginning.

"I'm really enjoying this class! It's amazing how they have hands-on virtual projects and interaction with other people."

Mark stiffened at her excitement but put on a smile that didn't quite reach his dark brown eyes. "You look mighty fine sitting there all studious. You're turning me on!" He said playfully, nuzzling her neck.

Karyn smiled and gently pulled Mark toward her by his tie. "I know what you want, and I'm about to give it to you."

She kept him happy, and he kept her happy. The children were blossoming into two brilliant and inquisitive little geniuses.

One night, after the children had left the dinner table, Karyn peered up at Mark. "Honey, now that I've completed my class, I'd like to try my hand at starting my own business."

Mark scratched his short-cropped hair, brow furrowing with confusion, "Start your own business?" he echoed. "Why?"

She opened her mouth to explain, but he didn't give her a chance. "Karyn, I'm your provider! There's no reason for you to be out in the world working. You already have everything." He glared at her. "Why would you want to work?"

For the life of her she couldn't understand why Mark was extremely paranoid of her being outside of their home. Every time she would bring up that fact of doing anything outside of the agenda he had planned he went from a kind, gentle man to one filled with anger and anxiety.

Walking over to him, Karyn rubbed his chest. "Honey, I know you make sure I have what I want, but I've always been an ambitious person. Remember, that's why you fell in love with me in the first place. You liked that I had dreams and goals. You would let me go on talking to you about them for hours. Now you want me to give that all up?" She shook her head, knowing that statement couldn't be true. "I just want to feel like I've accomplished things in my life."

"Well, you have," he said, barely disguising his anger. "You have a husband who loves you and two beautiful children. We need you."

She pulled away to look at him. "Mark, you act as if I'm going to leave and not come back one day."

"Well you just might," he retorted, shoulder tensing as he ground the words out. "You may get to a point that you'll feel you won't need us anymore."

Karyn just looked at him, wondering where all this insecurity was coming from. "It would be a business I could run from home," she said slowly as though speaking to a child. "The same way I took my class. It wouldn't interfere with our home life. And baby, I love you, so you don't have to worry about anyone taking me away, unless it's Denzel Washington."

Mark finally laughed. Even he admired the award–winning actor.

"Okay, fine. You can have your business as long as it all takes place right here in our home and doesn't interfere with you raising the kids or anything else that you do for the house or me."

Karyn hugged him, but she was perturbed at the same time. Why did it always seem like she had to ask permission to do anything? When did she become a child again? Even her parents had trusted her and her judgment. Mark didn't seem to trust her for any time that she was out of his sight.

She should have known that his paranoia surrounding this issue was just masking a deeper, hidden problem.

Karyn received the first wedding planning contract a month after advertising her new business, and it was huge! A local politician contacted her to plan his daughter's wedding for over five hundred guests. She would be responsible for every single detail—the bridal shower, the wedding ceremony, the reception—and she had to do it perfectly. She saw this opportunity as a great start to her business. She should have known that Mark would see things differently.

That night, in bed, she told him the good news. "Mark, you're going to be so proud of me!"

"Oh yeah, what is it, baby?"

"I landed my first job!"

His hand stilled along her rib cage, ending its journey toward her hips.

"And it's not just *any* job. Governor Robertson wants me to plan his daughter's wedding. It's going to be huge—literally. It's an amazing, once in a lifetime opportunity, and the best way to start my business."

Her smile and enthusiasm faded quickly under Mark's angry glare.

"Sounds like you're going to be extremely busy and away from the house over the next six months or so."

She decided to try and make him see the positive aspects. "Yes, I will be busy, but I'm going to make a lot of money from this job. It'll be a great start for the rest of the business that follows."

Mark hopped out of bed, stormed over to the dresser, yanked open the top drawer that contained an overflow of hundred dollar bills. "Why do you need money?" Pointing at the cash, "See here," he yelled tossing some in her face. "You have money, plenty of it. I provide well for you, don't I?"

Mark's mood changes frightened Karyn beyond words. "Baby, it's not about the money, it's about me pursuing my *dream*."

"Your dream isn't the point here. You're interfering with the life *I've* built for us."

By this point, he had worked himself up and was pacing the length of the room while she was trying, unsuccessfully, to quiet him before he woke the children. Completely throwing her off guard, he stormed out of the house and didn't come home that night.

Karyn, shocked and confused by his anger, made several attempts to call him on his cell, but he never answered. Each time she left a voicemail, "Mark, this is Karyn. Baby, pick up the phone, we need to talk. Please, call me. I'm worried."

She tried to go about her normal day, but it was tough not knowing where her husband was. She hoped he was safe and would call her soon. She dropped the kids off at school, and returned home to begin working on her very first wedding assignment in an effort to keep her mind busy and off Mark's disappearance.

Two days later, Mark stumbled through the front door at five in the morning, eyes bloodshot and he reeked of alcohol. In her sleep, Karyn could feel the presence of someone in the room. Stirring, she woke to see him standing over her, just staring. She was frightened by his demeanor, but even more by the dead look in his eyes.

Whipping off the covers, she got out of bed and stood in front of him, searching his face. "Where have you been? I've been worried about you. I tried calling you and you never responded." She gave him a once over, noticing that he was still wearing the same clothes he had been when he left days ago.

He just stood there, but when he finally spoke, his voice was as cold as his eyes. "How could you accept a job without asking me first? What about me and the kids? You didn't stop to think about *us*. You're not fucking doing it!"

A little shocked, she weighed her words carefully, wondering if she could reach him in his inebriated state. "Honey, I was thinking about us when I decided to take on this job. Imagine what we can do with two incomes. You won't have to work so hard anymore. You won't be gone so much of the time. It is an opportunity of a lifetime. I couldn't turn it down."

It was as if he hadn't heard anything she'd just said. Getting in her face, he grabbed both of her arms so tightly she could feel the bruises forming. "I don't give a damn! You're *not* doing the wedding and that's final. And we don't need two incomes, I make enough money in one year to retire and live well if I choose to. You're not doing it. Ever!" He released her so hard that she fell against the wall and slumped to the floor.

Instead of packing her things and running for the border, she decided to go ahead with the wedding on the sly, hiring a couple of students to do her leg work. She would keep the money in a separate account. What he didn't know wouldn't hurt him.

The demands of planning the wedding required her to work longer and more hours than she had originally anticipated. Though she enjoyed every minute of it, the stress of having to hide her activities from her husband overshadowed any happiness she felt from finally doing what she loved. There were times when the day would get away from her, but she was usually able to get back on schedule and be home and have dinner prepared before Mark was home and suspected anything.

One night, however, she wasn't so lucky. After a particularly grueling day of running all over town because one of her interns got sick, she finally got around to picking up the kids from her mother's house, but didn't arrive home until 10:30 p.m. When she walked through the door, Mark was already there, which was to be expected, but he was sitting in the dining room with the lights off, strange behavior for him. Karyn chanced a wary glance in his direction as the children ran up to him for their hugs. She was more hurt by the fact that he didn't even acknowledge them than that he ignored her attempts at saying hello to him. The tension in the room was palpable. She knew trouble was brewing. Then she saw the secret files that she kept tucked away in a open slot behind their dresser.

"Mary and Mark Jr., come on, let's go upstairs and get ready for bed," she urged, leading them away from their father and toward the stairs. The children were wise enough to sense something was wrong and went upstairs without protest, but still took one last look in their father's direction, hoping he would say something.

After Karyn had put them in bed and kissed them goodnight, she bravely headed back down the stairs, the entire time thinking, *I'm a grown woman. I shouldn't have to sneak around like this. He's not my father or my God.* Mark hadn't moved from his position in the thirty minutes she'd been upstairs. Sitting in a chair across from him, she took a deep breath, but somehow, the words still came quickly stumbling out of her mouth. "Mark, I know you didn't want me doing this wedding, but I've been managing, except for tonight, and I think you'd really be proud of the work I've done. I—"

Mark was out of his seat and across the room in the amount of time it took her to blink. The slap across her face was so hard that it sent her flying out of her chair. He then bore down on her landing a series of punches that made her head spin.

She could feel the moisture and taste the blood pooling in the corners of her mouth. Towering over her, he bent down yanked her body up from the floor lifted her by her armpits and pinned her to the wall like she was a rag doll so that they were eye to eye. His hot, whiskey-laden breath rushed over her like an inferno. Staring at her with eyes dark with fury and chest heaving with an effort to kill. She trembled in his arms, not recognizing the man in front of her.

"You'd better not lie to me again, bitch." He swiped at the blood, causing her to cringe. "That was just a small taste of what'll happen in the future. Your place is in this house taking care of me and my children. If you ever defy me again, you'll be sorry."

He let her go so abruptly that she fell hard on the carpet, skinning her knees in the process. She was sure that she had bruised her tailbone.

Karyn watched Mark stalk out of the room but remained seated, fear paralyzing her to the floor for several hours. Her face throbbed, and she had to stop herself from crying, a natural instinct to alleviate the pain, but something that would only cause her more with the growing welts from where Mark's hand had met her cheekbone and his fist connected solidly with her jaw.

Somehow, she managed to get herself into bed and fell into a fitful sleep. She woke the next morning to Mark's voice, warm and loving the way she remembered, and the smell of breakfast wafting through the air. "Baby, I took the kids to school so you could sleep in late."

She didn't bother to respond or move from her position. Bending down, he kissed her, and then made love to her, if she could even call it that since she didn't want to, but was too petrified of his reaction if she dared say no. Her walls were dry with fear and the pain was so excruciating she tried to let her mind go blank. *Is this rape? Is this what my life has become?* Questions swam in her head about what had happened last night, replaying his actions and his words in that cold, hard, unfeeling voice he had spoken them in.

He finished, recovered from his orgasm, and left her lying in bed. As she heard the shower turn on, she allowed herself to finally cry, the weight of the situation finally dawning on her. *This man is crazy.* The total turnaround in his behavior from last night to this morning had her believing this to be true.

After Mark left for work, Karyn showered, trying to scrub herself clean, then got dressed and called her father. Holding back the tears was impossible the moment the loving and caring sound of her dad's voice came through the line.

"Dad, it's Karyn."

"Hi baby girl! How are you doing?"

She began to sob so violently she had to struggle just to breath. Once her dad was able to calm her down with comforting words, she was finally able to say what she had called about. "Dad, I'm coming home."

"What's wrong? Do you need me to come and get you?"

"No, I'll be there within the hour."

Karyn packed things for herself and the kids, grabbed money from Marks' not quite "secret" stash and scrambled to the school to pick up the kids before Mark got the bright idea to do it himself trying to "make up" for the pain he caused.

When Mark called Karyn's parents that evening, he was the epitome of calm. "I'm so sorry about last night, baby. I'll never do that to you ever again. I promise."

Karyn remained silent, remembering the ugly bruises reflected in the mirror earlier that day. She couldn't forget or forgive what he had done that easily. Especially when little Mary and Mark Jr. stood before her asking what was wrong and Mary touching her face asking why did she look that way. Cringing from the pain of her baby girl's gentle touch she was only able to provide them with a lie–she had fallen down the stairs.

Mark interrupted her thoughts, pleading, almost crying into the phone. "You can do the wedding planning thing. I just need you and the kids back home with me. Please, I don't know what I would ever do without you."

For the first time in his life, Mark had resorted to pleading, which was shocking in itself, because Mark James begged no one.

Sighing, Karyn turned over in her old canopy bed, trying to rid herself of the headache that had started the day he'd hit her and was now throbbing with every word he uttered. "I need some time to think. I'll call you when I've figured things out."

Over the next week, Karyn's parents spoiled their grandchildren, buying them gifts and sweets and taking them on trips to the zoo and circus. Occasionally they would ask about their father, but Karyn only responded with short, vague answers. She definitely wasn't going to let him come and see them at her parent's house. There was no telling what threats he would make or the damage he would do that couldn't be undone.

After nearly two weeks of living under her parent's roof, Karyn sat down with them to discuss her options and her marriage. She expressed her concerns over keeping the children away from their father, and even though she would never verbalize it to them, time away from her lavish home and nice things had made her begin to question if she could leave everything behind and still be happy. Staying in her parents' modest home was cozy, peaceful, and relaxing, but nothing compared to the luxury she had become accustomed to.

Her parents thought it was obvious that she should never go back to him after what he had done. They argued that he would do it again, and maybe even to the kids. They couldn't stand the thought of their beautiful daughter being treated so horribly. What if he harmed their precious grandchildren?

"But I love Mark and despite what he did to me, he's always been good to me and the kids." Karyn said while thinking of her gorgeous, expansive home, brand new SUV, jewelry and closets filled with designer clothes—although she never got to wear them anywhere except inside the house. "This was only *one* time. He promised me it would never happen again."

They tried to talk some sense into her, but Mark had a way with her, that even she could not explain. By the next weekend, Karyn and the kids had moved back into the house with Mark.

When they first got there, his mood was relieved and happy, hugging and tickling the kids, causing them to laugh with joy. Karyn held back until he came to her, and when he planted a gentle, sweet kiss on her lips, the children giggled.

After a day of family time, which was spent watching the Cosby Show and playing a few board games, Karyn put the children to bed. The children being reunited with their father, and the happiness they felt, made her feel that she had made the right decision in coming home. She headed back downstairs, feeling optimistic that she and Mark could work through this and become stronger, unlike so many other marriages that allowed something like this to destroy it.

All optimism and hope left her body when she saw him sitting with a drink in his hand and the half empty bottle of liquor next to him on the end table. Mark tossed down the remainder of his glass of Martell, jumped from his seat, and lunged for his wife before she could even think of running away.

Dragging her by the hair, he made his way toward the basement. When clumps of hair ripped from her scalp, he grabbed her arms, a bit of a challenge since she was fighting him furiously. The entire time, he was spitting on her and calling her every vile name he could think of.

When they had finally gotten to the entrance of the basement, Mark picked her up and tossed her, literally, down the stairs. Before she was able to regain her bearings, he was down the stairs and standing over her. Swiftly, he kicked her hard in the stomach knocking the wind out of her. Karyn doubled over, gripping her stomach hoping the pain would subside. "If you *ever* discuss what goes on in *my* home again, I will make sure you never see the light of day again. If you *ever* try to leave me again, I will make your life a living hell."

She lay still on the basement floor, trying to be as quiet as possible, too fearful to speak let alone breathe.

"And since I have a feeling you aren't taking me seriously," he growled, with another swift kick, this time into her back, "I'm going to beat your ass every day until you get it through your thick ass skull—that you are mine! And you will obey me."

She lost sense of time, trying to leave her mind and body so that she might become numb to the slaps and punches he rained down on her body. She was jolted back to the present when she heard him say, "And since you want to work so badly that you would lie to me, then you can work for me. I could make a pretty penny selling your ass on the street."

She thought he was just saying it to be cruel.

Karyn would learn soon enough that Mark James did not make idle threats.

* * *

"Baby? Baby!" Carl said, shaking her gently on the sauna's wooden bench. He pulled the towel from her face. "Karyn, where were you just now? You haven't heard a word I've said."

Karyn sat up. She was trying to catch her breath and come back to the present, but it was so hard with the heat in the sauna and the fear that clutched her heart.

"I love you, but I can't help you if you keep shutting me out." He reached for her. "Talk to me, baby. It hurts me to see you this way."

She hugged him, laying her head on his shoulder. "Thanks honey. I needed to hear that. I just need some more time."

She had to tell him before one of the girls snapped and everything fell apart.

Chapter 12

Veronica Smith stared down at the gorgeous diamond engagement ring, wondering when she would have the chance to share the big news with her girlfriends. Anything that happened in her life had always taken a backseat to their drama and love lives. There was always something more pressing. She was either helping Sherry deal with another pregnancy or supporting Karyn through her abusive marriage, or Yvette, well Yvette always had drama to be dealt with. Once again, the other three women were all wrapped up in their own dramas, making it nearly impossible for her to find the right time to share her happiness.

Veronica had been very successful in her professional career, but had yet to accomplish what she yearned for most in life—marriage and children. Now forty–five, she felt her time for having babies was long gone, but that didn't mean she still couldn't find love and companionship that a great marriage could provide. Sherry and her pregnancies might have kept Veronica busy, but she couldn't place all the blame on her friend for her lack of a love life. Veronica's fast–paced, high pressure career as a fashion merchandiser for Donna Karan, required her to travel from one place to another, making it plenty difficult for her to find her Mr. Right or even Mr. Right Now.

From an early age, Veronica had challenged herself to strive for success. She had parted ways with her best friends and attended one of the most competitive fashion schools in Los Angeles, of course graduating at the top of her class and earning a coveted internship in Paris and then one in Milan. Between focusing on her education and working to help support Sherry's baby, there wasn't much time left for anything else, including finding love. Sometimes, when loneliness and desire consumed her, she would be filled with anger, but ultimately, she knew it was her own choices keeping her from finding true love.

But that was all in the past. Finally, after all of the years spent alone, she had met a wonderful man who wanted to marry her and wasn't against adopting children, if it came to that. William Butler, a handsome, wealthy, sophisticated man had approached her at a marketing conference in New York. For the past year, they had been secretly dating without anyone in her circle knowing a thing about it. But now that he had asked her to marry him, she wanted to shout it from the rooftops.

* * *

Veronica had just entered the conference room when she saw William, a sales consultant for Versace USA Inc, a prestigious New York fashion company specializing in high–end apparel and accessories and had also been on the cutting edge of the Haute Couture—a distinction and privilege only few design houses were given. He was wearing a conservative black Versace suit that was tailored for his muscular frame. He stood six–feet– two inches, with a caramel complexion and buzz cut so tight, he almost appeared bald. The icing on the cake for Veronica was the hair, trimmed close to his handsome face, mirroring that of a five o'clock shadow, but more finely tuned.

He was laid back and smooth, yet had an air about him that commanded the respect and attention of everyone in the room.

After the meeting, he strolled up to Veronica to discuss some of the selections of fabrics and textiles, as well as the marketing strategies to increase sales for the upcoming year. As he handed her a disk with the financial projections, he ended his conversation with a dinner invitation.

Veronica managed to keep her cool long enough to accept and hand him a business card with her cell number. Wanting to avoid doing or saying anything stupid, she made up an excuse so that she could return to her hotel room to rest and get ready for their date. Giddy with excitement, she wanted to call her friends, but resisted the urge. No point in jinxing it before she even had a chance to see where this would lead.

Maybe she should keep it a secret, the same way she kept her relationship with Simone Gaultier a secret, which wasn't so difficult since Simone still lived in Paris and would only come to the states a few times a year for modeling assignments.

Having learned from mistakes made in her friend's past relationships, she wanted to do things right her first time. That meant taking things slow, not jumping straight into bed with the guy, and most importantly, trusting that God had a plan and would lead her into a loving, lasting relationship.

Attempting to shake her nervousness, she flipped on the television, turning it to a suspense movie. She had almost fallen asleep when her cell phone rang on the bedside table next to her. She took a deep breath, shook out her hair, answering with a sultry, "Hello?"

"Well, hello to you," came the deep just above baritone voice on the other end. "Do you always sound this sexy in the afternoon?"

"I do when I'm expecting a call from you."

There was a pause on William's end for a brief moment, "Oh really?" She could hear the smile in his voice. "Well, I've made reservations at seven for us at Louey's House, a new Italian restaurant that just opened in the Upper East Side."

Veronica perked up, having heard the rave reviews for the place. It was supposed to be the new "it" place to be, very upscale with high class clientele, with cuisine that would make one's mouth water.

"Let's meet in the lobby at six for a cocktail or two beforehand."

"I'll be there, anxiously waiting to see your beautiful face again."

"See you then." Hanging up, she immediately went to the closet, contemplating what she should wear. She had packed two evening dresses, even though at the time, there was no obvious reason. Now it seemed that something—or someone—had wanted her to be prepared. Pulling them both out of the garment bag, she held each one to her slender body, trying to decide which one would be more appropriate for the night. The black, conservative, form–fitting dress was always classic and chic. She could make it stand out with turquoise accessories that would compliment her bronze complexion. Four inch black patent leather pumps would give her kissing height, and also accentuate her shapely legs.

At 5:55, she grabbed her purse and jacket, then headed toward the elevator. Moments later, she was standing in the elegantly furnished lobby. William was seated in a purple velvet lounge chair just outside of the elevator banks. When he saw her, a shining smile appeared giving him a boyish charm. He stood to greet her, extending his hand and saying, "Thank you, for having dinner with me this evening."

She inclined her head as a reply, allowing him to give her a once over. It was apparent from the flash of desire in his eyes that he appreciated how she looked, staring at her hair, which was pulled up in a love knot, then sweeping his gaze leisurely over her body. "You look stunning."

She looked up at him, testing one of her mother's favorite sayings, "You can tell when a guy is on the up and up if he can look you directly in your eyes." William had passed with flying colors. "Thank you for inviting me."

After their cocktail in the hotel bar, he led her toward the limousine that was waiting for them directly outside. A short drive through downtown traffic, and they were there. The driver parked in front of the restaurant, walked around to open the door, and offered his hand to help Veronica out of the car. She scanned the area, saying, "I heart New York," which only made William grin.

"I'm glad to hear that," he said, pulling in close to her. "I find that it's a place people either love or hate, and it's hard to change someone's mind once it's made up."

They passed through the front entrance, and it was like stepping out of New York City and into Tuscany. The restaurant was decorated with warm colors, bringing images of sunshine and the ocean to life. After taking in the beauty, they followed the maitre'd to their table, appreciating the delicious smells that wafted in the air.

Once they were seated, Veronica looked at William across the table, saying, "This place is truly wonderful. Thank you for thinking of me and inviting me."

"I've seen you at some of the past meetings, and I've wanted to approach you for awhile now."

She leaned back, crossing one shapely leg over the other, which was not missed by William. His gaze flickered over the smooth expanse of bronze flesh as she asked, "So why haven't you?"

"Would you believe me if I told you I was nervous?" he asked with a shy smile. "But I promised myself the next time I saw you,

I wouldn't let my nerves, or anything else get in the way of asking you to dinner. I didn't want to live with the regret of never getting to know you better."

She placed her hand on top of his and smiled. "I'm glad you finally asked."

He lifted the delicate fingers to his lips and kissed them. "So, now that I've finally got you to myself, tell me everything there is to know about you."

Veronica had to recover from the warmth and tingle that little action sent through her. "Well let's see, where should I start…I grew up in a small south suburban town in Illinois with my mom Carol, dad Earl and two siblings Sheila and Jessie I'm the youngest. Once I became a teenager they were grown, had been moved out of my parent's home, and were married with children of their own. So, basically I grew up like an only child. I guess that's why I'm closer to my girlfriends than my siblings. My girls are my partners in crime…" Veronica thought about what she had just said and it sent chills through her. How could she ever be close to anyone else with this secret lingering in the background? How did Karyn and Yvette manage with their husbands? "My parents worked hard to provide us with a good life. They constantly stressed the importance of education."

William reached across the table and took Veronica's hand in his. "Sounds like you had a good childhood. So how did you land in the wonderful world of fashion?"

"When I was a little girl, I was intrigued by the variation of styles that people wore. I practically lived downtown on the Magnificent Mile. Then after college I started my career in Paris, starting with my internship, then I moved to Los Angeles for a bit, and now I've settled in Chicago. All the people who matter most to me are there, so I wanted to put my roots there, but it means I travel a lot to make up for it."

Their conversation was interrupted by their platinum-haired waiter, Richard, who came to take their order.

Veronica passed him the menu. "I would like a porterhouse steak, medium rare with all the trimmings."

"A woman after my own heart!" William said, giving her a wide smile that softened his chiseled features. "I'll have the same and bring us a bottle of your best red."

"Yes sir," Richard said with a slight bow, then quickly disappeared.

"So, you travel a lot? It's been all work and no play?"

"I've dated but nothing serious." Veronica shifted in her seat. "I want to get married and have children someday, I just haven't found the right guy yet. And since I believe in only marrying once, I want to make sure I get it right the first time."

Before William had a chance to respond, Richard returned with their bottle of wine, pouring a sample in William's glass first, then into Veronica's.

Veronica took a sip before asking, "What about you? You're single, right?" It had just hit her that she should have asked that question *before* they had gotten to this point. If she had learned anything from Sherry and her mistakes, it was to avoid falling for men already taken, something Sherry did on a regular basis.

"Well, I was married for eighteen years to my college sweetheart." William took another taste of wine. "I have one son, he's twenty, and finishing up at Morehouse right now. The moment he went off to Atlanta, my wife decided she wanted out of the marriage. I later discovered she'd been having an affair with one of our neighbors who was going through his own divorce at the time. She was...*consoling* him."

Veronica placed a hand on her chest releasing a small sigh to express her sadness.

He shrugged. "That was three years ago. We've been able to remain cordial for our son's sake, but it kind of took the wind out of my sails that I was traveling too much to notice that it had started while we were still married."

"I'm sorry things didn't work out."

William looked up at her. "Now that I've met you, I'm not."

After dinner, they sat and relaxed talking a bit about the industry and comparing notes on upcoming trends, finishing their bottle of wine while a stocky, gray-haired man played romantic melodies on the piano. The restaurant closed around them, but instead of going back to the hotel, they decided to enjoy the clear night and take a walk along Fifth Avenue, admiring the boutiques, the mom-and-pop shops and the street vendors. They didn't lie when they said New York was the city that never sleeps.

From their conversations, she learned that they both enjoyed some of the same things, including going to the theatre, jazz concerts, traveling to exotic places, reading James Baldwin and Richard Wright novels, and a love for all places near the ocean. The thing that did it for her was that they shared similar spiritual beliefs, something she thought was critical for a successful relationship.

After a couple of cocktails, a wonderful and delicious dinner and a hand-in-hand walk through the city on a warm, beautiful night, she realized that he was a strong, but kind spirit and felt incredibly comfortable with him. She was having such a great evening with him, she ignored the calls coming into her cell; didn't bother to even look and see who was making an attempt to reach her. When his driver pulled up in front of her hotel, a sense of sadness enveloped her.

Turning to her in the car, he took her hand, looked into her eyes. "Veronica, I don't even know if I can put into words how much I've enjoyed my time with you tonight or how disappointed I am that the date is coming to an end."

Veronica wrapped her arms around William, hugging him tightly. "That's so sweet of you, William. I've had a fabulous time."

"When can I see you again?"

She tried to play coy, not wanting to appear overeager, even though inside, she was screaming with joy. "Well, I'm not sure when I'll be back to New York again. It probably won't be at least until the end of the month for fashion week."

"I can't wait that long!" he whispered, stroking his fingers over her more delicate ones. "What if I fly you out here on the weekend? Or I could come and see you in Chicago?"

Still trying to keep her cool, she responded calmly, "Let's talk once I'm back home."

They walked up the steps and into the hotel, but feeling her resolve weaken, she stopped him at the elevator and kissed him on the cheek, then waved to him as the doors closed.

She only allowed herself to dance and sing a happy tune once she was on her way up to her suite. Again her cell began to ring. She pulled it from her purse and her heart clinched when she looked down at the name on the screen—Simone. She had received five calls from Simone tonight and one text message which read... *Veronica why are you avoiding me? I've called you five times and you won't answer. We were supposed to spend this weekend together. This is not like you, I am concerned baby, please call.*"

After reading Simone's message she turned off her phone and placed it back in her purse. Simone was a relationship that she never wanted to revisit. The woman was needy, almost cloying, but she had ushered Veronica into the highest levels of the fashion world, something that would have taken Veronica years to do on her own. The tradeoff was the relationship that Simone had desperately wanted to have with such a gorgeous Black beauty—as she called her. She found Veronica "exquisite" and her virgin status an absolute treat. She had always said that they were meant to be together forever. Forever ended for Veronica the moment she landed back on American soil. Simone had served her purpose and so had Veronica, having been traipsed all over Europe on the arm and in the bed of one of the richest women in the world, whose influence was far–reaching, had always remained steadfast about the fact that she wanted children someday.

The next day after the date with William, Veronica returned to Chicago, happily surprised to find two dozen long–stemmed red roses waiting for her in the lobby of her city condo. Tucked inside was a note from William, thanking her for a wonderful evening and expressing his hope that they could see each other again soon. She had the doorman bring them up and place them on her marble table in her dining room. Somehow, her luxury one–bedroom condo, done in an art–deco style and was filled with so many wonderful things, felt empty. The moment she pictured William Butler, her heart was overflowed with delicious expectations.

A week later, William invited her to visit him at his home on Staten Island, sending her a first–class roundtrip ticket along with a driver to take her to the airport in Chicago. William's driver waited for her at the baggage claim on the New York end and assisted her to the car. Before long, the beautiful skyscrapers of the Manhattan skyline were behind them, replaced with trees, grass and grand homes that were absolutely breathtaking!

The moment Charles, who she learned had been in William's employ for ten years, pulled up to Williams' estate, Veronica's jaw dropped. It was one of the biggest houses she had ever seen, sitting on acres of land that seemed to go on forever. The door to the home itself was richly made of steel and mahogany and led into a place that looked as though it had been designed and furnished for a magazine spread. It had character, warmth, and style—not a small feat to achieve in such a wide expanse of space. The great room had two walls of cathedral windows allowing sunlight to beam throughout the entire first floor and highlight the magnificent marble fireplace. A quick glance to the right showed an atrium that lead to an outdoor pool and looking upward to the second floor overlooking the great room.

"Welcome to my humble abode Veronica."

Veronica stood silently for a moment, still in awe. "You can't be serious. Your *humble* abode? You live here all alone?"

William nodded, "Most of the time, unless the housekeepers or chefs stay over when I have a gathering. Sometimes my son stays with me when he's home for a long weekend, but for the most part, yes, I'm here alone."

He pulled Veronica close to him, gently kissing her on the lips. "But if you moved in, I wouldn't have to be a lonely old man any longer."

"You're not old."

He grinned, "I see you didn't comment on the lonely part."

"Because that makes two of us." Veronica smiled, avoiding more of that conversation by steering it in another direction. "Your home is truly amazing. Whoever decorated did a stellar job."

William smiled at her compliment, planting another soft kiss on her lips. "I've missed you. Come, let's go to the great room and sit for a bit."

After catching up on their week, which included more snuggling and kissing, William continued the tour. He took her hand and walked her up to the master bedroom which had a fireplace and a balcony overlooking the patio.

Veronica stood in the bedroom window, taking in the view and breathing in the fresh air. "Now I could get use to this, not another house within miles. No blaring horns. No sirens off in the distance."

"I could get used to you being here," he said in a low tone that sent shivers of pleasure up her spine.

William let her rest in his room while he prepared dinner. She awoke to the smells of something delicious, and allowed her tastebuds to propel her downstairs into the dining room where there was a spread of seafood and pasta. William had remembered, from one of their many conversations, what her favorite foods entailed.

After a leisurely dinner, they went for a swim under the night time sky, talking and laughing, then ending their night lying in each other arms under the stars.

William, who had always seemed so calm and confident, suddenly appeared a tad bit nervous. "Veronica, I'm really, and I do mean really, feeling you. I'd like to spend a lot more time with you."

Veronica didn't respond, but placed her head on his chest so that William could wrap his arm around her.

"I enjoy your company," his deep, baritone voice said, washing over her. "You just seem to fit perfectly right here with me, in my arms, in my life."

Her heart was pounding with the nerves that had been building all day. Trying to keep it light and casual, she responded, "Yeah, you seem to be okay for a guy who lives all the way out in the boondocks."

"Just okay?" he inquired with a sad puppy dog look on his face.

"Well, maybe more like fantastic," she said grinning and accepting another kiss from him.

He held her closely and this time the kiss turned so intense, fear clutched her heart. How could she be into someone like him, and so fast? He had so much and she came from more humble beginnings. She felt the stirrings of desire and wanted to take his hand and lead him to the master bedroom, but she remembered her promise to herself. From now on, God, not sex, would lead and guide her relationships. It was where she felt her friends had made their biggest mistakes. That night, despite the fact that her body was screaming for completion, she slept in one of William's exquisitely decorated guest rooms.

After four months of dating, Veronica finally invited William to Chicago so that he could see where she lived and she could take him out on the town. Her date, while not as extravagant as his, started with a tour of the famous "Magnificent Mile" on a horse–drawn carriage, followed by a visit to Millennium Park, the Art Museum, and lunch at Gibson's.

That evening, she prepared a mouth–watering meal for him. Candles burned throughout, and red rose petals led to the most intimate places in her condo. It was a beautiful night in Chicago; the temperature played nice and hovered at seventy–five degrees—perfect weather for eating on the balcony and taking in a warm breeze. After enjoying their meal, they lingered at the table, listening to contemporary jazz and watching the sky become an artist's masterpiece of colors, starting with pink and orange, changing to light purple, and finally ending with dark purple blending into navy. They were still outside when the sky had become sprinkled with stars and the bright white moon.

As William prepared to leave for his hotel for the night, Veronica grabbed his hand, looking him directly in the eyes, she abandoned all thoughts of holding out as she said, "I'd like it very much if you spent the night with me."

William stood staring at Veronica, lost for words. She pulled him close and began to kiss, at first gently, than harder and deeper. Then the moist tip of her tongue explored the warmth of his mouth in a smooth sensual way that made William groan, and then groan again. Veronica pressed her body so close to his she could feel his erection swell with need.

She slipped her warm hands into his, and led him along the trail of rose petals to her bedroom. William's strong hands undressed her slowly, savoring every moment as he caressed her skin as though he had never touched a woman before that time. He kissed her face, trailing kisses all the way down to her toes, leaving no part of her body untouched. The tenderness ignited a passion within her that far surpassed any she had felt before that time.

Veronica's body was hot under the warmth of his lips and the touch of his hands. His breathing became shallow with passion, desire and lust. Feelings that she had buried began to resurface, and the need to have a man, to feel him inside her, made her anxious. She crooked a finger, beckoning him and he obliged, nestling his head and tongue between her legs, making her body tingle and shake with pleasure. With perspiration making her body slick to the touch, she pulled him up toward her, wanting him inside her *now*.

He was slow, tortuously slow, when he entered her, then paused at the resistance and pulled away to look at her.

Veronica looked away, unable to take the surprise that registered on his face. "You're the first man I've ever been with."

William placed his fingers on her chin, turning her face to meet his. He placed a gentle kiss on her lips. "I am so honored." He embraced her, holding her to his chest as she allowed the anxiousness that had crept into her mind to dissipate.

Moments later he kissed her gently, then more passionately, as he poised to enter and was soon exploring her body with a stroke that seemed to go on until her head rolled back and she released the moment he hit her g–spot. Veronica's eyes rolled into the back of her head, her body trembled, and she let out a scream the moment the orgasm slammed into her and she damn near blacked out. She had never experienced anything so powerful before and her pleasure excited William even more. His erection never left as he continued, ushering another wave of pleasure that left her breathless. She held onto him, crying out his name, knowing that this was the man she wanted to spend the rest of her life with.

Chapter 13

Sleeping with her best friend's husband was one sin. To know that she could possibly have spilled their secret to Derrick was a sin that was just too much for Sherry to bear. She swallowed down the remaining Crown Royal to help ease her mind of the dilemmas facing her at the moment. How could she have betrayed their trust? How could she have let things get so out of hand? What was wrong with her?

In a drunken state, she sat at the kitchen table dazed, realizing the past had never been kind to her, the present was a total mess, and the future wasn't looking to good either. Someone just shoot her and get it over with already!

* * *

Sherry had been single for several years when she struck out in the game of love for a second time. Two years after college she had earned an internship at Cook County Hospital. She sat in the lecture hall on the first day of orientation, trying not to be intimidated by the size of the place. There were one hundred other interns seated around her, all seemingly as nervous as Sherry felt. As everyone spread out toward the front rows, the director of the program approached the lectern where she adjusted the microphone so that it would be level with her short frame. "Good morning new candidates and welcome to the Cook County's internship program for nurses."

After two hours of being inundated with information, she wrapped it up with a question and answer section. "On your way out, please grab a package containing all of the materials you'll need to get you through this program."

"Hopefully that includes some weed," a brunette mumbled, eliciting chuckles from everyone nearby.

"Once everyone has their packet, we'll begin the tour of the hospital."

While learning her way around, Sherry's focus got sidetracked by a handsome young doctor in the Coronary Care Unit. She made a mental note to circle her way back to that area once the tour was over, but soon realized it would be unnecessary.

Sensing her stare, he looked up and smiled. He walked over to her and held out his hand while studying her. "Hello, I'm Dr. Washington."

Oooh! He's so cute! Sherry quelled her hormones long enough to say, "I'm Sherry Lakeside."

Dr. Washington, whose slender frame belied his strong, solid build, kept a firm grip on Sherry's hand. "I hear you're doing your internship in the ER unit?"

Sherry's imagination didn't disappoint her. The man was actually flirting with her. "Yes, yes I am."

He released her hand, showering her with a smile that was all perfect white teeth. "I'm sure I'll be seeing you around. Remember to stay focused, study hard, and when you have some down time, which won't be much," he said with a wink, "party like a rock star."

Sherry was touched by his encouraging words and amused at his advice to 'party hard' which was so not what they had heard in the boring lecture that morning. "Why thank you, Dr. Washington. This is a tough program but your words just put a little more fight back in me."

She was about to walk away when he slipped a pad of paper and pen from his medical coat. "Here's my number. Call me, anytime, if you ever need advice or more...encouraging words."

"Don't be surprised if I take you up on that," she giggled and walked away with a little pep in her step.

And did she ever! After that day, Sherry began seeking Dr. Washington's *advice* as often as she could, making up all kinds of excuses to stay in contact with him. After some time, he became a mentor, and they began spending time together away from the hospital, but always seemed to keep their conversations professional and about the hospital, much to Sherry's dismay.

One night, after an especially long shift, she was surprised to see a missed call from him on her cell. Dialing his number, she wondered why *he* had called her when from day one, it had always been the other way around. After three rings, his warm voice came through, "Hey, Sherry, I know you just finished up a long shift, but I wanted to see if you'd want to grab a bite to eat? I'm not in the area but, I could meet you at Miller's Pub for some ribs."

Trying to keep her composure in check as she placed the last of the charts on the desk, Sherry replied evenly, "That'd be great! I need some food and possibly a drink, after the day I've had."

Thirty minutes later, they were in the famous Chicago pub enjoying some good food, and strong drinks while sharing a few laughs as they talked about their day. She never realized how funny he was. Maybe it was because they were finally hanging out in a social setting rather than a professional one. Signaling for the waiter, he asked,

"You up for some shots?"

Sherry shook her head. "No, I can't handle the tough stuff. That's for you hairy chest men."

Julius laughed at her, taunting. "Awwww, a little liquor never hurt nobody. Live a little!"

"Nah!"

He shrugged and signaled for the waitress. "Well, if you can't handle the tough stuff, you're not going to be around for long."

Sherry was having a great time, and since it had been a while since she'd let her hair down, she said, "Sure, why not? It's the weekend and I don't have to work until Monday." She laughed. "Bring it on!"

As their tall, leggy waitress walked toward the table, Sherry thought she heard him mumble, "Damn she's fine." She was hoping that he meant her, and not the blonde that was giving him a thorough once-over. Once the waitress was within earshot, he was a polite gentleman. "Can you bring us some of your top shelf tequila with lemons and salt?"

"Sure, Dr. Washington." Sherry noticed how the woman swayed her hips as she walked away from the table, letting him have an eyeful of her tight behind. Something within Sherry's heart crumbled. The man was acting as if she wasn't even there. As if she wasn't beautiful, too. So it was all about work for him. Maybe she had mistaken his earlier flirting for something else.

"Wow, you must frequent this place often. She knew you by name," she said in a breathy whisper that masked her disappointment.

"Oh yeah, I love eating here," was his absent reply.

Five minutes later, their waitress returned, shot glasses and liquor in hand.

"Thanks, Angie." He handed her a solid hundred. "Keep the

change. And did I tell you how beautiful you look today?"

Angie blushed, walking away with a huge smile on her face as she flickered a quick, dismissive glance in Sherry's direction. Sherry focused her gaze on her bare hand, void of any ring, wondering if Dr. Washington thought she was taken or something. She didn't notice that he took other interns out for lunch and dinner or the fact that he has never spent any time with her until now. Maybe he wasn't into her.

They topped off their night with a sixth and final shot. After that, everything became a haze to Sherry with one view blurring into another. She vaguely remembered a nightclub, flashing lights and dancing on a table and taking off her favorite long–line bra.

The next morning, Sherry woke up in an unfamiliar room on top of an equally unfamiliar bed. As she tried to put together the pieces of the previous night's puzzle, her head pounded to the point she couldn't see straight. Her gaze swept the room until it came to her own body. She was stark naked.

Slowly turning her head, the man lying naked next to her in all his handsomely naked glory was Dr. Washington.

Oh shit!

A soft groan of horror escaped her lips, she managed to bring the rest of room into focus. Clothes were thrown haphazardly about the floor. Her body ached in places that were too numerous to mention. *Damn, we must have had a good time. Too bad I can't remember any of it.*

Next to her, Dr. Washington stirred, clearing his throat before saying a groggy, "Morning sweetheart."

Sherry reached for the cool white sheet to cover her naked body. "Good morning," she replied, unable to make eye contact with him.

Rolling toward her, he kissed her on her forehead and cupped her full breasts. "Last night was incredible! I had a good time. Guessing by the sounds you made last night, you had fun too," he said with a devilish grin.

Sherry couldn't remember anything after that last shot, but she wasn't about to tell him that. Instead, she replied dryly, "Yeah, last night was great. Where are we anyway?"

"We were so hammered last night that I got us a room at the hotel next to the club. Shortest walk to a bed," he said with a husky chuckle.

And then Sherry knew. This was a normal thing for him. He had probably taken Angie and several other women on that short walk as well. Miller's Ribs? No, it was all about the ass for him.

"Well, it's back to work for me," he said, slipping out of bed and hitting the shower. "See you around."

Sherry swallowed hard against the pain swelling in her chest. She felt empty, used, and there wasn't much she could say about it. She was grown. He was grown. He hadn't forced her to do anything.

Sherry prepared herself for Dr. Washington to disregard her after their one night stand, but to her surprise, the exact opposite happened. Instead, they began spending every free minute together. Their dates, if one could call them that, consisted of partying, lots of drinking. and ended with plenty of mind–blowing sex.

There were times when their days together included bringing her daughter. Watching him interact and play with KeAnna made Sherry hope and believe that she might have finally found a good man to be a father to her little girl. Even if she had reservations on whether he would be a good man for her in the long run. The man had a wandering eye that roved so severely one would think it was its own planet.

One night she and Julius–she still felt weird calling him by his first name—had finished a great night of love–making and she had finally found the courage to say that she wanted to slow things down for a while. He turned to her and fixed his eyes on hers. "Sherry, I love you, I don't want this to end. What do you think about us having a baby of our own?"

For a minute, her heart soared. Smiling, she responded, "I think KeAnna would like being a big sister." She finally believed that after all she had been through, things were finally going her way. She'd get the happy ending she'd been dreaming about for so very long.

Once again, her vivid imagination had skipped over the fact that the man had only made one reference to love, but had put more emphasis on having a child. She was blinded by her love for him, and possibly all the alcohol, so she heard things she *wanted* to hear rather than what was actually said. She was convinced Julius Washington, the most handsome doctor, and eligible bachelor at Cook County Hospital, wanted to marry her and start a family. Somehow his flirtatious behavior whenever they were out in public was swept so far under the rug it had become a permanent part of the fibers. She never stopped to think that the high and mighty Doctor Washington was just like any other man and simply saying what he needed to in order to keep enjoying things the way they were.

Later that year, she took a pregnancy test—actually three of them to confirm what she already knew. She had expected him to be shocked, but also elated. Wasn't he the one to suggest they have a child?

She found him eating his dinner in the cafeteria with a book in tow. "Julius, I need to talk to you. I have some great news!" Her eyes were glistening with excitement and happiness.

Looking up from the medical journal, he asked, "What is it sweetie?"

Going over to him, she sat down and grabbed his hand. "Your wish has come true!"

"Oh yeah?" he said, his lips parting in a warm smile "And what wish is that?"

"I'm pregnant! We're going to have a baby!"

The grin on her face quickly melted away as she realized that his warm smile soon turned downward and was followed by an angry glare that turned his handsome features into something that was hardly recognizable.

Snatching his hand away, he growled, "What? How? I don't *want* a baby. How could you possibly think this is good news for me?"

Sherry's heart practically stopped. "But...well...remember, you said it the same night you told me you loved me."

"Back up, I *never* said that Sherry. You must have misunderstood."

Seeing the crumpled and pitiful expression on her face, he attempted to soften the blow. "Look, Sherry, I love spending time with you, but I don't *love* you. I thought we were, you know, friends with benefits." He scanned the area, noting that her tears were drawing unwanted attention to their private conversation. "I can't deal with a relationship or a baby right now. I have too much going on in my life, and frankly, so do you with your internship and the kid you already have."

Sherry just stared at him as though he couldn't possibly be saying what he was actually saying.

"I suggest you think long and hard about whether or not you should have this baby, because if you do, you're on your own." His gaze, filled with disdain, flickered over her as though she were some bug he wanted to squash. "I want no part of its life...or you."

He grabbed his white lab coat, angled the book and files in his arm, and stormed out of the door.

Somehow she'd screwed up. Again.

From that night on, he avoided her at all costs. Not knowing what else to do, and feeling slightly batty at being dumped on her ass the same night she found out she was pregnant, Sherry stalked him. She would go by his home and sit on his front porch, trying to get him to see her and talk to her, and would only leave when he threatened to call the police. She would call him several times a day, leaving messages that went unanswered. After all of her attempts at communication had failed, she decided to go against her better judgment and talk to him at the hospital. He couldn't leave the grounds if he was the on-call doctor, which was the case this night when she finally cornered him.

Walking through the emergency room doors, she was thrown off balance at the sight of Julius talking animatedly with a pretty intern. Like Sherry, she was a thick, curvy girl and had that same star struck look in her eyes that was familiar to the now disenchanted woman.

Sherry walked right up to them, tapped on his shoulder. "I don't mean to break anything up," she said, her tone dripping with sarcasm, "But I need to speak with you, *Doctor* Washington."

Turning to the young intern, he shot her one of his charming smiles and asked her to excuse him for a minute, then turned toward Sherry, giving her one of the dirtiest looks she had ever seen him give anyone.

Grabbing her by the elbow, he ushered Sherry into his office. Slamming the door behind her, he turned to look at her, his face flushed with anger. "First you call me incessantly, then you come to my home, and now *this.*" He gestured to her, meaning her presence here in the hospital on her off hours. "This—showing up at the hospital like this…is totally inappropriate! What the hell is wrong with you?" he barked.

"Well, I've been trying to reach you, Doctor Julius Washington, but you won't *return* my calls." She hated herself for it, but she started to whine. "I thought we had something. You told me you loved me."

He placed a firm grip on her shoulders and looked her square in the eye. "You're right, we *had* something, and now, it's over. You need to move on with your life because I've definitely moved on with mine."

"What about your baby? The baby *you* wanted me to have?"

"I never wanted anything serious with you," he snarled. "And I especially didn't want a child. I never wanted this kid to begin with, so if you choose to keep it, you're on your own for anything else."

Stunned that he could so easily forget that he was the one to suggest she have his child, she gaped at him. "That's all you have to say? You're going to leave me high and dry?"

Avoiding the question, he gave her an indirect answer that confirmed he was just another asshole. "I don't want you and I don't want any kids!" He opened his office door. "We have nothing left to say here, and I don't expect you to keep calling me, showing up at my house, or at the hospital confronting me. If you dare, I will file a formal police report and get a restraining order. You will lose your job."

"And if you don't do right by your child, you will lose yours," she shot back. "I'm sure a disciplinary hearing can be brought up if I levied charges against you my damn self. I'm sure that I'm not the only intern you've roped into sleeping with you. Maybe a few tests to show that you don't have a problem drinking then showing up for work might do the trick."

His face registered alarm that she could have any amount of bite. He had pegged her as some stupid little woman that he could use and push aside, and until that day he had been right. But from this point on, she would not allow any man to use her that way. She would be the one to call the shots. She was so angry that tears blurred her vision.

"I'll give you money to get rid of the child, but no more."

"Oh, no, Doctor Washington, you're going to give me more than that—a lot more," she countered, turning him to face her. "And just because I was irresponsible in believing that you loved me, and listened to your drivel saying you wanted this child, doesn't mean I'm going to compound *our* error and have an abortion." She leveled a stony gaze at him as his hands curled into fists as though he was about to hit her. "Touch me, and it will be the last thing that you do."

He turned his back to her, began pacing his office. "I'll have my lawyer draw up papers and give you money to take care of the child." He turned, held up his hand to ward off anything she was about to say. "But I want a paternity test first, and I don't want anyone at this hospital knowing that I had a child by you. Bottom line."

"Works for me. I definitely don't want anyone knowing that I fell for your line of bullshit. That will never happen again," she spat. "And though your lawyer may put it in writing, the moment the paternity test pans out, trust me, *my* lawyer will make the necessary adjustments to make sure I and your baby get exactly what's coming to us. You're not getting off so easy on this one, *Doctor…Julius… Washington.*"

She swept from his office with an unnatural anger building inside. How could she have been so stupid? Now, until everything worked itself out, she would have three mouths to feed instead of two, and she could ill–afford the weariness that pregnancy would bring on. She had barely made it through school the first time, now this internship was critical to the rest of what she wanted to do with her life!

Once again, Sherry turned to the only people she could always depend on–her best girlfriends. They rescued her. They helped her find the best family lawyer and fought Dr. Washington's ass in court. When they were through with him, he was required to pay more than his fair share of child support and medical expenses–and he was so angry that he resigned from Cook County and took a position at another hospital out–of–state. Good for him, cause she never wanted to see him again anyway. But she certainly wanted those checks filling up her bank accounts as taking care of this new child, with the medical issues that ensued because she was a preemie and the lungs hadn't developed quite the way they would have with a full birth, was more demanding than she would have thought possible.

Now, seventeen years later, Sherry sat at her kitchen table, sipping a strong cup of coffee hoping it would sober her up as she thought long and hard about her two wayward daughters, KeAnna, nineteen, and Jaynene, seventeen. The youngest was two months pregnant, and the oldest was steadily on a pathway to nowhere, drinking, partying and sleeping with every Tom, Joe and Ricky that aimed his dick her way.

Sherry, no real role model herself, was trying, unsuccessfully, to keep her life from falling apart at the seams, when the threads hadn't been sewn all that tight to begin with. She was sleeping with one of her best friend's husbands, and needed to find a way to end it. Every time the guilt washed over her and she brought up the fact that they needed to stop seeing each other, he threatened to tell Yvette. He wasn't worried about the fallout in his life because he was so angry with Yvette for what she'd done to him, that this was just the catalyst he needed to force her hand. And he didn't mind hurting Sherry in the process. And what could she say? She was already hurting Yvette in the meantime. She could see no way out without losing what little respect she had of the people she needed most in her life.

Feeling desolate, trapped with her hands tied behind her back, she could do nothing but sit there all alone, and let the tears fall into the bitter cup of coffee.

Chapter 14

Veronica finally mustered up the nerve to call Simone Gaultier. She knew it wasn't right to keep avoiding her and now that she had realized what she really wanted in a relationship, it just didn't seem fair to keep stringing the woman along. It had never occurred to her that she should have done that months ago, the moment she decided that the relationship was not going where she ultimately needed to be—a wife and a mother.

. She stood before her bathroom mirror rehearsing what she would say to the gorgeous, but very possessive and manipulative woman. After dialing the number several times, she finally allowed it to ring. A sultry voice came on the line with a simple, "hello" that spoke volumes to Simone's anger. There was never a time she didn't answer in her native French tongue.

Veronica took a deep, calming breath as she made one more pass in front of the mirror. "Hey babe, what's wrong? You're not happy to hear from me?"

There was a gasp on the other end as Simone released a long sigh that tinged on Veronica's nerves. The woman was more than angry. She was downright furious. "What's up!" she spat, her thickly accented English didn't hide the sarcasm. "I have been trying to reach you for four months," she said through her teeth. "I've left messages and you haven't returned a single one. I even sent two telegrams. Am I supposed to be happy to hear from you now? What kind of foolishness is this?!"

Veronica knew there was no other way to tell Simone about William except to be totally honest at this point. "Well, I–I–I really didn't know how to tell you, but I hope you'll be happy for me…"

"What exactly are you getting at?"

"Well, I haven't been able to get back to you because I've been preoccupied with work. Then I met this wonderful guy. We have been dating for four months and it's…serious."

Silence expanded between them and Veronica's heart clenched with fear. She was stupid for not bringing this up long before now. Simone still had the power to destroy her career.

"And you didn't have the decency to tell me?" Simone asked in a low tone, that hid barely controlled rage. "I thought I meant more to you than that. We've been seeing each other for how many years now? And I had to threaten you by saying I was coming to Chicago in order to get you to return my call? If I had not said those things, you probably would have never called me.

Veronica winced at the truth of that statement.

" Now that you have a *man*," she spat in a tone that made Veronica wither. "You want to treat me like I am a total stranger. Like I, Simone G, is *nothing*? Who do you think you are you little twit!"

"Look Simone, you're getting a little too sensitive," Veronica shot back, chancing a glance in the mirror which showed that her skin was flushed with anger. "You knew as well as I did that there were never any demands on our relationship. You also knew I wanted to be married and have children. Can you give me children?"

Silence.

"Frankly, I don't owe you anything."

Simone cleared her throat, drawling, "All right, so that is how you want things to play out, eh? You didn't feel that way when this relationship benefited you."

Veronica parted her lips to protest, but wasn't given a chance.

"You used every piece of information I gave you to further your career. I did it because I loved you. No way would a woman like you have made it in Paris. You would be *nothing*–nothing! If it were not for all of *my* contacts I provided you that put you with the right people at the right time."

Veronica felt the tears welling in her eyes. She knew that Simone spoke some words of truth. She would still be chugging along, begging for the opportunities that had come when Simone opened the doors for her. But she would like to think that with hard work and determination that she would have made it all the same.

But thanks to Simone, Veronica had started at the top–in Haute Couture, rather than just working on someone's ready–to–wear fashion line. Someone in Simone's family had always been an official member of the Chambre Syndicale de la Haute Couture, the body which was responsible for drawing up the list of companies who were entitled to avail themselves of the label haute couture–a coveted distinction for any fashion house worth its salt.

Veronica soon learned from Simone and her never–ending knowledge of the fashion world that even though many houses could not afford to produce a full Haute Couture line, since the financial benefits were far less reaching than the more mass marketable ready–to–wear lines; being labeled as a house with at least a showing of a high end line of made–to–order fashion for private clients, helped to separate the old world fashion houses like Chanel and Yves Saint Laurent, from the newer lines that did not have a workshop—an atelier—in Paris that employed at least fifteen people full-time, and could not present a collection to the Paris press, with at least thirty-five runs or exits with outfits for both daytime wear and evening wear.

To say that Simone had helped her to navigate that eclectic world, where Veronica would have been lost, would be putting it mildly. The woman had personally directed her career, helping to steer clear of any missteps that could have landed Veronica on the wrong side of the fabric, which could end a promising career before it even began.

All the woman wanted in return was for Veronica to love her, and even in that she had failed. She loved her, but loved the idea of the fairytale—her crown prince, a man who would sweep her off her feet and then some. It was one of the main reasons she never fell for anyone in high school or college, she knew starter husband material when it crossed her path. And the men she came in contact with, before William, could keep it moving.

"I thought we meant more to each other," Simone whispered in a tone so filled with hurt that Veronica clutched a hand to her heart. "But I see now you were just using me?" Simone's sobs came across the line with crystal clarity, "If this is how you want things to play out between us, so be it. Common courtesy would have meant telling me immediately rather than playing with my emotions."

And that is where Veronica had erred. She knew it to the bottom of her soul. Telling her early on would have hurt, but it would have provided a cleaner break than avoiding Simone had created.

"You haven't heard the last of me." Simone disconnected the call letting the threat linger in the airwaves.

Fear gripped Veronica like no other time she could remember. Simone was a dynamic lover. But she was a formidable enemy. She had seen what the woman had done to others who had crossed her. Why hadn't Veronica remembered that fact when she had sought ways not to have to tell Simone anything at all? Mostly, because she was afraid. What if one word from the scorned woman closed doors for Veronica that it took a decade to walk through. What if what she had with William was the illusion? What if it was just a passing thing? What if she only wanted him because he was safe and didn't require that she keep him hidden from the friends who would surely have something untoward to say about her relationship with a woman?

"She knew the deal, I never lied to her," Veronica said to her tear-filled reflection, without bothering to add the truth of the matter, *before now*. "She knew I wanted to be married, wanted to have children. Those were the things she could never give me."

And the truth be told, Simone tried to make up for that little fact in every way possible. Veronica had soaked up everything and had given much less in return.

* * *

"Thank you for flying Air France, Flight #47. We hope your flight has been pleasant and please come back and visit us soon. Welcome to Paris, France and enjoy your stay," the flight attendant's warm voice echoed throughout the airplane.

Veronica grabbed the red carry-on bag from the over head rack, exited the plane to make her way to the baggage claim area. There were at least ten bags that circled the carousel with her name on them. She had brought everything that might be important as she didn't know how long she would have to stay in Paris to achieve her goals.

Circling around the airport pushing a cart full of heavy bags, for what seemed to be hours had Veronica exhausted and agitated and so ready to turn tail and go back to America. All the excitement of being in Paris had waned.

She bumped into a tall blonde as she maneuvered the cart to an area that she hoped would land her in a taxi. "Pardon me," Veronica said, reaching into her purse and pulling out a French translation book. "Bon jour, Je m'appella, Veronica."

That little phrase was met with a blank stare that made Veronica's heart skip. She had tried to learn a few French terms before coming to Paris, but whatever she was spouting didn't sound anything close to the French language–which was a telling sign since her word for taxi stand, must have been close to sounding like departure gate–as everyone kept pointing her back into the airport!! To a frustrated Veronica, it seemed like everyone was saying, "Go home, you silly American."

She peered up at the woman who had to be at least six feet even in low heels and smelled of the classic Chanel No. 5, "Par ah par lez vous ang lais." Could that be translated as ... Help!!!

The beautiful woman, with classically chiseled features, laughed at Veronica's stricken expression. "It's actually pronounced, pahr–lay Vooz Leh." She extended her hand, which was pale and delicate despite her tall stature. "My name is Simone and actually, I do speak English."

Veronica released a sigh of relief. "Thank God! This is my first time to Paris and I need help, seriously. Can you please direct me to the taxi–stand?"

"I'd be more than happy to," the woman gestured toward the area directly behind them, with a big sign that stated that it was exactly what Veronica was looking for.

Veronica threw back her head and could only laugh, which was mirrored in the sweet smile of the woman standing before her.

As they walked toward the taxi stand, Veronica flipped out the sheet which had the address to her new apartment. "Are you familiar with this area?"

Simone's gaze flickered over the page. "Yes I am, In fact I don't live far from there." Then she pointed to the black stretch limousine waiting at the curb. "You can ride with me, if you would like."

Veronica felt her day was getting better. Catching a ride in a luxury vehicle far outweighed trying to find her own way in a place that was totally unfamiliar to her. "Sure, if you don't mind, I'll pay you for the ride."

"No," Simone said, frowning as though she had been insulted. "You Americans. Don't know how to accept hospitality when it is offered."

Veronica parted her lips to get in a word, but Simone carried on, "Your money will not be necessary. I truly understand how intimidating Paris can be. When I came to America so many years ago, I was only fourteen and it certainly would have been nice to have a friendly face help me."

Simone signaled and the driver came out to greet her with a warm smile, and then a curious expression at the woman standing near her. "Hello Pierre."

"Mademoiselle," he replied warmly, tipping his hat to her.

"Veronica will be riding with us," she said, sweeping into the limo. "Please take care of her bags."

The short, stocky man moved forward, inclining his head in Veronica's direction. "Mademoiselle?"

It was more a question than anything. Veronica smiled and gave him a nod. "Bon Jour, Pierre."

He grinned. Finally she had said something right!

During the drive to Veronica's apartment, Simone pointed out some places along the way and then noted that she should visit: of course, the Eiffel Tower, The Notre Dame Cathedral, The Louvre Museum, Tuileries Garden, The Champs-Élysées Avenue, The Sacred-Heart Basilica, Latin Quarter, and for the brave at heart-The Catacombs of Paris.

Veronica shared a glass of wine with Simone as the limo moved smoothly through the City of Lights. Simone shared her background and some amazing stories of her life as a model. The woman was a world traveler, but Paris always called her home, especially since her family had such strong ties to the fashion world. Veronica could not believe her good fortune.

Once Pierre pulled up to the four story, stone building with an arched courtyard, Simone placed a small sheet of paper into Veronica's hand. "Please call me anytime and I will be more than elated to show you around."

Veronica embraced Simone, and felt a stirring of something she couldn't quite name as the woman held onto her. "Thank you so much, who knows where I would've ended up without your help. And believe you me," she lifted the small slip of paper. "I'm going to take you up on showing me around town. Have a good night."

Three months in Paris and thanks to Simone, Veronica was getting around the city that held a world of mysteries, art, architecture, fashion, cuisine and Veronica having a love for all things rich and wonderful, felt like she had been destined to live in this place all of her life.

Simone was a top model for Ford Models Europe. Her long, curly blonde hair complimented a chic slim frame with sexy legs that seemed to go on forever. She was outgoing and confident and definitely turned heads wherever she went. Veronica was always proud to be in her company. Simone took Veronica under her wing, she taught her everything there was to know about the fashion business as well as a full command of French. They spent so much time together, learning about the differences and similarities in each other's lives, that Veronica let her guard down.

One evening after dinner Veronica went back to Simone's place which was located in the chic Parisian suburb of Neuilly sur Seine. Veronica strolled over to the stereo, slid in a CD that she brought with her and soon the sultry, contemporary sound of Alex Bugnon filled the air.

"Ahh, you would like someone like him," Simone purred. "He was born in Montreux, Switzerland. But he studied here at the Paris Conservatory and the famous Mozart Academy in Salzburg, Austria. Speaks French like a native. I love his work. Great choice, Veronica."

Simone sat beside Veronica, who was so relaxed by the glasses of red wine that she nearly slipped off the elegant settee. "Veronica you are nice," Simone said in that thickly accented English Veronica could never tire of hearing. "I'm glad we are friends." Fingers that had fed Veronica a symphony of cheeses that nearly melted on the tongue, accompanied by wines that she would never be able to pronounce, followed by French delicacies that were designed to titillate the most discriminating palette; were now thrumming along Veronica's collarbone, eliciting a moan that escaped before the American woman could close it off. "I like you a lot." She pressed her lips to Veronica's cheek, then trailed it until she reached the pouty lips that opened, welcoming the delicious, but forbidden intrusion.

Veronica's mind shut off for only a few seconds, but it was enough that Simone took that as a sign to continue with a kiss that was so soft in its delivery, so passionate as it built steam and became intense the moment Veronica rose to the challenge.

Finally, reason returned and Veronica pulled away, sputtering, "Why did ...what are you..."

Then Simone kissed her again, trailing lips that had been seen the world over to a place no woman–or man–had ever touched Veronica before. They went to her hardened nipples, before Simone released the bra that held rounded breasts in a lace prison. She suckled them, teased them, parting Veronica's thighs slightly to give her the range needed to explore the woman in depth. She hesitated only a moment before slipping off the black lace panties, waiting for Veronica to say something that would put an end to something that Simone had wanted the moment she laid eyes on the beautiful Black woman.

Veronica was speechless, afraid, but soon all of the fear was swept aside as Simone leaned in, draping a gentle tongue across her moist center. She cried out from the sensations that ripped through her, gripping the blonde curls as Simone's tongue created a whirlwind of pleasure that saw no immediate end. At that moment Veronica lost control and gave in to the passion that engulfed her.

Spent from the first wave of orgasms, Veronica made no protest when Simone reached for her hand, then lead her down the hallway to the bedroom.

The passion between them was nearly unquenchable. Only the fact that Veronica would one day have to leave and return to America was a sad factor in a relationship that had blossomed into something that was shunned in America, but an everyday occurrence in more advanced cultures. If Simone could give her children, then it would have been a forever thing. But the moment Simone tried to lock her down into something more permanent, Veronica made it known that marriage and children were the end all and be all as far as long term commitments would go.

Saddened by this fact, Simone did everything in her power to keep Veronica in Paris, even foregoing some major modeling assignments to help Veronica land positions in one of the more prestigious fashion houses. Though she knew within her heart she should turn down the woman's help, especially knowing the premise behind the offer, the call of doing what she loved won out over common sense.

Years later, when it was obvious that Veronica would need to return to the states, having ended the term at the current house, and being homesick for her family and friends, she could only stare at the woman she had come to adore, if not love. "Simone, please don't look so sad, you're making me sad," Veronica said in a breathy whisper. "You knew it would come to this."

Tears rolled down Simone's face, "I am going to miss you so much. I did not know it would be this difficult for me."

Simone wrapped her arms around Veronica, holding the smaller woman to her breasts.

"I know sweetheart, it's hard for me too." Veronica kissed Simone softly. "But I will keep in touch." She reached up to stroke a hand through the woman's curls.

"Au revoir, my love." Simone whispered as she released Veronica to board her plane.

After returning home, Veronica missed Simone so badly she ended up catching a flight back to Paris at least six times a year. Though, Simone had suggested on many occasions that she wanted Veronica to show her what there was to love about Chicago, Veronica was dead–set against the blonde bombshell visiting her home town. She would always manage to be "traveling" or come up with some other excuse to avoid having to see Simone when she came to the States on assignments. The woman was still very much in demand, especially after a nude photo shoot that had all those gorgeous curves outlined in grayscale detail with only a set of exquisite diamonds around her neck to display the latest line of must–have jewels. Even though she loved Simone dearly, she was ashamed of their relationship. Her religious background spoke against such liaisons. And her girlfriends, who were raised Baptist just as she had been, would never fully accept that Veronica loved a woman. So she blew off their inquiries about her love life in Paris, letting them believe that she had been with this man or that one, when it was so far from the truth it hurt. Because honestly, she wasn't thinking "religious" anything the moment Simone made love to her. She wasn't feeling ashamed then. She loved the woman, plain and simple, but the woman, despite her ability to take care of her in grand style, could never give Veronica what she sorely wanted–children.

And now that William had come along, and he was the perfect man for her, worldly, sophisticated, and rich, she knew there was no way to tread a fine line with Simone.

Simone Gaultier was part of her past. One that she could never share with William or anyone else.

Chapter 15

BANG...BANGGG...BANGGG!!!

Sherry couldn't imagine who could be at her door. Her daughters had been gone all weekend and they knew the drill—if you don't have your key, don't come calling for me.

Despite every attempt Sherry made to block out all sounds, the pounding on the door continued. Sherry ignored it, hoping whoever it was would leave. Then it hit her—what if it was the police? What if something had happened to one of her hard-headed daughters while they were out doing God knows what, with God knows who?

"Who could that be?" she whispered, noting that the phone was still off the hook, as she still wasn't up to talking to anyone.

BANG...BANGGG...BANGGG!!!

Sherry stormed to the door, jerked it open, parted her lips to scream at whoever was on the other side. She wasn't given the chance. She could feel the strength leave her body as the person on the other side stared back at her disheveled condition.

She blinked once to clear her vision. Twice to get her bearings. A third time to still the anger that welled up the moment she realized that the man in her doorway, was exactly who she thought he was.

Raynard Cosey's dark brown eyes widened in alarm, as a huge

smile spread out over his handsome features. "Sherry! Is it really you? I've finally found you."

"Finally found me?" Sherry shot back, getting over her shock. "I haven't been lost. Can't say the same for your tired ass."

Sherry glared at him as he pursed his lips to formulate a reply. There were many emotions whipping through her that she couldn't count them all, but the one that dominated was anger–something that she had every right to, given the situation.

Raynard broke the silence by saying, "Can I come in, Sherry?"

"For what?"

"We need to talk."

"We did enough talking, say, ooooooh, about what? Nineteen years ago?" Her gaze flickered over the tailored suit that fit his muscular frame to perfection, the well-groomed hair and goatee, the set of perfect white teeth–that showed his life was going a hell of a lot better than her own. "You said all you needed to say then–absolutely nothing!"

She turned to walk away, closing the door behind her.

The tip of his shoes blocked the closure. "Sherry, just give me a few minutes. Then if you want nothing to do with me, I'll totally understand."

Sherry gestured for him to move on, but he slipped inside the door, closing it behind him as he took in the surroundings. His quick glance was all it took for her to feel ashamed. Clothes littered the living room, trailing to the girl's separate rooms. The kitchen hadn't seen dishwashing liquid, a sponge, or a dishrag for a few days. Mop? What mop? It was probably holed up somewhere next to the vacuum cleaner, wherever the hell that was. She was tired, tired of trying to do everything alone, tired of trying to get help from her daughters who scoffed at any idea of boundaries or discipline; tired of trying to make ends meet and never seeing the middle; tired of just every damn thing. Raynard could judge all he liked, but right now she could give a good goddamn.

Sherry gathered up some of the clothes scattered around the couch and didn't even bother to take them to the hamper. She was working double shifts to pay off the balance of bills that seemed insurmountable. The weariness went all the way to the bone and this motherfucker shows up looking like nothing had ever touched him. How unfair was that?

Sherry moved the pizza boxes from the sofa and pointed toward the now–empty seat. "Since you're not too keen on leaving, have a seat."

Raynard looked at her a long moment, and she was so ashamed that she couldn't keep the tears from welling up in her eyes. Earlier she had thought of just packing up and leaving everything–just to go somewhere where no one knew her name or her background. To hell with the two little sluts, to hell with a job that never appreciated her–just piled on longer hours, to hell with Derrick and his threats to destroy the friendship that had survived adversities they couldn't speak about, but was certain not to survive her betrayal.

"Sherry, you okay?"

"No, Raynard," she spat, realizing that the beginning of her hard times started when she believed that he, the man who was supposed to love her to the ends of the earth, had not only abandoned her when she needed him most, but had made no effort whatsoever in all these years to cover the distance. And now he wanted to show up after all the hard work had been done, looking like he had stepped out of a GQ magazine and like he had his life together in a way she never had? "I'm not okay. How could you do this to me? To our daughter? Not even a call. I had no one." She wiped the tears away with the back of her hand. "My parents disowned me because I was pregnant with *your* child." She grimaced as another thought hit her. "And where in–da–hell did you get those weak ass condoms from anyway?"

Raynard reached out for her hand, but she snatched it away.

"And when I reached out to you, you were nowhere to be found. You told me you loved me and you promised me you would help support our daughter. You even promised we would be married right away–I could understand that wouldn't happen. But our child? You lied to me!" She stood, walked the length of the living room, which is what it took for her to voice the next sentence. "Now you come to my doorstep twenty years later. How dare you!"

Raynard stood, stepped over a mountain of beer cans. "Sherry, please hear me out. I'm sorry for what happened, sorry for what I've done to you."

She avoided his reach.

"But I freaked out. Becoming a father at eighteen scared the shit out of me."

"And I wasn't scared, too," she shrieked.

He looked away from her stricken expression. "My parents didn't help the situation either. When I went to them for advice, they put me in another college that next day. They forbid me to have any contact with you if I wanted to finish my education."

"Oh, so that's it," she said with a snap of her fingers. "You've been *in cooooollege* for the last twenty years! They've been supporting you *all this time*. Damn, I didn't know that it could happen that way." Especially since her parents had cut her off at the first sign of adversity. She still didn't have a relationship with her dad, and only had a halfway decent relationship with her mother only because they were now divorced.

"No, I ..." he let go of a long, weary sigh.

"I know you didn't expect this to be easy, right? I know you didn't think you were going to walk in here and just what?" She gestured to his professional attire. "Take up where we left off…nineteen years ago? Damn, I know people think I'm stupid, but not this fucking stupid. Like it would be really stupid for me to believe that what kept us apart all this time was your parents and that you had to finish college. You could at least tell me the truth."

Raynard settled back down on the sofa, waiting for Sherry to take the place across from him.

"After college I met a woman and we married for all the wrong reasons. It lasted only six years. I was miserable; my heart was still missing something."

Sherry folded her arms over ample breasts, trying to hold in a laugh. She could only shake her head.

"Finally, I realized it was you and my child. No one has ever made me feel the way you made me feel. I called your parents countless times and sent letters to their house. They told me that you never wanted to see me again. Each and every year, they said the same things over and over again. They would never tell me how to reach you, would never give me a lead on how to find you. They only told me that you had a baby girl. That's it."

To this Sherry looked away. Yes, it sounded like something her parents would do. Her father had felt seriously betrayed by what they had done. The "Deacon" would not like to have anyone at church find out that he hadn't kept the only child he had in line. So of course he would make Raynard pay. Just as he had made Sherry pay.

"And I accepted that for years. But that didn't help the pain go away. Having a child in this world and not knowing anything about her was unbearable. And missing you, it was overwhelming. I wasn't going to be satisfied until I heard it from your mouth. That's why I'm here today."

Sherry couldn't keep the tears at bay. "What do you want me to say?"

"Tell me what I can do to make things right between us."

"It's way past time for that." This was too much for Sherry to handle. She needed a stiff one–and she didn't mean dick, either. She went to the kitchen and grabbed two glasses. "Would you like a glass of wine?"

He shook his head, and so she went straight for the hard stuff. A gift from Dr. Washington. He'd left her with a child and a taste for 100 proof all in one swoop.

Raynard's frown was the only thing that made her pause, but it didn't stop that liquid from topping off the glass.

"Sherry, I know a lot of time has gone by and your life is completely different from when we were together in high school. You're probably married. Maybe you have other children."

She used the bottle of whiskey to gesture to her floral housecoat, and the hair all over her head, "Does it *look* like I'm married, Negro?"

"Sherry, despite what you might think, what I see right now is a woman who has given up. What I see is a woman who has let life beat her down. I know I have some part in that, but I ... wonder what happened to the Sherry who would fight me tooth and nail on even simple things. What happened to the Sherry that would debate anyone on a point so minor that they would forget what started it all?"

Sherry broke out in sobs and at that moment Raynard came forward, timidly gathered her in his arms that tightened when she didn't resist.

"That Sherry is tired. She's so tired." The wail that tore through the air rent her soul. "That Sherry has done so many things that she's ashamed of, that she just wants to crawl into a corner and die." She pulled away and looked up at him. "I'm tired of doing this. Nothing I do is right, nothing I do matters to anyone anymore. I've failed as a mother. I've failed as a friend. I'm just so…tired."

Raynard just held her, rocking her as she cried in sobs that tore through her and came out in waves. After several minutes he led her to the coach, but didn't remove his arms from her as he continued to hold her and allow the tears, the frustration to come out the best way it could.

"I have no excuse," he whispered. "I could have come long before now. I could have found a way to contact you besides going through your parents."

"They never told me anything," she said sniffling back the last of her tears. "We didn't even speak for a long time. But they could have told me about you. They knew how hard I was struggling."

"I know it'll be tough, but I hope one day you will forgive me and forward my information to my daughter. What is her name?"

"KeAnna."

"Does she look anything like me?"

Sherry smiled through her tears. "Just like you."

Raynard's head lowered to his chest. "I'm so sorry, Sherry. Nothing has mattered in my life, not the degrees, the jobs, the marriage, the cars, nothing has been right for me since I didn't stand up for you."

Sherry took his hand in hers, "It might take a while, but maybe I can find my way to forgiving you."

Raynard let out a long, slow breath and didn't bother to hide his relief.

"Your daughter might be home sometime today, if not

tomorrow," she said, confused about how much more she should tell him at this point.

He paused at that declaration. "It's like that, huh?"

"Yeah, it's like that. I haven't been here to really enforce the boundaries I've set. Neither one of my daughters," she looked up at him. "I have two, by the way." Raynard gave her a nod. "Neither one of them listen to me at any time. I've had to work to keep a roof over their heads. Getting them to clean up is like pulling my own teeth. I just don't have it in me anymore to fuss, scream, or say anything."

"First, let me check you into a hotel and I'll call a maid service to whip this place into shape."

Sherry's shoulders squared. "I can't just up and go off somewhere without letting someone know. And I'm not letting some strange woman come into my house and–"

"It's either that, or I hang around to help. Your call."

"Maid service it is. We'll leave a note." No he was not going to see the rest of the house or help wash her dirty drawers.

"We'll get a good meal into you, a nice hot bath, and a nice warm bed, and work from there and come up with a plan that can get your daughters back on track, and help establish a relationship of some sort that everyone can live with."

Sherry's shoulders relaxed as she surveyed the messy surroundings. "And by the way, I'm not married. Really"

"Oh, so you're telling me that because you want us to share a room, instead of having one of your own?" he said with a wide grin.

"Negro, it is definitely not going to be that easy," she shot back with one hand riding up on her hip.

"Now that's the Sherry I remember."

Chapter 16

Even after a year of long-distance dating, Veronica still felt as giddy as a school girl when William would call. Her love for him had grown stronger and deeper with every passing day. Yet, even after it was clear that William wasn't going to be a short lived fling, Veronica still hadn't told her friends about him for reasons unknown to her. They thought nothing of her constant trips to New York, attributing them to her job, but the mere mention of a man in her life after all this time was sure to bring questions she wasn't ready to answer, at least not right now.

As always, they were busy with their own lives and wrapped up in their own issues. Yvette was preoccupied with trying to save her marriage and Sherry's hands were full with both of her daughters' madness. The oldest, KeAnna, had dropped out of school and was on a one way road toward destruction, and her youngest, Jaynene, was pregnant–although Sherry didn't realize that Veronica knew and she hadn't shared the information with the group. As much money as Veronica had sent to help with their upbringing, she felt a profound sense of disappointment where Sherry's children were concerned. And for the reason Jaynene now stayed with her, with no mention of it to Sherry. Jaynene felt that Veronica's condo was the only place she would be safe.

Veronica seemed to have a connection with all of her friend's children. Ironic, since she had no children of her own. Though Karyn was practically set with the money Mark had left behind, Veronica insisted on establishing a college fund for both Mary and Mark Jr. They sent her progress reports and pictures of events going on in their lives. She looked forward to them. And though she had offered to send KeAnna on trips to Paris, Spain and Brazil, if she finished high school, the girl turned her nose up at the idea and dropped out. Nothing Veronica did from that point could reach her. So she just kept her in prayer. To her dismay, Yvette's twins were like phantoms. She had only seen them a few times in their young lives. It was unreal how Yvette foisted them off whenever she could, but would never allow Veronica to keep them. After a while she stopped asking.

Meanwhile, Karyn was so into Carl that she certainly wasn't finding time for anyone but him, all of which made it easy for Veronica to keep her happiness a secret. After her conversation with Simone, and how their relationship abruptly ended, she was no longer an issue. Or so she thought.

One evening, Veronica was at home reading over recent marketing strategies when William called. He could barely contain the happiness in his voice. "Honey, I'm sending a car for you so that we can have dinner at our spot."

Their favorite place was Louey's House, the Italian restaurant where they'd had their first date. Since that memorable night, they'd tried several other restaurants and cuisines, but it seemed that for milestone occasions—their one month anniversary, sixth month anniversary, their first year together, they always came back to this place. William found any reason for them to be together as much as possible. And she also noticed that if he invited her to New York, he arranged for everything. If she invited him to Chicago and tried to return the favor, he would have all charges reversed to her credit card and picked up his own tab. The man took chivalry seriously, and made her feel that she deserved no less than the best.

"Sure sweetie, I can fly out tomorrow morning."

"I'll be working late, so I'll have Charles pick you up and take you directly to the restaurant."

"Sounds great."

The next afternoon, she boarded the plane dressed in a red strapless chiffon dress, and her hair pinned up the same way she had worn it on their first date. Diamond earrings, a gift from William, and a matching necklace completed the outfit.

As promised, Charles was waiting for her at his usual place near baggage claim. They joined arms, making small talk as they headed toward the car.

Once at the restaurant, the host directed her to the table where William was already sitting, waiting with a wide smile as he stood to greet her.

She gave him a kiss before he pulled out her chair. "I thought you said you were working late?"

He smiled down at her, "Hello to you, too. Aren't you happy to see me?"

She leaned over and offered her lips for another kiss. "Of course, I am. I'm ecstatic!"

"It seems like a life time since I last saw your beautiful face."

"William," she said in a chiding tone. "It was just last weekend."

She waited for him to take his seat. Instead, he lowered to one knee, reached into the hidden pocket of his blazer and pulled out a small velvet box. Soon a few gasps echoed around them as a range of smiles flashed over the faces of nearby patrons.

"Veronica Smith, would you be my friend, my wife, my confidant, my love, for the rest of my life?"

He flipped back the lid from the box, exposing a two caret princess cut diamond that glittered even under the dim, romantic lighting.

Veronica jumped up from the seat, nearly knocking the box from his hand as she squealed with delight and wrapped her arms around him. "Yes! Yes! Yes!"

Applause rang out around them and she finally pulled away, feeling the heat flush her face. But that soon went away the moment he slipped that ring on her finger.

Later that night, after a heated love making session, she lay in William's arms, basking in the glow of love and the astonishing sparkle and beauty of her engagement ring. She had finally accomplished one of her lifelong goals. Nothing and no one would destroy her happiness. She deserved to have a good man, a good life and all the best that life had to offer.

Next to her on his nightstand her cell vibrated so hard and loud it almost buzzed off to land on the floor. At first she felt it might be one of the girls checking in on her. But a sinking feeling deep in her gut forced her to look at the display. Simone Gaultier's number came across, followed by a text message that said, "I hope you have not forgotten about me. I certainly have not forgotten about you."

Chapter 17

The four friends met the following Saturday afternoon for lunch at their favorite neighborhood restaurant. Squeezed into a booth at the Perfect Place Café and Bakery, they enjoyed gourmet salads, soups, and sandwiches while carefully avoiding the main issues brewing between them – mistrust, betrayal, and the reoccurring mentions and references to Mark's murder.

Sherry, having finished the last of her oven roasted turkey sandwich, was the first to start a conversation about something more than the superficial nonsense they'd been trying to amuse themselves with. "Ladies, I have some bad news."

Yvette gave Sherry a long, hard look and shook her head. "What now?"

Sherry frowned. "What do you mean, '*what now*? Damn! That was a cold thing for you to say. Aren't friends supposed to be the ones you can share the good and bad with?"

Yvette was just pissed that Sherry had been the first to break the small talk. She had something she needed to get off her chest too, and she'd be damned if any one of them stood in her way this time. "Well I'm just saying, what's special about your problems? My husband's cheating on me, has been for a while." Tears filled her eyes as she looked at each one of them, saying, "Can any news be worse than that?"

Veronica and Karyn shared a quick, knowing glance that went unnoticed by Yvette who was wiping away the tears she had summoned at will. They all sat there in silence, playing with the food on their plate or taking in their surroundings.

Sherry quickly released the pain that had sliced through her as she took in the venom in Yvette's voice, but it was instantly replaced with fear that maybe the woman's anger stemmed from the fact that she knew who Derrick was sleeping with. *Could he have told her? He told me he wouldn't. That asshole!*

A few moments of silence went by, and when Yvette didn't say more about the subject, Sherry gave a sigh of relief. She was in the clear, at least for now, as long as Derrick held his side of the bargain. Especially now that Raynard was trying to make amends, dating her while waiting for the right time to meet her daughters. He was also looking into properties as he realized that remaining in the area where Sherry now resided would continue to provide a world of seedy delights that his daughter now favored.

The time away had given Sherry and Raynard an opportunity to catch up, but there was an obvious strain between them at times that made it seemingly impossible for them to try to rekindle a love lost. Though she appreciated his efforts, the whole knight in shining armor, coming in to rescue her, but the save the day thing was not sitting as well with Sherry. His help had come at the right time, but how was she to tell her best friends that the man who had abandoned her and her child was now back in the picture? How was she really going to be able to cut things off with Derrick when he became angered whenever she brought it up? What a mess!

Sherry fingered the potato chips on her plate, mustering the courage to say something, anything, to Yvette. "Wow, I'm sorry. I thought I was hurting, but you've got me beat this time. I just learned that my baby girl is pregnant."

Two of the three chorused, "What?" as Veronica just shook her head and turned her gaze to focus on the artwork strategically placed on the white walls around them. The fact that the fashion queen had summarily zoned out made Sherry's heart sink. Veronica had always been the one to support her, even when the other two were a bit more reluctant.

Karyn didn't bother to mask her disapproval as her lips set in a grim line as she muttered. "Not again."

Sherry turned to her. "What the hell do you mean *not again*? Jaynene's never been pregnant!"

"I'm sorry," Karyn said smoothly, realizing how her words had been perceived. "I was just taken by surprise." She ventured a look at the other women who still hadn't made eye contact with her or Sherry, then looked down at the table. "It's just that you were around her age when you got pregnant. I guess the apple doesn't fall too far from the tree."

"Yes, Karyn, I remember like it was just yesterday," Sherry spat, glaring at her friend. "I also remember *you* being pregnant around the same age."

Karyn lifted her head, fixing a hard look on Sherry. "Yes, but I was *married*."

"Yeah, to an evil bastard who kicked your ass and sold you on the streets. Do you remember that?" she shot back, eyes flashing with anger. "Or how about when you got fed up and asked us to help you take care of that problem ... permanently? You didn't seem to think twice about asking for our help then. So if you're saying that my daughter is just like me, you might also want to remember that your mother isn't so squeaky clean, either."

Veronica's head whipped around as she reached out to pinch Sherry, growling, "Shut your mouth."

"What? You know what I'm talking about."

"But there are some of us who don't need to be reminded of that." She gripped the fleshy arm and held it tight. "My mother was there that night, and so was yours. Don't let your mouth overload your ass on that one, too. Because then you're going to put something on the table that can't be scraped away."

Sherry took in the hard expression on Veronica's face, then chanced a quick glance at Karyn, whose bottom lip had been captured within her teeth. Yvette looked at all of them, peering as though she didn't understand what was going on. And maybe she didn't. If something so traumatic that had happened to Yvette as a child had happened to Sherry, she, too, wouldn't want anyone to bring it up again. Lord, she needed a drink.

"I'm just asking for a little back-up and encouragement every now and then. It's not like I'm asking you to *kill* anyone."

A collective gasp was followed by an icy silence. No one dared to speak first. All of a sudden, Karyn stood, causing all gazes to fix on her. Looking at each one of them with a stare that could melt driven snow, she lowered her voice to just above a whisper. "I see you're going to keep throwing Mark up in my face. You just can't let the whole thing rest, can you?" She pushed the drink in Sherry's hand until it fell on the woman's lap. "Fuck you, Sherry!" she said through clenched teeth. "Fuck you all! If I had known you were going to play me like this I never would have asked for your help."

Sherry rolled her eyes, grabbed a handful of napkins to mop up the mess. "Give me a break," she taunted. "Poor sensitive little Karyn. You can say cruel things to hurt someone else but when it comes back at you, you can't handle it. Get a grip."

"I'd *never* bring up something we promised never to discuss especially knowing it could destroy us all. And now you've made reference to something else that should be long forgotten. There's just no understanding you." She glanced at Veronica, who had closed her eyes to block out whatever she could and to Yvette who was now rubbing a hand on Veronica's shoulder. "I'm really not feeling up for this bullshit today."

Before Karyn could walk away, Veronica had grabbed her hand, which was shaking so badly the thin bracelets were rattling. "Please Karyn, don't leave like this. We go back too far to allow these things to break down our friendship. Something's going on and I don't understand it. Lately everyone has been on edge for whatever reason–I'm sure they're good ones, but we can't let this tear us apart. These angry swipes at each other–I'd swear we've become enemies rather than friends who grew up together. This is the kind of thing that breaks Black women down. I thought we were above the petty jealousies, and snide remarks and the cattiness! We didn't even do this when we were teenagers. Get it together people. I've been there for you all, now I need you to be there for me."

All heads turned in her direction as Karyn lowered to her seat. "All we've been doing is sharing bad news when we get together or making some strange demands." She looked at each of the other women. "Ladies, I have some good news. I mean, *really, really* good news that I've wanted to share with you all for awhile now. And every time I want to say something, all this madness jumps off. "

"What is it," Sherry asked, placing the wet napkins back on the table.

"First, you all do something about what just happened here."

Karyn locked gazes with Sherry as Yvette folded her arms over her ample breasts, waiting.

"I'm sorry for what I said, Sherry," Karyn ground out.

"Me too," came Sherry's mumbled reply, though it was obvious from her tight expression that she didn't quite mean it.

Veronica sighed and looked off at the abstract painting that was just over Yvette's head. Disappointment stabbed her heart at the fact that none of the other women had noticed the huge rock on her finger. The only time women didn't comment on jewelry that size was when people thought it was fake. She was certain this wasn't the case. Once again, they were so caught up in their own egos, that they hadn't noticed anything new going on with her. When had they become individuals rather than the four musketeers—one for all, all for one. Evidently it had become every woman for herself these days. That did not sit well with Veronica at all. Maybe her news was just what was needed to pull them back together.

"I'm getting married!" She held out her hand, displaying her sparkly two– carat princess cut engagement ring.

Sherry gaped. Yvette's jaw dropped. Karyn's left eyebrow shot up. Despite the earlier frowns and anger, squeals of joy erupted from the other three women and Veronica sighed with relief. Stares from the people around them failed to quiet the friends in any kind of way.

Sherry grabbed her hand to get a closer look at the ring. Yvette plastered a smile on her face, which faltered seconds later as she took a quick glance at the ring on her own finger and then another look at the diamond that Veronica sported on a French manicured hand. "Damn, now that's a rock," she muttered, and that little green demon flashed in her eyes for a minute. Veronica looked away, then tried to focus on the animated conversation between Sherry and Karyn who were speculating on what type of man would give her such a wonderful declaration of his love.

"I can't believe we didn't notice this huge thing," Sherry said with a light laugh.

"I'm so happy for you girl," Yvette finally said, but her voice was so void of emotion that Veronica just flashed her a smile, but then peered at her a moment longer before giving a mild shrug. There was nothing she could do about Yvette's sullen behavior. She turned to Karyn and Sherry and told them a few details about William Butler and their year long relationship.

"A whole year," Karyn whispered, pushing the empty plate away. "And you never told anyone of us? Why!"

"That's typical Veronica for you," Sherry said with a sly grin, "always had more secrets than any of us."

Veronica grimaced at the meaning behind those words. Sherry, more than anyone had always tried to pry in Veronica's personal life, but Veronica valued her privacy, and she valued their friendship. She knew, with their religious upbringing that they would still love her, but they would never accept or understand a relationship as deep and forbidden as the one she had with Simone.

Despite the fact that neither of them could cast the first stone to begin with and as far as she knew one sin was no greater than another, but somehow her sexuality would have been deemed more of a sin than Sherry's fornications, Yvette's gold digging ways–that Veronica speculated had separated Derrick from the woman he was supposed to marry. And it definitely would not overshadow that mortal sin of thou shalt not kill. Unlike Sherry, Veronica would not point out these facts to her friends as she knew that everyone had faults, so she kept her thoughts and her relationship to herself.

"Look, just be happy for me," she whispered to the group who had now looked at her with expectant expressions. "I had my reasons. And I'll need all of your support to help me plan my engagement party, and Karyn," she said, smiling at the mother of the group. "I want you to do my wedding."

"Most definitely!" Karyn beamed. "I'd be pissed if you went to someone else." The obvious thing was that she didn't have to hide her flourishing business from her husband. "It will be an event you'll never forget." Looking to Sherry and Yvette, she added, "And you guys can help me."

Veronica laughed as she leaned back in her seat. "Yeah, you might need their help because we've set a date for six months from now."

Karyn's dark brown eyes widened with disbelief. "Six months? Have you lost your mind? We need at least a year!"

"Well, you only have six months," Veronica countered smoothly. "That's why you're the best, right? You can pull this off with no problem, Mon Cheri!" She flexed her fingers, admiring the diamond perched on her hand. "I'm not letting this one get away."

Chapter 18

A month later, Veronica strolled into Karyn's gorgeous, California-style home, which was perfect for the empty-nesters with its spacious great room with fireplace, formal dining room overlooking a large deck, full bath and guest bedroom on the first level and the spacious master suite and comfortable third bedroom nestled side-by-side on the second level.

The minute she stepped inside, the scent of vanilla filled her senses. Everywhere she looked, there were white rose petals scattered even on the tables. Scented candles floated in glass vases and calla lilies were beautifully arranged, emanating elegance, class and romance. Soft jazz—the preference of the happy couple—played in the background. She took the stairs two at a time, pleased with her decision to let the girls plan her engagement party. Everything was beautifully laid out, obviously done with the happiness of the soon-to-be hitched couple in mind.

Veronica hoped that planning something as special as a wedding would bring the group together and finally put an end to all the fighting, blaming and darkness that seemed to permeate every conversation these days. Looking around the room, she was filled with elation and excitement, but also anxiety. This would be the first time the couple's immediate families and close friends would be meeting. She could only hope it would go smoothly and that everyone would get along.

Smiling, she turned to her three best friends, who were all dressed in cream outfits like hers, and wrapped her arms around all of them in a group hug. "Everything looks amazing and so beautiful. You've really outdone yourselves. William is going to be so pleased."

Peering over the rail leading to the foyer, Sherry asked, "Where is the man of the hour, anyway?"

"He's parking the car. I can't wait for you all to meet him!"

They heard the front door shut and an unfamiliar voice, echoed throughout the house. Looking to Veronica, who was smiling like the proverbial Cheshire cat, they tore down the stairs, tearing up the space between the second landing and the front entrance. Karyn, Yvette and Sherry stopped short when they saw the regal male specimen in front of them who was dressed in an off-white suit that draped his muscular frame like a GQ model. Veronica had lied when she said he was good looking. He was *fine* with a capital "F!"

Veronica gave each one of them a sly look as she sauntered toward her mate. Then she winked and gestured for them to pick their tongues up from the floor and get themselves together. She leaned up, pressed her lips to his, then looked at her friends.

Karyn gave her a big thumbs up. Sherry nodded as though someone had asked her a question. Yvette's gaze traveled over his body as though she wanted to sop him up with gravy and a biscuit. Veronica placed her arm around his waist and pulled him closer.

"Baby, I'd like for you to meet my best friends, my sisters." Veronica pointed toward the group, singling out the woman with a warm smile on her face. "This is Karyn."

Karyn came forward, extended her hand to William, "It's a pleasure to finally meet you."

"The pleasure is all mine," William answered in a husky voice, giving her a smile that matched hers in warmth and sincerity.

Veronica gestured to Sherry, but before she had the chance to introduce the baby of the group, Yvette stepped forward, brushing past Sherry as she thrust her hand out. "Yvette Glover, nice to meet you, William."

Veronica's gaze narrowed, noticing that her voice had taken on a sultrier tone than warranted for the moment.

"Hello, Yvette," William replied, then dismissed her by fixing his gaze on the woman standing behind her, as though sensing Veronica's discomfort at the woman's bold actions.

The last woman moved forward. "I'm Sherry. We've heard so many great things about you," she said with a grin, which immediately turned into a deadpan serious look. "And speaking on behalf of all of us, there's only one thing we'll ask of you…"

William's eyebrow shot up as he waited for her to continue.

"And that is to treat our sister right."

His shoulders visually relaxed as did Veronica's. "Now that's something you won't have to worry about." His gaze focused on his lady love. "But I promise you, I will."

Once introductions were over, the girls bombarded him with questions, each sometimes speaking at the same time until a mellower baritone voice interrupted. "Hello there, I'm Carl. These ladies can be a bit much sometimes, but you'll learn that they're not so bad," he said with a hearty chuckle and giving a hearty handshake.

"Oh, stop," Karyn gave him a light slap on his chest. "William, this is my husband. Why don't you take William into the family room while we finish preparing for tonight? You two can get more acquainted and relax with a drink or two."

Even though they had just shared a wonderful kiss mere minutes before, William gave Veronica another scrumptious one and a possessive pat on her behind before following Carl to the next room.

Once he was out of eyesight and ear shot, the four women shared a giggle, sounding more like girls in junior high than women in their forties.

"Damn he's fine," Yvette said, still looking in the direction that William had just walked away from. "Girl, he's most definitely a keeper."

"Now where did you say you met this fine ass brother again? New York?" Sherry rolled her shoulders as though preparing for a championship fight. "Shoooot, I'm purchasing my ticket *today*,"

Veronica just laughed at their antics. "Please, y'all need to quit it before he hears you."

Karyn crooked her fingers, "Come on girls there are a few more things we need to do before everyone else arrives."

Veronica couldn't imagine what more needed to be done since everything looked so beautiful and perfect. Vintage champagne chilled in buckets made of crystal. Exquisite hors d'oeuvres had been prepared and were being placed on sterling silver serving trays by the catering company Karyn had hired, who were also preparing the three course meal. The dining room table, draped in a formal black and white cloth with matching linen napkins had been set with Karyn's finest china. Karyn had thought of everything – literally – even making travel and lodging arrangements for all the out of town guests. All Veronica and William had to do was show up.

Three hours later, the party was going well and everyone seemed to be enjoying themselves. Veronica was happy to see that her parents, who were laid back and personable and William's parents, who were formal and proper, connected instantly. Each set of parents stood to give the obligatory toasts, offering congratulations and best wishes while mingling in a few embarrassing childhood stories.

While the dinner plates were being cleared, Veronica approached the girls to thank them for their hard work and for throwing such a fabulous party. Across the room she noticed Yvette and Karyn huddled together in a corner talking quietly. As she approached them, the first thing that stood out was Yvette's red eyes and the glisten of tears that were threatening to fall at any minute. Either she had consumed more than her share of the champagne or the drama queen was back in action.

"Hey girls, why don't you take this conversation upstairs to the privacy of the bedroom."

Karyn whirled, crossed the distance without seeing if anyone followed.

Sherry, who was speaking with William's equally as dashing uncle, saw the girls going upstairs and quickly excused herself.

Veronica's happiness dwindled with every step. The tension between Karyn and Yvette were as if they were two magnets repelling each other.

Once in the bedroom, Sherry closed the door behind them and it wasn't a moment too soon.

Yvette started crying, then screamed at the top of her lungs, "I want him dead!"

Sherry and Veronica looked at each other, their expressions showing their confusion. How the hell did they get to this point when such a wonderful event was going on downstairs? They had to calm her down before someone heard her and came looking to see what was going on.

After a few moments, they managed to get Yvette to talk in a mostly "indoor voice," as if she were some grammar school kid who needed to be reminded of that fact. It was the best they could do under the circumstance and they weren't going to argue with the drama queen for fear that she'd just start screaming again.

Veronica and Sherry were confused at what was going on. Veronica took a spot on the bed. Sherry stayed near the door. Both switched their gazes between Yvette whose shoulders heaved in sobs, and Karyn who was fuming to the point that smoke could come out from her ears at any moment.

Yvette ended her whiny diatribe with her current mantra. "I want him dead." Yvette spat, pacing the area leading to the master bath. Veronica thought about pushing the belligerent woman into the Jacuzzi and turning on the cold water full force. How dare she taint this engagement party with her histrionics. All of Veronica's and William's relatives were downstairs having a great time. It took every effort not to storm out and just leave these three women to handle this mess. She should be with her family, not trying to calm an overindulged woman who couldn't seem to get a grip on life. Pullease!!!

"If he thinks he can just leave me and take my children to be raised by some other bitch, he's got another thing coming!" She stopped pacing long enough to look at them. "He's not going to get away with it."

Karyn moved to block Yvette's path. "You're not thinking straight. Only a court of law can have your children taken away. You can't just kill your husband because he doesn't want to stay with you."

"I beg to differ," Yvette responded in a pitch that was levels above her normal alto range. "You did! No, wait, *we* killed Mark for you." Yvette walked straight up to Karyn until she was as close as conventional space allowed. She spoke so quietly, the other two women thought they had misheard her when she said, "Now it's your time to return the favor, Karyn. Derrick must die." Yvette turned her back and walked away as if the problem, at least for her, had been solved.

Karyn bore down on the psychotic woman. "Look, I'm sick and tired of hearing this shit about him! We killed him because he was going to *kill me*, not because he was leaving me for some other woman." Karyn pushed Yvette a few steps backward. "Just because you can't keep your shit together doesn't mean I'm going to kill for you. I'm done hearing about what happened. Don't you ever dare go there with me again."

"What are you going to do, Karyn?" Yvette shrieked, moving forward as she advanced, forcing Karyn to stumble backward to have some type of space.

Karyn heaved, finally found her footing and stood her ground. "I will fuck you up just on general principle," she growled, then let that threat whirl around them. "Trust me, if Derrick's ready to walk, there's a damn good reason. The main one is you and your bullshit." Then she looked at the quiet woman standing near the door. "And that goes for you too, Sherry."

For once Sherry remained unusually silent.

"You want to threaten me?" Yvette screamed. "I really don't think you can risk having me on your bad side."

Veronica, furious that this insane argument would happen on tonight of all nights, swiftly moved from the bed to the middle of the room and stood in between Karyn and Yvette. "This is going too far. You need to calm the hell down, both of you." She turned to the hysterical woman on her right. "Yvette, what the hell is your problem? You act like you've lost your damn backbone."

Yvette tore her angry stare from Veronica, taking a long, steadying breath. "My husband wants to leave me, take my children and everything I've worked so hard to achieve." She looked at each of the women. "He's sleeping with some other woman, I know it! And I'll be damned if he takes everything just to give it to some other bitch."

Veronica shook her head. "And you want to take his *life* for that? How stupid can you be," she spat. "You had a way of making money before you met his ass, so suck it up and get over yourself."

"And wait just a minute, Yvette," Sherry said moving forward to stand next to the four poster bed. "You need to tell them the *whole* story. Tell them exactly why he's pissed at you. Like what you'd done to get him to marry you. Or all the things you did to destroy his relationship with Lisa."

"How do *you* know *he* found out about all that?" Yvette said, peering suspiciously at Sherry, who didn't have the presence of mind to know that she'd slipped up.

He called me one day upset!" Sherry shook her head. "He even knows you're sleeping around on him now. I wouldn't stay with your tired ass either. Who knows what disease you have right now."

The room became so silent each woman could hear her own heart beating. Not even Veronica or Karyn knew those minor details.

Yvette's tears had dried with every bitter word that came out of Sherry's mouth. Suddenly, her arm drew back and she released it, slapping Sherry in the face with a force so hard she staggered backward until she bounced off the nearest wall.

"How could you have talked to my husband and not told me? The only way Derrick could know any of that is if *you* told him!" Yvette screamed, pushing Karyn away from her who had failed in an effort to hold her back. "I trusted you when I confided in you and now you're conspiring with Derrick? Why?" She barreled forward, pushing Sherry to the ground. "What's in it for you, slut?"

Sherry jumped up from the floor, grabbed Yvette by her neck, and tossed her to the bed, slamming a fist in her face. "You've always been a spoiled, selfish bitch. Now all your shit has backfired. You deserve just what you get. He should leave you! Your gold digging ass doesn't deserve a dime."

Karyn and Veronica tried in vain to pull the fleshy woman off Yvette, who had plenty of fight still left in her. "Now you see what it feels like to be on the receiving end of pain. This is what you get for getting pregnant to trap a man," Sherry huffed, still fighting off blows.

Veronica and Karyn eyes bucked in disbelief as they tried to keep the two women apart.

"Don't be jealous of me because your life is so miserable. Because your ass is always struggling. Never have two nickels to rub together to make smoke," she said with a harsh laugh. "Or is it because you don't have a man in your life to love you the way Derrick loved me? So let's fuck with Yvette, right? Let's destroy Yvette's life?" Her lips lengthened into a long, bitter smile. "You'll *never* have a man, you jealous bitch!"

"That's where you're wrong," Sherry shot back from her place behind Veronica. "I do have a man who loves me." Her lips spread into a smile that matched Yvette's viciousness. "Your husband."

Chapter 19

Veronica's eyes widened in horror. Karyn released her grip on Sherry's body as if she had just been burned by fire. Sherry stood stock still having realized that, once again, her mouth had gotten her into hot water!

"What, did you say?" Yvette said in a low tone that caused everyone to freeze. "Your stinky ass is fucking my husband? *You're* the bitch he's leaving me for?"

Yvette lunged toward Sherry, grabbing a fistful of hair. She pulled her to the floor, straddled her hefty form and smashed a fist into her face. "Bitch, you are dead! I'm going to kill your fat ass, then I'll take care of Derrick!"

For a moment, neither Veronica or Karyn moved as they locked gazes, unsure as to what they should do. Hell, Sherry did need her ass kicked for this one.

They allowed them to duke it out for a few minutes before Veronica finally moved forward, pulling Yvette away from Sherry, who in turn, sprang out, reaching for Yvette. Karyn pushed her back then managed to pin Sherry to the bed.

Yvette swung out, almost hitting Veronica instead of her intended target, screaming, "How could you do this to me?"

Veronica shook Yvette underneath her saying, "Now if you miss and hit me, I'm going to whip *your* ass. Calm the fuck down!"

"What have I ever done to you to deserve this?" Yvette said, sobbing her frustration. "I loved you like a sister! Why?"

Karyn and Veronica exchanged glances, both at a loss for words. First Yvette's madness, now Sherry's betrayal. It was all too much for one evening. People were still downstairs celebrating. And it probably hadn't escaped anyone's notice that the four women were missing in action.

Yvette managed to escape Veronica's grip. The others braced, fearing she'd go after Sherry again, but instead, she turned and left the room, slamming the door behind her. Storming down the stairs, she grabbed her purse, and walked straight past the guests who turned her way, taking in the torn state of her clothes as she flew out the front door, slamming that one behind her, too.

Veronica and Karyn wanted to go after Yvette, but they also didn't want to cause more of a scene than Yvette's abrupt departure.

Karyn looked at Sherry who was still lying on the bed, clothes ripped from around her shoulder. "How could you have stooped so low? You've allowed the alcohol to take over. You're letting something else make your decisions for you, and honey, they ain't good ones." She peered down at the woman who was using a hand to wipe the blood from her mouth. "Whatever happened to…I am my sister's keeper. That's the kind of friendship we had. Now you've destroyed that."

Veronica shook her head as she slumped to the floor. *What had happened to them? How had they gotten to the point where all they did was scream at each other and hate one another?*

The party ended the moment a haggard Sherry, a worried Karyn, and Veronica's tear–stained face came into view. William stood, leaving her parents on the couch and went to Veronica, but she held her hand out to keep him from asking the questions that she was sure everyone wanted answers to. The vibe went from festive to anxious in a matter of seconds.

William nodded to Carl, who went to turn the stereo down. William said, "Everyone, thank you for coming and I hope you have a good night and safe trip back home." With that he crossed the distance to Veronica, who gripped his arms and leaned on his chest. He just held her, throwing a questioning glance in Karyn's direction. Carl lifted his wife's chin, waiting for her to give some type of explanation, but she, too, remained mum.

Murmurs erupted around them as the guests made their way to the door. Veronica gave William a kiss and told him, "I'm going to stay and help Karyn clean up." He simply nodded, thinking she meant the remains of the party, when it was clear there was so much more that needed to be fixed. One night certainly wouldn't repair the damage that had been done.

Karyn turned to Carl. "Why don't you and William go out to Floyd's Sport's Bar for awhile? Have a few drinks while we get things squared away here."

Carl swept a glance at each of women's faces, and asked, "Sweetie, is everything okay? Yvette almost laid me out when she stormed out of here."

"I need a ride home," Sherry said in a voice so mild that almost no one recognized that it came from her. Except Karyn who managed to shoot a death glare in Sherry's direction before turning back to her husband and giving him a hug that was as devoid of energy as she was of strength. "Oh, baby, everything's fine. Nothing for you to be concerned about. She had to leave because she has an early morning meeting."

Carl cupped her face in his hands, forcing her to look him in the eye. "She looked upset, actually more than upset. She looked... crazy. Welts on her face, clothes all torn up. Baby, what happened up there?"

"I'm not sure," Karyn replied, trying to politely brush him off. "Didn't you notice that Derrick wasn't here?"

Carl simply nodded.

"They're having some marital problems, but she'll be fine."

He just looked at her without voicing the obvious. None of what Karyn had just said explained what had gone on in their master bedroom.

William took one last look in Veronica's direction, who tried to playfully shove him toward the door to follow Carl, insisting that it would be all right when in her heart of hearts, nothing could be further from the truth.

When the men had finally left the house and all the guests were gone, the three women gathered in the kitchen. Veronica took a seat at the table, Karyn leaned on the kitchen counter, and Sherry snagged a glass from the cabinet, and naturally, turned to hit the bar.

"Oh, no, my sister, your ass won't be drinking anything else tonight," Karyn said with a voice that let the woman know she meant business. "That's the main part of your problem. Your mouth—what you put in it and what comes out!"

Sherry placed the glass on the table and slumped into a seat next to Veronica.

Karyn stilled her mind, then turned to them. "I can't believe Yvette wants me to kill Derrick."

There she goes again, Sherry thought, I can't believe this shit, if it's not about Karyn it's not worth talking about.

"I can't believe she practically threatened to land our asses in jail if you don't." Veronica added which snapped Sherry to attention.

"Yes, I picked up on that too." Karyn stood, grabbed a few of the remaining plates and went to the sink. "Doesn't she realize that if we go down, she goes down? She has just as much to lose as we do."

Karyn's shoulders heaved in an effort not to cry. One of the fine china plates slipped through her fingers, crashing to the floor.

Veronica went to her, guiding the sobbing woman back to the chair, leaving the shattered pieces where they were.

She couldn't stop thinking about what had just transpired. One best friend was sleeping with another best friend's husband. And as a consequence, said husband wanted to leave the wife, which had angered the woman to the point she wanted him dead. And the wife wanted Karyn to kill him because she had killed on her behalf before. How unreal was that?

Sherry, more frustrated that the women were ignoring her than the fact that she was the catalyst for all of the dark happenings in their recent misfortunes, flipped her hand in the air, a scowl marring her normally pretty face. "Forget about her! She's just pissed because Derrick finally sees her for who she really is."

Veronica turned to Sherry, mirroring Karyn's disappointed look. "What you've done is unforgivable! You've broken the cardinal rule! Friends don't sleep with friend's husbands!"

A chilling thought came to Karyn. She stilled the candle in her hand as she looked over at Sherry. "And I hope you didn't tell Derrick anything about Mark. Since that's been your only topic of conversation lately."

Sherry lowered her gaze trying to filter through that flimsy network of memories which had become foggier as of late. She finally spoke the words that made Karyn's shoulders slump with defeat. "I don't know. I really don't know!"

"Why would you sleep with him in the first place?"

Veronica handed Sherry a napkin to wipe away the sudden onslaught of tears.

"He told me he loved me." She couldn't very well tell them that she had tried to cut things off with Derrick, long before Raynard popped up. But his threat always lingered over her head and whenever she flat out refused, he would play his trump card. She had no choice but to go to him when he demanded to see her. She'd had an easier time since she had been honest and told Raynard about it. She passed the phone to Raynard on the last day Derrick called and that had ended things. At least she thought it had. Raynard had told her time and again that she should come honest with the other three as she had with him. Unfortunately, she had never found the right moment.

"He said he loved you? And you *believed* that?" Karyn screamed, moving out of her seat so that she could stand in front of Sherry. "Do you really think he *loves* you? That he would leave Yvette...for you?" She shook her head, "You're dumber than I thought."

Veronica, who was always the one to keep her cool, released a weary sigh. "Baby girl, he just played you to get back at Yvette."

Sherry sat up, grabbing her heart. "No, no, I don't believe that."

"You don't *want* to believe it, but you know it's true," Veronica shot back. "And this affects more than just Yvette. How are we supposed to look at you the same way after treating one of us as shitty as you've treated her? While you had your legs in the air, you might've slipped up and told him something!" she said with a glare that told how she felt inside. "And you" she crooked her fingers as quotes. "Can't even remember! I don't believe this shit."

"I'm really sorry."

"And are you sure he said he's leaving Yvette for you?" Karyn snapped, gaping at the woman who was so dense that she might be holding onto a pipe dream even though evidence bore out the truth. "Did *he* tell you that? Or is this just another imagined story you want to believe?"

"Think about it," Veronica said slowly. "Did he say those exact words to you?"

Sherry just looked at them, then lowered her gaze. "Well no, he didn't tell me those *exact* words, but who else could it be?"

Veronica's anger had hit an all time high. "Have you ever stopped to think that maybe, just maybe, you aren't the only one he's sticking his dick into? She told Karyn that he stays away from home days at a time. Is he spending days and night with you?"

"No, of course not," Karyn taunted. "She does actually work, double shifts. Right, Sherry?"

Sherry eyes filled with tears. "No, he hasn't been spending any nights at my house." She couldn't rightfully add, because I've been seeing Raynard. But then again, maybe now was the time. "Actually, I—"

"You weren't thinking of anyone but yourself," Karyn said, her voice dripping with disdain. "You never once stopped to think about the effect that this would have on your friendship with us, did you?" Karyn gritted her teeth. "If you could sleep with Derrick, what's to stop you from going after Carl? Or William?"

Veronica blinked wide at that thought. She was aware that Sherry slept around but didn't think she'd creep so close to home, but now it was a valid concern.

"I would never do that to either of you," she protested, trying to reach for Karyn's hand. "You've already been through so much, and Veronica, you've never been anything but kind to anyone you've met." Then her gaze narrowed on the floral centerpiece on Karyn's glass table. "But Yvette," she spat. "That woman can be evil. She got what was coming to her."

Karyn slammed her hand down on the kitchen table, causing everyone to jump. "You know, you are lower than low. He wanted to get back at Yvette. And thanks to you, his mission's accomplished."

Sherry's face tightened with her effort not to cry again. "Karyn, Veronica, I've made a mess of things. I hope you can forgive me. I love Yvette. I didn't mean to hurt her. I was lonely, and Derrick played on that. And I have cut it off. I haven't seen him in at least a couple weeks." She buried her face in her hands. "Will she ever be able to forgive me?"

Karyn locked gazes with Veronica who shook her head and mouthed the words, "I don't think so."

"We need to talk to her. I'll call her tomorrow, give her some time to cool down and hope and pray she'll agree to see us."

Karyn fixed her gaze on the outside deck that Carl was painstakingly restoring to its former beauty. "Yvette might get her wish after all. If Derrick knows, which I have a feeling he does, we need to keep him quiet before he lands us all in jail."

Chapter 20

Karyn placed the last of her dishes in the sink, having already stacked up the items that would be picked up by the caterer in a couple of hours. Carl was still out with William, a good thing since Karyn needed to be alone with her thoughts. She hadn't even tried to call Yvette. Anger at that woman didn't bode well for peaceful conversation. If she had known that things would come to this point, that her happiness could be taken in a fleeting moment, then maybe it would have been better if Mark *had* killed her.

Dead was certainly better than living in fear.

***

Once she moved back in with Mark after leaving him for a week, she became a prisoner in her own home. It seemed as if he enjoyed her tears, her screams, reveled in her pain. Mark knew she'd never leave the house bruised, bloody, and battered, so he made sure there was a steady visible stream of welts and bruising, forcing her to stay secluded from her friends and family. His beatings became so frequent that she would jump at any slight movement he made.

At one point, she went weeks without stepping foot outside or speaking to anyone from the outside world. Even though she wanted to, she knew she couldn't involve her parents for fear of what Mark would do to them. She could never forgive herself if he hurt them because of her. He would do exactly that if she defied him.

One afternoon, when Mark normally stayed away for hours, Karyn snuck out to Veronica's house which was only a few miles away. Luckily, Yvette and Sherry were there, too.

The moment Veronica opened the door, she shrieked. "Oh my God, who did that to your face? I hardly recognized you, sweetie!"

Yvette pushed Veronica aside and ushered Karyn in and planted her into a seat next to Sherry. "What happened, Karyn? We haven't seen you since whenever!"

Karyn, trying to catch her breath, struggled to talk. After the beating she'd gotten the night before, breathing, especially after a three-mile run was a bit of a challenge. She didn't doubt that he might have broken a rib this time. If he hadn't, it certainly felt that way.

The three women stopped with the questions long enough to hold her, even if timidly so they wouldn't aggravate an already bad condition. Veronica went away and came back with a cool towel for her face.

Yvette, who had practically worn a hole in the carpet as she stole sideways glances at their wounded friend. "Who would do this to someone?" She stopped and turned to face the trembling, frail woman on the sofa. "You need to tell us what happened."

"Mark," Karyn said so quietly that her friends almost wondered if she had even opened her mouth to respond.

Sherry ran to Veronica's front closet, finding the softball bat tucked way in the corner and returned to where the rest of them sat. "Let's go!"

Karyn reached for Sherry's hands, screaming, "No! You can't go over there, Sherry. If he found out I told you, he'll kill me. I love you and I'm touched that you would go to bat for me, literally," she said in a dry tone as her gaze swept to the other women, "but I can't put you in that kind of danger. I have to be there for my kids and if he keeps going the way he has lately, I'm going to die before I see them grow up." She held on tightly to Sherry's arm whispering, "Please, I just needed to see your faces. I need to get away…even if it's just for a little while."

"Are you actually protecting him?" Yvette responded angrily. "I told you we should get you someplace out of state! If we go over there right now and beat the living shit out of him, he'll think twice about putting his hands on you ever again."

"That's right," Sherry replied wielding the bat in her right hand. "He's a punk! Any man who puts his hands on a woman is nothing. I bet if a man got up in his face he would tuck his tail between his legs and run like a little bitch."

"No, you don't understand!" Karyn cried, uncontrollably. "It's not as simple as beating him up. Mark, well," she swept a gaze across the women she had known all her life, wondering how much information she could share. "He's a big time drug dealer and pimp. He takes ruthless to a whole new level. He might go after my parents, or do something to my children too, and all of you as well. He would never let anyone, especially three *women*, get away with beating him. It'd ruin his reputation on the streets. "

"You need to get your kids and leave the state *now*," Veronica said yelling. "I'll help you. You can go stay with my momma until we sort things out. Or I could send you to my friend in Paris."

"I can't," Karyn replied with a weary shake of her head. "Mark's always picking up the kids and he's the one who deals with anything to do with their school. They haven't seen me in ages. Everything was fine until my stupid ass decided to start this event planning business.

Mark's always been a good husband and father. "

The other three women stared at her, stunned and appalled. Did she realize what she had just said? How could she possibly think that it was *her* fault that Mark smacked her around for breakfast, lunch, and dinner?

Karyn would never tell the girls this, but deep down inside, she still loved him, and wanted things to go back to the way they were, even after everything he had done to her. Karyn was afraid and confused, maybe she deserved some of what he'd done. All he wanted was for her to stay at home. How could she make it without him? She had been with him since she was seventeen, her entire adult life had revolved around being married to him. Would she be able to survive on her own in some other state? In another country? Her decision was made for her a long time ago. "I'm going to go back and fix my mistakes. I'm going to be a good wife and mother. Then everything will go back to the way it was. We'll be happy and things will be fine."

"Stop! Do you hear yourself?" Sherry frowned as she looked down at the woman rocking back and forth on the sofa. "Mark's brainwashed you. He wants total control of you, and if you go back, he'll have it."

"I can't understand you." Veronica yelled. "How can you justify staying with a man who's done what he has to you?"

"Until I can find a way to get out with my children and without Mark ever finding me, I have to stay and at least pretend things are fine. It's actually the safest thing for me to do right now."

Despite their protests, she tore away and returned home. Mark never found out about her trip to Veronica's, and things, as the girls had suspected, went back to normal, which for her meant taking a beating every now and then. She began to find ways to slip out and see the girls, if not her family—and they would say the same things each time, but she was too afraid to act on the very things that would save her life—and her children's lives.

One morning, he walked into the bedroom, yelling, "So you've been sneaking out with some nigger?" He jerked the covers from around her frail body. "Wake-up bitch! Is your lazy ass going to sleep all day? Fix yourself up. We have somewhere to go." He held out a red mini dress and a pair of three inch heels. Tossing them at her, he growled, "And wear this."

Still in a daze, she wondered why he would think she was sleeping around? She barely wanted to sleep with him! Had he followed her? Why would he want her to put on such slutty looking clothes, especially so early in the morning. Karyn rubbed her eyes trying to focus her vision, "Where are we going?"

"Don't question me! Just get dressed."

They drove to her parents' home and left the kids with her mom, who parted her lips to question Karyn, but Mark didn't give her the opportunity to say a word as they tore out of the driveway. She knew the children would be safe and happy to escape the military style discipline received at the hands of their father. She also knew that her parents had not seen the children in so long they would be happy for that at least. But to leave and not say anything was uncalled for. What did Mark have up his sleeve?

The silence between them was cold and eerie as he hit the expressway at top speed. She kept her body tight and still so he wouldn't lash out at her for the slightest movement she could make.

"You're going to learn what it means to appreciate a good man," he said as he exited the highway and turned into a neighborhood known for violence and drugs. Karyn's stomach churned and her body began to tremble. What could be worse than the things he had already done to her? Karyn knew this time she was about to die. But why did he have her in such horrible clothes?

"I want you to see what it's like for me when I'm out here in these streets providing a good life for my family, only to have my wife show me that it's not good enough."

They walked toward an abandoned building where a burly man stood just inside the steel door. As they approached, the man opened the door and bowed his head saying a respectful, "Good morning, Mr. James, how are you today?"

Mark didn't bother to answer, brushing the man aside as he dragged Karyn with him inside the dilapidated building.

They went up a set of stairs to the second floor, down an infested hall that smelled of piss and garbage, sidestepping the rats that scurried their way before turning into an apartment at the end of the rickety hallway. They had barely managed to get through the door before men's voices chanted in unison, "Good morning, Mr. James. How are you this morning Mr. James?" She froze, taking in at the range of mangy–looking and weary faces of men who treated her husband as though he were a king.

They didn't acknowledge Karyn, whose heart fluttered with worry. What she saw in that room caused her to grip Mark so tightly, it would be impossible for him to leave her behind. Her enemy had suddenly become her protector.

Mark looked down at her and could only smile at her fear–stricken expression. "You're with me. You have nothing to worry about. Nothing goes down here unless I say so."

Karyn moved further into the room behind Mark, where another set of men who looked a lot like city cops were guarding the place. They patted down the young kids with school backpacks rushing in and out of the door, past her, some almost knocking her over in a quest to hurry to their destination.

The authority and power Mark exhibited made everyone take notice, especially Karyn. There were towering mounds of white powder on a table that had been coated with clear plastic sheeting. Scales in several different forms littered the table along with small plastic bags. There wasn't a female in the room. Karyn was afraid to wonder why.

"Now that you have gotten a taste of my life inside," he snarled. "I want to take you to the streets where all the action happens."

He got in the car and he began driving, heading down Rush Street and passing scantily clad women on the sidewalks, some of which leaned into the car windows to proposition the drivers who had stopped to check them out.

Mark pulled over to the curb, got out of the car, motioning for Karyn to follow. She was too frightened to move. He walked to the passenger side and yanked her from her seat. She staggered, and almost hit the ground, but recovered just in time. Just as she had managed to smooth out her dress, two men pulled up and offered Mark money to sleep with the "pretty lady" on his arm.

Mark looked down. His lips spread into a sneer. It was then Karyn understood exactly what his plans were.

She tried to release his grip from her arm. "No Mark, please no! I'll do whatever you say. I won't question you ever again. You'll never hear a complaint out of my mouth."

"And you won't leave the house again without my permission?"

"No, I promise, I won't. Mark please don't do this to me," she cried out.

"I want to make sure of that."

Shoving her toward the men, he took their money, but gave the men a warning. "Make sure you use a condom, like I told you." He watched them hop in their car and head toward the shady motel a few blocks away. Karyn's cries fell on deaf ears. Vagabonds and crack addicts stood in front of the building begging for money. The sheets were stained and bugs were running rampant around the motel room.

Karyn kicked, trying to get out of their reach. Screams for help went unanswered. One of the men slapped her, and then forced a small white pill down her throat while the other one continued to hold her down. Soon, everything became a blur. She vaguely remembered being tied up and both of the men having their way with her for hours. Everything good within her died in that cheap, vermin-infested motel room.

Mark returned once it was dark, and found the room where Karyn's lifeless form laid, her hands still tied to the bedpost. He sat on the edge of the bed, took out a cigarette, and lit it before looking down on her. "This could be you, bitch, but I decided to put you in the big house because you were my queen." His eyes narrowed to slits. "You changed. You wanted to have dreams," he spat. "you want to *pursue* shit."

He untied her hands and grabbed her by her hair and pulled her up so that her face was nearly touching his, spit flying from his mouth and landing onto her tear-stained face as he said, "Bitch, *I'm* your dream and that's all you need, got that? You need to go back to being that sweet, obedient girl I met so many years ago, 'cause if you don't, this is what you'll get. Everyday. Understand?"

Her throat, tight with stress and fear, made it impossible for her to talk, making her resort to a nod to acknowledge his threat.

She thought he was done threatening her, but before leaving the motel, he threw down his trump card—her children. He would only give her so many chances before he'd teach her a lesson that she knew she couldn't live with. She could handle the beatings. She could even deal with being forced to have sex with those strange men, but having her children taken from her permanently was out of the question. Just the thought made her breath catch and her heart stop.

After that awful night, Karyn made every attempt to muster the strength and courage she'd always had, but had somehow been lost between the worlds of fear and shame. She had to find a way out for herself and her children. She knew she would need her friends help to organize and execute her escape to freedom. If anyone could do it, she knew they could help her get out of the mess she had found herself in. But as so often was the case, Karyn found excuse after excuse to delay leaving her husband.

On days when he managed to treat her like a human being, she thought there was hope for the two of them. And on the days when he only gave her an occasional slap, she reminded herself that she could live with that so long as he continued to pay the bills, put food on the table, and provide for her and the kids. Then there were the days when he beat her so badly she couldn't get out of bed, she feared for her life and knew if she tried to leave, he would hunt her down and kill her. She could never leave him. She couldn't protect everyone that would be affected if she did.

Then one evening, something happened that made her decision an easy one. After dinner, she went downstairs to the basement and was shocked and appalled to discover Mark standing just behind Mark Jr., saying, "You need to grip the handle like this. Make sure you focus and have the gun pointing on your target, then pull the trigger."

Mark Jr. was doing his best to do as his father commanded, but it was clear from his tense shoulders and dilated pupils that he was anything but interested. In fact, the minute he sensed Karyn's presence, he instinctively looked in her direction for help.

Mark Senior, having not noticed that she had slipped into the room, continued with his lesson. "And always be alert."

"Yes, Dad," her son said in a weary tone.

Disgust filled her mouth. She wanted to throw up the last remnants of dinner. It was like a bad accident where you didn't want to see the results, but you couldn't look away either. *Not my children.* She never thought she could hate someone as much as she hated her husband at that moment. Watching him teach her baby boy how to hold a gun, she knew she wanted him out of their lives forever. Mark had crossed a line that there was no coming back from.

Weeks later, when her girlfriends had set the wheels in motion to take Mark out of the picture, she sat holding her Bible and praying. The door bell jarred her out of her stupor as she rocked back and forth on the sofa. Two officers were standing at the threshold of her front door, their faces solemn, their stance respectful.

She took a deep breath, swallowing back a sudden onslaught of fear. "Good evening officers. What can I do for you?"

The taller of the two presented a badge, before asking, "Are you Mrs. James?"

"Yes, I am." She looked from one officer to the other. "Is there something wrong?"

"Mind if we step inside for a minute, ma'am?"

Nodding, she opened the door wide, allowing the two men to stand just inside the entryway. "Is Mark James your husband, ma'am?"

She blinked a moment, then peered up at them. "Why?"

The stockier one released a small, sad sigh. "We're sorry to inform you ma'am, but your husband was murdered this evening."

Karyn's hands began to tremble, tears rolled down her face and she bent over thinking, *My God, they actually pulled it off!*

The officers probably thought nothing of her reaction as it was what anyone would expect from a woman who had just found out her husband was murdered. It only helped her cause when she screamed, "No! he just left here a few hours ago. Mark can't be dead. We just had dinner and we... He can't be dead!" She was shocked at her reaction.

She didn't think she would be able to pull off the role of a devastated wife. What she thought she would feel is happiness and relief. Some of it wasn't acting. Karyn was actually sad that it had come to this.

Mark was dead! As she stood there looking at the officers, she suddenly let out a howling scream and they had to catch her before she hit the ground. Deep down inside, joy filled every part of her body.

Freedom. Finally, Freedom!

* * *

At the funeral all Karyn could do was stare straight ahead and try to keep what remained of her composure. Pimps, hustlers, gangsters and prostitutes decked out in the most outlandish attire she had ever seen, filed into the funeral home as though they were as welcome as the family, pastor, choir members, and police officers who were already seated.

One masculine–looking woman shocked Karyn by screaming at the head of the casket, "Mark I love you! It isn't fair! Now my kids will have to grow up without their daddy!"

Karyn looked over at her teenage children whose hands the woman held. The children looked just like Mark, looked just like Karyn's own two children!

Three other women came forward to confront the screaming woman, and an argument ensued about whose children were really Mark's and whose were just ho's trying to cash in on his untimely death. They almost tipped the casket over when the argument escalated to blows.

That bastard! Karyn thought, calculating that there were at least ten other children Mark had fathered without her having ever finding out anything until he was somewhere she could no longer confront him. As if she would have if he were still alive.

She thought that in his death, she could finally find some peace, but instead she felt more hatred toward the man who had made her life a living hell. And now, even in his death, he had left a legacy of embarrassment. She never invited these people! How had they even found out?

Karyn played the role of the grieving widow to the best of her ability, saying the right things at the right time and crying at the right moments, when all she wanted to do was have it all over and done. Her family was appalled at the developments before and during the funeral. Veronica, Yvette, and Sherry sat in the back of the church wearing dark shades, keeping to themselves, but from the tense set of their shoulders—she could tell that the other women's antics were wearing on them, too. Occasionally one of them would chance a small smile or a nod in Karyn direction. She returned it in kind.

Karyn's mother approached her, with a wary glance toward the commotion behind them. "Honey, we're here for you if you need anything. Just call us and we'll be there."

"Thanks Mom." She leaned over and kissed the woman's weathered cheek before she turned to hug her grandchildren.

Karyn's dad, shorter and more humble than she remembered, embraced her as he whispered, "You know this is for the best. Sometimes, God has a way of rescuing us from our enemies."

"I know, Dad," she said, while silently adding with a look at the back of the church, *and sometimes our friends can help things along.*

She turned away from her father to look at her children who were taking Mark's death exceptionally hard. Going to them, she gave them each a hug and kiss and let them know that everything would be okay.

Mary looked up with tears falling down her face, playing with the white bows on the red dress she wore. "Mom, why did this have to happen to daddy? Was he a bad man?"

Mark Junior scowled. "And who are all of these strange people saying they knew dad? And what's with these kids calling him daddy? He wasn't their daddy!" he yelled.

Karyn put a calming hand on his shoulder. "We'll talk about it when we get home, okay?"

Both of the children nodded, but neither looked comforted by her vague words. There was no comfort to give. She could only be grateful that she hadn't been one of his whores. They looked worse for the wear. What was she saying? She had been his whore. He just didn't keep her out on the street like the others. They all feared him. Some adored him. But one thing was for certain, he owned them mind, body and soul—just like Karyn.

* * *

Everyone who attended the repast following the funeral had left. Her children were with her parents. Karyn poured a glass of wine and sat back and thought about what was next for her life. She decided that for her sanity she would get rid of everything that belonged to Mark. Then on a second thought, picturing all of those strange people at the funeral, it would be best if she moved into a new home and a totally different neighborhood. That would help keep them safe from all of Mark's illegal dealings. What would happen if one of those whores showed up demanding money. Only those she loved would know her new location.

After a couple of months had gone by, true to her word Karyn began unpacking in her new house, a long way from the house that had brought her so much pain. She was focusing on rebuilding her life and as if life itself wanted to make sure things stayed that way, she had found evidence that Mark had actually made some sound legal investments that would benefit her and the family.

Picking up the phone, she called one of her friends to discuss her newest discovery. "Veronica, I'm glad you're back in Chicago." Karyn said, lounging on the beige sectional set she had purchased for her new home. "You would not believe that man. He really was a financial genius." She threw her head back and released a victorious laugh. "And I really do believe he loved us in his own sick way, because he made sure we would be set for life. I'll never, and I mean never, have to work again. His lawyer–"

"What?" Veronica said with a mild gasp. "Mark had a lawyer?"

"Yes, girl, his *lawyer* called and updated me on his finances." She brushed a finger over the document on the top of the pile. "He had additional insurance policies on himself, on me, even the kids. He even had investments in stocks and bonds of companies I'd never even heard of. I knew nothing about any of it."

"The man had many secrets."

"You don't know the half of it." She kicked off her shoes and lit a vanilla scented candle and poured herself another glass of wine. "Lord, I'm glad none of those fools from the funeral have tracked me down."

"I thought it was like something out of a circus."

Karyn could hear Veronica catching her breath from laughing so hard. "I'm glad I had on shades, because some of those outrageous outfits had me dying. I knew it wouldn't look right if I let it go. But damn, how could he associate himself with those types of people?"

"Girl, he was one of those people, it was his way of life, but thank God it's all behind me now." She exhaled. "I'm going to enjoy what he left because after all the misery he put me through, I deserve it all."

"You deserve all that and more. Maybe the bastard will be able to rest in peace."

"Yeah, you're right! I just want to get myself back on track. And when I do, I'm taking my girls on a trip," she smiled, warming up to the idea. "It'll all be on me. It's the least I can do."

Sure enough, a few months later, she treated the three women to a holiday in Hawaii for a full week. She scheduled spa dates for pampering, treated them to dinner and nights out on the town. She did notice that Yvette was more sullen, and at times she zoned out as the women discussed the trip, their lives, and what they wanted to do in the future.

For the next several years, Karyn focused on going back to school, building her business and on the children. She wanted to get them all in a better place mentally so that they could move forward and live happier lives. Among the first changes she made was joining a church. There she gained the spiritual support and guidance she, and her children, so desperately needed.

Months after joining Life Saving Nondenominational Church she met Carl Johnson, the man of her dreams and from there, everything had finally fallen into place.

Mark James, pimp, drug dealer, abuser and fraud soon became a thing of the past.

Life could only get better for Karyn and her children.

Chapter 21

The next day, following Veronica's engagement party, Karyn woke up hoping she had dreamed the nightmare that had happened in her master bedroom, only to discover that wasn't the case. The fight between Sherry and Yvette had been very real. There was still a swatch of blood on the lower edge of the Egyptian cotton comforter draping the bed. The Lalique vase had a cracked edge and the plush white carpet was peppered with spots of blood that she was certain would never come out. It had taken all of her acting skills to dodge Carl's questions after he had dropped William at Veronica's place and came back home. Finally she just broke down in tears and that shut him down—always had. She hated to deceive him, but she had no choice in the matter.

She threw the covers back, slipped to the side of the bed and tried to hold her head up. Her heart was still racing from all of the drama. Yvette had threatened her! Despite everything that happened between Sherry and Yvette, the thing that would have her world falling apart right before her eyes was if the woman gave even a hint of what they had done to Carl.

Carl was already up and out of the house which gave her a chance to try to pull herself back together. She had feigned sleep when he had called out to her, then grumbled as he left for work at the construction site not far from their home. All she wanted to do was to take a long hot bath to calm her nerves and clear her mind.

While soaking, she tried to let it all go, but Yvette's voice kept pushing its way in: *I really don't think you can risk having me on your bad side.* Karyn was sure Yvette wanted to land her ass in jail. All because Karyn was now happy in her life, and Yvette had fucked up her own. Life just wasn't fair.

Karyn thought the steaming hot water would siphon away the fear, the pain and her confusion, but in doing so it only made things clearer. By not following her first instinct and leaving Mark that first time and staying gone, she had caused so much pain for everyone else. It was her choice to go back, fearing that she wouldn't be able to make it on her own, fearing that she was so far behind her girlfriends in her life's path, only had a high school diploma, and had two children to take care of, that she was stuck. Nothing could have been further from the truth. Even Veronica had spent out thousands for her to leave the United States. She had to face the hard fact, that her mistakes were the root cause of everyone's problems. They were even costing Carl the benefit of an honest wife.

"God Please," she whispered, tears streaming down her face. "I don't know what to do. How can I make things right with my girlfriends? It's all my fault, I never stopped to think about how this would affect them. My selfishness has caused too much pain and it's destroying our friendship, destroying our lives. Lord please help me to bring peace. Please show me what to do."

Karyn stepped out of the tub, dried off, then swiped a hand across the mirror to remove the steam before taking in her reflection in the mirror. What stared back at her was an image she barely recognized—eyes reddened from crying, expression devoid of happiness, confusion in the dark brown depths of her eyes that matched the pain filling her heart. How had she come back to this place again? She had everything now. The children were doing well living their lives, though they didn't call as often as she would like. She had a feeling it had a great deal to do with the fact that they were still effected by how Mark had treated her and subsequently, them as well. Her business was going well—she could pick and chose her clients. Carl adored her. Why did it seem as though Mark James was reaching out from the grave to take away all that was so wonderful in her life?

"No more pity parties, Karyn," she whispered. "Pull yourself together and fix this." Karyn realized in order to reach complete healing from her past she must first start by being honest. First she would pull things together with her friends. Then she would tell her husband and take the consequences. If she lost Carl by opening up her soul to him, then she never really had him to begin with.

She picked up the phone and dialed Yvette's number. After several attempts to reach her, she was forced to leave a message since the woman was clearly screening her calls. "Yvette, honey, please give me a call. We need to talk baby girl. I love you."

Chapter 22

Sherry hadn't heard from Karyn or Veronica in over a week. She certainly didn't expect to hear from Yvette, though she had called and left messages apologizing for what she had done. That was the most she could do.

She woke up at 5:30 a.m. to prepare breakfast. She wanted things to be perfect when KeAnna met her dad for the first time. But she also wanted to make a better second appearance and to show Raynard that she was wife material. She had to admit, the cleaning crew had done one hell of a job, and there wasn't a single thing missing either. The moment they had come home from the hotel, she ran straight to her bedroom and checked the jewelry case. Only then, after everything had been accounted for, could she appreciate the fresh scent of pine and bleach wafting through the air.

The fact that all of her laundry had been done, everything was in its rightful place and thanks to Raynard, a fully stocked refrigerator and pantry. She had to be thankful for his support. But despite the perks of all that, from this point on, she would be on top of things herself. She never wanted anyone to believe she was too lazy to clean her own house. Things had just become so overwhelming and sometimes she'd step through the door and didn't know where to begin.

Even the girlfriends had stopped making references to having at least one gathering at her place. When she came up with one excuse after another it had become an unspoken rule that Sherry's spot was off limits.

She had been ignoring Derrick's calls. Lord, she had made a serious mistake there. In a moment of weakness she had allowed her attempts to be a listening ear and a shoulder to cry on which ended up falling for his charm and him laying the dick on her. It was wonderful to believe that someone like him, rich and handsome would choose her over the always so pretty and together Yvette. But now she could see it for what it actually was, not for the love he had touted it to be. He didn't love her. Her friends were right. No one believed it anymore than she had. No matter what happened with Raynard, she would not be seeing Derrick Glover again.

Jasmine scented candles burned around the room. Fresh cut flowers—roses, daises and lilies, had been set on the dining room table dressed with fine china and covered by white linen tablecloths, a gift from Karyn. Fresh ground coffee brewed in the percolator and fresh squeezed orange juice was chilling in a carafe in the fridge. She had prepared homemade biscuits, hickory smoked bacon, grits, potatoes and onions, salmon croquettes and would whip up the scrambled eggs the moment the girls walked through the door.

She had texted KeAnna and Jaynene, demanding that they be home this morning. She wasn't sure if they would comply, but on two other occasions when she had demanded they come home and they hadn't shown up, she cut their cell phone service off. Boy, did she hear about it later, but it got the desired response—they had their tailbones in the house. And the only reason she didn't turn them off completely, is that the little electronic gadgets were really her only communication with them most times. Though she had laid down some rules, unfortunately she wasn't home enough to enforce them.

Breakfast had always been her specialty, despite the fact that bagels, muffins, and donuts had been the mainstay of her diet for a while. To actually have a fully-stocked refrigerator felt nice. To have her girls at the table for a change would be even nicer. She wondered when and how she would address the issue of Raynard's return, since a lot of their problems over the years was all due to his untimely absence.

Exactly at 8, a hoodie wearing, slouchy jean sporting KeAnna stumbled into the house and came to stand at the kitchen door. The sienna skin beauty of her features pulled into a serious frown. Jaynene came in a few moments later, the aroma of food leading her straight to the kitchen to stand timidly behind her sister. Sherry didn't miss the glimpse of fear in Jaynene's eyes, and for a moment it made her pause. Soon it was swept away when surprise registered on their faces as they watched Sherry smoothly navigate the dynamics of finishing a full breakfast.

"Mom, what's going on?" KeAnna said, still glued to her spot between the kitchen and the dining room threshold.

They both scanned the kitchen, then as if they had become synchronized swimmers, both spun around, took a look at the rest of the house in their view, noticing how beautiful everything looked. They glanced at each other, then to their mother.

Sherry was dancing around the kitchen, humming a song they couldn't make out while placing platters of heaping food on the table. She could barely contain the excitement that Raynard had come back for her and at the prospect that they could possible build a life together—a good one. Maybe he'd been the only thing missing in her life. Fuck Derrick Glover. And the horse he rode in on!

"Girls, I have some good news," she crooned, placing the carafe of juice next to the creamer, then she locked gazes with her oldest. "Especially for you KeAnna."

KeAnna finally moved forward deciding that the dining room where all the good stuff was on the table had won out over the kitchen, the place where all the action was happening. She pulled the hoodie back to expose her face, which now had a small piercing in her nose that Sherry didn't remember her having a week ago. "What, Mama. What is it?"

"Well girls, we have a house guest," Sherry stated cheerfully, clasping her hands together trying to hide the nervousness that caused butterflies to flit around in her stomach. "Guess who it is?"

Jaynene folded her arms over her chest, the red sweat suit lifted, exposing the bright white t-shirt underneath. Somehow her youngest had managed to keep it together—and well. Even the sweat suit had creases! "Mama, would you tell us already?"

Sherry placed the platter of bacon on the table. "Raynard Cosey, your dad." She let that hang in the air as she turned back to retrieve the biscuits from the oven, then lathered them with butter. "He's upstairs in the bathroom right now. He wanted to meet you so badly he couldn't wait."

Before KeAnna could say a word, Raynard came down the stairs, stood a few feet from them, smiling as his dark brown orbs swept over both girls, then locked on his daughter. "Good morning, ladies."

Jaynene's gaze traveled from his short-cropped hair, to the blue polo shirt, to the black slacks, ending with the bare feet. She grimaced, realizing that the handsome man wasn't her father. That tidbit of information stung since KeAnna had never wanted to see her father, but Jaynene had secretly harbored hope that her father would be thrilled at the prospect of meeting her. It was a fact that Dr. Julius

Washington never wanted to hear from her at all. He made it abundantly clear the day she tracked him down at Philadelphia General.

* * *

She had taken the Greyhound by herself to Pennsylvania, trying to find the one person no one could give her much information about. Her mother had been brutally honest about his intentions, but somehow deep in her heart, Jaynene had hoped that it was all a lie. Did she have brothers? More sisters? Grandparents?

She approached the tall, barrel–chested man as he shared a laugh with the women at the nurses' station on the 8th floor of the hospital. Jaynene told him her name and asked to speak with him for a moment. His features twisted into something that made even the nurses wince at its unsightliness. "Come this way," he ground out, gripping her arm and practically dragging her down the hall of the cardio unit, then the stairs and down another hall to his office.

He shoved her inside. The door didn't close all the way before he growled, "Did that bitch send you? What? She needs more money or something?"

At that moment, with his vicious tone and deadly expression, Jaynene knew she had made a big mistake. The man had called her mother a bitch? What had she done to him that he could say that about her?

"She doesn't even know I'm here," Jaynene whispered under his hard glare, holding back tears as she tried to avoid looking his way. Instead she ended up sweeping a look across the plaques and awards on the wall behind him. "I just wanted to see the man who is supposed to be my father. I thought she was lying to me about you not wanting to be with me or see me."

"She wasn't lying," he spat, moving away from her to take a seat behind the big oak desk. "We had a deal. But seeing that you're here, it's obvious that she couldn't keep that straight. The bitch."

"Leave my mother out of this!" she shot back, finally finding an anger of her own. "And you shouldn't call her that name."

"Well, that's what she is," he countered, sounding more like a whiny teenager than a full grown man.

"Then what does it make you?" she snapped, covering the distance between them in five long strides. "You were older—and a *doctor* and didn't use protection. And you got her drunk, too. Right? You knew better even if she didn't. And she did the more responsible thing, and *you're* angry?"

Dr. Washington only glared at her, but as reality sank in, hearing it so bluntly from his own child's mouth, his actions did seem childish from that vantage point.

Jaynene, realizing that nothing more could be gained from the visit, walked to the door, but turned back to him saying, "I'd rather be like 'that bitch' who stuck it out, than the pussy who ran away."

That night as Jaynene made her way home, determination penetrating her heart. The moment she stepped off the bus, she knew when she saw her mother, she would give her the biggest hug. And she would go to school every day, finish and do the right things—no matter what. She'd become the doctor her mother always wanted to be. She would be a success. She would show her no good father exactly what she, Sherry Lakeside's daughter, was made of.

Jaynene traveled the trash littered streets, totally unaware of the footsteps echoing behind her. She was so bent on getting home to show her mother how much she appreciated all she had done, that she didn't realize that she had picked up a shadow from the moment she hit 39th Street.

The second she put the key in her door, hands grabbed her from behind, tossed her on the ground, and punched her repeatedly in the face. The man, who she instantly recognized as one of KeAnna's friends, despite his attempt to hide his face, ripped her jeans, pinned her to the ground, and managed to dodge the blows from her attempts to fight him off before he raped her.

Jaynene called out for her mother. She called out for God. She screamed Sherry's name over and over as he continued thrusting into her, and the pain ripped through her like nothing she could ever have imagined.

Her silent sobs rent the air the moment he pulled away, kicked her in the side and ran. Sirens blared off in the distance. So close and yet so far—and none of that meant they were coming to her rescue. For a moment, the pain was so excruciating, she thought she may never see her mother again. But still, hours later after he had ravaged and beaten her, she could only manage to say her mother's name, then it lead into the only thing she knew to do—something that Veronica had instilled in her long ago…"Our Father, who art in Heaven…"

In daylight, the hallway was silent and empty. Jaynene had crawled the rest of the way into the apartment, hoping against hope that her mother *wasn't* home and that was the reason she hadn't come to help. Sherry lay across the bed, sprawled in the same position that they always seemed to find her in, an empty bottle of Crown Royal on the carpet. She still had on the bright blue nurses' uniform from the day before and her makeup had smeared onto the bedclothes.

Vision blurred by tears, Jaynene trudged to the bathroom and soon showered the remains of her torture away. Scrubbing in vicious strokes as she tried and failed to keep the sobs from coming and waking her mother. Her mother worked so hard all the time—and everything she did was for Jaynene and her sister. This bad thing was her punishment for not believing her mother. She should never have gone to Philadelphia. It was all for nothing!

She walked down the hall, stumbled past her own bedroom and to her mother's, crawled into bed next to the fleshy, nearly comatose, form and curled into her arms the best way she could manage. Silent tears streamed down her face, soaking the bed sheets, as the pungent scent of liquor permeated the air.

The next morning she awoke alone and called Veronica, who told her she would come as soon as she could. Veronica left a meeting in New York, picked up Jaynene from the apartment and took her to her condo after all efforts to get the young girl to file a police report had failed, and a visit to the hospital had found that Jaynene had washed away all evidence that could be used in a rape case. They had at least given the girl the series of medications that was to ensure that she didn't get pregnant, or that she was less susceptible to any diseases the attacker might have had.

Against her better judgment, in order to keep Jaynene's trust, she reluctantly agreed that she would not say a word of what happened to Sherry. The young woman was so filled with pain regarding the incident and worry over her mother's anger if she found out that she had tried to see Dr. Washington. Veronica's first inclination was to locate KeAnna, get the information she needed on Jaynene's attacker and confront him her–damn–self. Now for *this*, a man deserves to die. She could make him disappear with no help from her friends. Which is where Karyn had made her first mistake. If you're going to do some dirt, you go solo. Veronica found that she couldn't go vigilante if she was to maintain Jaynene's trust and be there for her Godchild in the best way that she could. And at this point, it meant remaining silent about such a tragic event. All while wondering what the hell was Sherry doing while all of this had transpired.

* * *

KeAnna had pushed past her younger sister, but froze as she took in the meaning behind her mother's words. "This is Raynard Cosey, your father."

The young girl's features pulled into a frown as she glowered angrily first at the man who she had never seen before this day, then at her mother wondering why she would have this *stranger* stay here at their home.

She swished past him, going straight to her mother. "Mom, how could you? This man has never done anything for me and you let him walk in here and demand to see me. And you didn't ask me if I was okay with it?" Her gaze flew up to meet his. "And you," she spat, hand riding high on her hip, "Walking around here like you have the right to be here." Then she looked back at her mother, whose brown eyes flashed with the rage building inside her. "Smiling and singing over this man who didn't even drop you a call. Upstairs *in the bathroom*, my ass! Don't you think more of yourself than that?"

Sherry's smile had already went south, along with all hopes for at least a somewhat cordial gathering, if not happy reunion. "Hold up, girl, you're not going to talk to me that way. At least hear what he has to say. He's here to make things right with you and with me. Don't be stupid," As soon as the word stupid came out of Sherry's mouth, she wished she could cram it back in. The word itself was one that caused her to cringe inwardly, having heard it so often from her own father. Along with how she was never good enough, would *never* be good enough, no matter how well she did in school. She had been called fat and stupid at every turn. And now she was doling out that same negativity to her daughter.

"I'm stupid," KeAnna said in a low voice, raising an eyebrow. "All dressed up, cooking breakfast and shit," she scoffed. "You have no idea how *you're* looking right now."

Raynard moved forward to stand between the two. "KeAnna," he said softly, "Please don't be angry with your mom. It's not her fault. I begged her to let me see you. I know I'm looking like a really bad person right now, but if you'll just listen, we can at least start a friendship of some type, even if you can't accept more than that. There's no excuse for what I've done, but give me a chance to make it up to you now."

KeAnna's hands were balled into fists at her side. "Never!" she spat, dodging his attempt to touch her. "I have no dad. He's dead! You're dead to me!" She pushed past her sister and stormed out the door.

Raynard slumped down into a seat at the dining room table, stared at the scrumptious meal, then looked up at Sherry with an expression that let her know that all of her hard work was in vain. Like her, he didn't have an appetite after that exchange—and a relationship with his daughter might be out of the question.

Sherry looked at Jaynene, who took off her jacket, slipped into a chair next to Raynard then picked up a plate and said, "Hmmmm, that went well," and started piling on the food as if nothing out of the ordinary had happened.

Jaynene poured Raynard a glass of juice and said, "Mr. Cosey, my sister's hurting right now. We both are. She'll come around." She took a bite of bacon. "You might as well eat this wonderful breakfast mom made. I don't remember the last time she cooked. And this looks gooooood!"

Sherry glared at her, but inwardly she was thinking that she had done more bad than good. It hurt even more when KeAnna slapped her in the face with the truth. She had just expected everything to be fine now that Raynard was in the picture. She was under the misconception that Raynard could be their savior, that all her dreams had come true with just him coming back. But now, she realized for her daughter's sake, there had to be more to it than just that. How could she make things right in her house again?

"I made a really bad mistake," Raynard's baritone voice broke through her musings. "I've made a lot of bad decisions in my life. The worst was abandoning your mother, and then abandoning my child. I was young...and dumb."

"We all make mistakes," Jaynene said with a shrug, continuing with the meal. "I can understand how frightening it can be when you're a child yourself and you're still trying to figure out who you are. Then you get the news that you're gonna bring a child into the world and have nothing you can give to it." She paused, placed the fork on the plate and looked over to the man whose eyes were so filled with worry. Her heart went out to him. He actually wanted to be with his daughter. And after all this time, whereas her father could give less than a damn. "I was raped."

Sherry's gasp echoed throughout the room.

"I was on my way back home," she whispered, swallowing against the pain. "I tried to find my father and I'm sorry that I did. I doubted my mother and what she had said to me. So I went to Philadelphia and I saw him and when I came back home..." She shook her head. "A man raped me in front of our door." Tears pooled in her eyes as Raynard reached over and pulled her against his chest.

"Oh baby, why didn't you tell me?" Sherry said, her horror–

stricken expression nearly matching the one on Raynard's face. She stood frozen, afraid to move; as though Jaynene couldn't be saying what she had said.

"I called out for you, but you didn't hear me," Jaynene said in a voice just above a whisper. "You were too drunk to hear me." Then her expression crumbled. Sobs tore through her. Each heave of her little shoulders was a stab to Sherry's heart.

Raynard folded the little girl into his arms, looked over his head at Sherry who had placed a hand over her chest to quell the pain. She could only stagger under the weight of that admission. She had been home when it happened? This had happened right outside her door? And she didn't hear a thing! Oh, God!!!

"I screamed for you, mommy," Jaynene wailed. "Why didn't you come for me? I needed you. I needed you!"

Moments passed before Sherry could move a mere inch. The tears ran down her face unchecked. She couldn't utter a word if she tried. What could she say? What could she do? She had tried to be the best mother and father for them, but it seemed she had failed at that; and failed at being a friend to her girlfriends, too. No wonder her baby girl never wanted to be home. This place held a world of nightmares for her.

Jaynene pulled out of Raynard's embrace. "You never asked me what happened, mommy. It was easier to let you believe that some thug had gotten me pregnant, because you wanted to believe the worst of me."

Raynard kept his hands around her shoulders and said, "I may not be your father, but I can be the next best thing. Whatever you need, I'll be here." Jaynene looked up at him, the hope in her eyes caused Sherry's heart to slam in her chest. Raynard was fast becoming very important to her youngest child. Could she trust him to keep his word to her?

"What do you want to do?" he asked her.

Jaynene released a long, slow breath and replied, "I want to finish school. Veronica's been helping me with that. I've been staying at her house." She took a look at Sherry, but seeing the confused expression, she looked away. "I want to be a doctor. I want to be safe." Tears pooled in her eyes. "I know the guy who raped me. KeAnna hangs out with him all the time. I want to visit Paris, like Aunt Veronica." Then she lowered her gaze to her not–quite–flat stomach. "I don't want this baby. Every time I look at it, I'll remember what he did to me."

Raynard got up, lowered to his knees as he took her hands in his. "First we're going to do whatever it takes to get that monster who did this to you."

Jaynene nodded as she looked down at him, then he said, "Then we'll get you into some counseling. And rest assured that whatever you're trying to achieve in life, I *will* be around to help this time. That's my promise to you." He ventured a long look at Sherry. "No matter what happens between me and your mother."

"But I'm not your daughter," she said quietly.

"Blood doesn't matter," he said, wiping the tears away, then extending his hand to Sherry who ran forward into his arms. "Love matters."

Chapter 23

Veronica placed the phone on the cradle, slumped down on the red Nimrod chair in her space-age styled kitchen to gather her wits. She wondered how Simone could possibly think to threaten her that way. Veronica now had ties of her own to the fashion industry that had nothing to do with Simone. Simone Gaultier may have given her a start, but it was Veronica's dedication that pushed her to the top ten percentile of her graduating class at FIDM in Los Angeles. Then it was her hard work and the reputation she built interning in Paris and Milan that had propelled her into a coveted position at Chanel, then landed her a position as a buyer for Christian LaCroix.

The conversation had upset her to the point that she probably shouldn't make the visit out to William's this weekend. Her spirits had plummeted and he always was perceptive when it came to her, and would certainly want to know the reason. And she hadn't heard from Jaynene. She worried for the little girl's safety, especially once she mentioned that she was returning to the scene of that vicious crime. It had been especially hard to juggle work, William, and help Jaynene navigate school and doctor's appointments now that it was painfully obvious that the meds the hospital had plied her with were ineffective.

William had made a passing reference to the fact that maybe she had some other guy she was dating since it was quite often now that he was unable to come visit because she had "company." Though she knew that William would never cross paths with anyone in her world, she knew the moment she mentioned Jaynene was staying with her that she would have to tell him more than she planned. She would want him to understand why she had opened her home to the young girl.

On second thought, she rushed to gather her luggage, realizing that she shouldn't jeopardize her relationship with such a wonderful man, just because everyone else decided to pencil themselves in on her agenda. Being with William would be the exact thing that would help her unwind from all the drama. Jaynene had keys to the condo and could come and go whenever she liked. And she tidied up after herself like a pro. What she also admired about the young girl was her strength and resilience in dealing with an issue that had caused grown women to fold in and give up. But she sorely wished that on this visit home, Jaynene would open up and tell Sherry what had happened. Keeping the secret was weighing heavily on Veronica's conscious. If it was her daughter, she would surely want to know. She was certain that Sherry would feel the same. It was possible that Sherry would be angry with Veronica when she finally found out. And that was bound to happen, as Veronica would be the first to tell anyone, secrets have a way of outing themselves, against everyone's wishes and at the wrong damn time.

She nearly tripped on the Coach luggage as she pulled the first two pieces to the door so they would be on hand when the driver arrived. The doorbell rang once, then twice, and a third time in succession as though someone wanted her to move faster than she had planned.

"Damn," she said out loud, checking her Bvlgari watch, a gift William said she shouldn't do without. "He's thirty minutes early. Why is he laying on the bell that way?"

She ran to the bedroom, grabbing the final bag. "I'm coming," she yelled out as the doorbell rang another few times. "Ease up!"

Now irritated by his actions, she went to the door, snatched it open and began, "What the hell—"

The words died on her lips the moment the person who stood across the threshold came into view.

Simone Gaultier pulled off her shades, gave Veronica a slow, easy smile and said, "Hello, darling. Going somewhere?"

Veronica's heart dropped, and she nearly stumbled backward. "What? What...what....what are you doing here?"

The option of slamming the door in the woman's face and making a run for the back door ended the moment Simone sauntered past her and into her condo slowly turning to take in Veronica's flushed face and stricken expression.

"What? You're not happy to see me, darling," she drawled in that thickly accented English that once sent shivers of pleasure up Veronica's spine, but now made her shudder with anger.

"Actually, I'm on my way out." Veronica went to the door and gestured to the other side. "After you."

"Oh, no sweetheart," Simone said, slipping onto the suede sectional couch. "I think you should cancel your little *rendezvous*." Her gaze swept over Veronica's with a sly smile. "We have *sooooo* much to catch up on. Do you have any wine?"

"Have you lost your fucking mind?"

Simone's face, which had been insured by Lloyd's of London, was now screwed into an expression that was a far cry from what had always been splayed on the pages of Vogue, Vanity Fair, Elle, and other high fashion magazines. The cold glint in the sky blue eyes was enough to halt Veronica's movements. What could she possibly do to get this woman out of her house; better yet, her *life?*

Simone took the liberty of strolling through the living room, then the dining room, inspecting the artwork, and the Lalique and Baccarat figurines, then did a quick sweep of her gaze across the marble coffee table where the latest of Williams fresh flowers were proudly displayed before turning up her nose as if the place did not quite meet with her standards.

Veronica tried to trail her movements, wondering what the woman had up her sleeve.

"So *this* is where you live?" She inquired in a tone that left no question on exactly what she thought of the one–bedroom condo. "So this is why you never wanted me to visit? Hmmmmm, very small, so beneath you." She brushed a delicate ivory hand over the arm of the couch. "And you left a promising career in Paris for this."

Veronica stormed to the door, pulled it open for the second time and said, "When I was in France, it was all good between us. But I'm home now, sister. And it's a totally different ball game." The sweat pooling in the palm of her hand made it difficult to keep a grip on the knob. "What we had was great. And don't misunderstand me, I appreciate everything you've done for me. But our relationship is over."

"You *used* me," Simone spat, pulling out a cigarette and relishing the fact that Veronica cringed at the action. "Pure and simple."

Simone perched on the edge of the sectional, lit the tip of her Virginia Slims, took a pull, and let the smoke curl around her. "You need to call…what is his name? Wilbur? Wilson? And tell him you will not be making your flight. I need answers."

Veronica closed her eyes and tried to summon some type of meditation technique to keep her from strangling the woman and tossing her over the balcony. Hey, not a bad idea. Accidents happen every day!

Instead, she crossed the room, picked up the phone and watched as Simone's award–winning lips lifted in a wide, victorious smile. Veronica returned it with one of her own, as she said, "Security? Could you please come up to my apartment? I have an *unwanted* guest, who needs your assistance in leaving the premises." Her gaze never left the blue eyes which now flashed with anger. "I don't know how you let her up here in the first place. But fix this."

Simone slipped off of the sofa, bore down on Veronica so that she was toe–to–toe. "And this is how you treat me? After everything I did for you. As if I need to be taken out like common trash?" She took a deep breath, trailed a finger across Veronica's flushed cheeks and leaned in to whisper, "Trust me, dear, this is not the end." She sailed to the door, opened it, flicked the cigarette back into the room for it to land on top of one of William's fresh flowers.

Veronica lunged forward, snatching the taller woman by the collar and pulled her face down to meet hers. "You don't know me like you think you do. I will whip your European ass."

She shoved the woman toward the door into the arms of the beefy security guard who appeared at the threshold. He gave her a nod as he gripped Simone's arm and led her forward. Curses in every language rent the air on the model's trip to the elevator.

Veronica closed the door and sighed with relief, went to the marble table and scooped the smoldering cigarette from the petals, and extinguished it. She coughed as the smoke curled into her nose, leaving an acrid stench behind along with worry in her heart.

Evidently, Simone Gaultier wasn't going to go away so easy.

Chapter 24

Five hours later, KeAnna stumbled through the door, eyes as red as sun dried tomatoes, laughter springing from her lips. She came to a complete halt when confronted by the scene on the living room sofa. Jaynene's head was resting on Raynard's shoulder. Sherry's hand was linked in his as they all stared forward at the flat-screen television.

"You still here? Damn!"

Sherry, Jaynene and Raynard were watching *First Friday*. A bowl of Chex Mix on the coffee table and three glasses of fruit punch next to it.

"Isn't this just lov–er–ly," she said with a rock of her little neck. "Family time? What's that 'bout, Sherry? We always doing our own thang while mama's out getting her swerve on with some old ugly dude. And now you want to try for a li'l faaaaaaamily time. Hmph!"

Sherry gasped, causing the girl to give her a sloppy grin. "Yeah, I know 'bout that. You think just 'cause you don't bring it home, we ain't gonna know?" she slurred, losing every single command of the King's good English, causing Sherry to cringe.

KeAnna switched off the set, swaying in front of the flat screen as though she was dancing to some unheard of music. "Can't believe you," she said to Raynard this time. "Can't believe you'd want a woman like her. She sleeps with eeeeeeerb'dy. I mean eeeeeee'r'body." She swerved back, couldn't catch her bearings and crashed into the cocktail table.

"Think we don't hear that in da streets," KeAnna spat, shrugging off her sister's attempts to help her stay upright. She leaned forward, gripped the edge of the sofa instead. "Don't think we don't hear it when we show up at your job? They're laughing at you. Laughing at us. Think we're like you." She gave Sherry a sly grin. "Why do you think all the fellas want to get wit' me? Why they be asking 'bout my little sister? They think we're ho's just like you."

"KeAnna watch your mouth, girl," Sherry said, getting to her feet, trembling with a rage she couldn't voice. Shock had her rooted to the floor. Had things really gotten that bad? She always thought that she covered her tracks and kept her business as far away from the girls as it could get.

"Why? I'm only telling the truth. What?" she said, raring back on her sneakers. She looked at Raynard, then back to Sherry with a sad shake of her head. "Awwwwww, you don't want him to know what's really going on? I thought it was all about making things riiiiiiight. Don't that start with telling the truth and shaming the devil!"

"I don't care what your mother's done. I care about her. I care about you," Raynard said coming to stand near his daughter who swerved again. "She's worried about you and after what happened to your sister, she very well should be. The moment your mother gives the word, I'm moving you all away from here."

Suddenly KeAnna sobered a little as her gaze shifted to Jaynene who slumped down on the sofa. "What's happened to my li'l sister?"

"Maybe she'll tell you in her own time," he answered softly, catching the pleading gaze in Jaynene's eyes. "But right now it's all about you."

KeAnna's glance flickered from her sister to the Monopoly set in the center of the floor, noticing the game was still in progress. She kicked out, causing the pieces and the money to fly everywhere, but landed flat on her ass for her efforts.

Raynard went to his daughter. Though he refrained from touching her as he said, "I'm sorry, KeAnna. I'm sorry for not being there for you. I'm sorry that things have turned out the way they have. Maybe if I had been here a lot of things would be different." He locked gazes first with Jaynene and then Sherry as he said that. "I can't change the past, but I can do something about the here and now. That's all I can do, baby girl. That's all I can do."

"So you're going to be a permanent fixture around here?" she demanded, looking first to Sherry then to him from her spot on the floor. "I'm so done with this scene." She pushed past him, swayed into the sofa as she walked through the living room, then ambled toward the hallway leading to the bedrooms.

"Regardless of what he did before, he's still your dad. He just wants to be a part of your life, please give him a chance," she pleaded to her daughter's back. "I didn't raise you to be disrespectful."

KeAnna waved off those words with a flick of her wrist and stormed up the hall. "I don't have a fucking daddy. Let Jaynene have him."

Sherry jumped up, aiming to go after her belligerent daughter. "KeAnna, get back here!"

Jaynene gripped the edges of Sherry's dress which was effective enough to hold the woman in place. "Mom, let me go talk to her," she said with a look in Raynard's direction, who gave her an encouraging nod.

Sherry took a seat next to Raynard, stared ahead at the dark screen. "I'm sorry things aren't going well. I just thought that she needed you, needed a man to kind of take a firm hand."

Raynard wrapped his arm around Sherry's full–figured frame and said, "Baby don't worry. It's just going to take time. I can't come up in here all roughshod like gangbusters. I have to take things slow. Why do you think I insisted that I don't move in here," he whispered, trailing a hand across her face. "I'd rather have my own place, and take the time to get back into things slowly, even with you. That's why we're still dating. That's why we haven't moved to getting to the good wood." He gave her a small bitter smile, which she returned, reluctantly.

Then he stood, moved into the kitchen and opened the right hand cabinet. "But there's one thing besides my not being here that has impacted them." He gestured to an array of liquors in the cabinet. Then he opened the lower cabinet to display even more. Then moved over, opening the cabinet under the sink. He shifted to the pantry and opened that door, too. Then he moved the garbage can from in front of another cabinet to display another hidden stash.

"This right here, Sherry, is like the elephant in the room. No one wants to talk about it, but it's there." He grabbed a single bottle of Crown Royal. "KeAnna's moved from the liquid stuff to stuff she can smoke. If we don't do something soon, she'll be on cocaine, or heroin or even crack. Then her not accepting me will be the least of our worries. We might lose her altogether. I'm a chemist, I know what those drugs do to people. It doesn't take seeing it in the news or watching it on television to know that the stuff she's doing and the stuff you're drinking is destroying your lives."

"Hold up one minute brother," Sherry snapped, getting to her feet. "You have lost your rabbit ass mind if you think you can walk right back into my life twenty years later and take jabs at what I've built here."

Raynard shook his head, "Sherry," he closed his eyes as though trying to find the right words. "But from the looks of things the foundation is shaky. Things can't last when it's not built on solid ground. One of your daughters doesn't respect you. The other loves you, despite how hurt she feels that you weren't there to help her when she needed you most. Trust needs to be rebuilt there. And it will take time." He leaned against the sink, locking a sad gaze with Sherry. "And though she's not my daughter by blood, I still feel just as responsible, because if I had been the man I should've been, she *would* be my biological daughter and she would have been as safe as we, and I do mean *we*, could have made her."

Sherry winced at the harshness behind that statement.

"Sorry for being so cold, but it's the truth. We've both made mistakes here, but they are the ones paying for it." His eyes watered, but the tears refused to fall. "Do you know how it feels to realize that if I had been in your life, Jaynene would never have been raped? Do you know what it feels like to know that you've been empty all these years and looked everywhere trying to fill that void? Do you know what it feels like to know my own daughter would rather consider me dead than have anything to do with me?" He stilled his mind against the pain. "I feel like such a failure and I owe it to you, I owe it to Jaynene, I owe it to KeAnna to keep trying no matter what. I was already that man who didn't handle his responsibility. I'm not that man any more. I will *never* be that man again. And if I have to face hard facts about my life, then it's damn sure time you faced yours."

Sherry glared at him, trembling with rage.

Raynard remained silent, waiting for her to get over her ego and see the truth.

Then slowly, almost halfheartedly she walked to the kitchen and grabbed the remaining bottles of Crown Royal. She paused, allowing her gaze to roam the myriad of bottles lined up like soldiers—tequila, vodka, gin, brandy, rum...

Sherry looked over at him, leaning over the sink as she said, "There's so much of it. I can't...I can't..."

"I'll help you, mama," Jaynene whispered from the doorway. She crossed the distance and linked her hand in Raynard's, then gripped the neck of the bottle Sherry held as all three of them turned it downward, their tears mingling with the liquid pouring down the drain.

Chapter 25

A couple of weeks had gone by without a single peep from Yvette. Karyn rescheduled a few client meetings so she could plan a complete ambush.

She arrived at Yvette's home at the crack of dawn, parking alongside a neighbor's house and waited with a cappuccino in hand and a bagel lathered with fattening cream cheese to keep her mouth busy. She was on a mission, but she relished the time alone to indulge in these forbidden little pleasures. Carl would kill her if he knew. But what he didn't know…

The moment a slight movement could be seen through Yvette's living room window, and a trail of one tall image followed by two smaller ones in rank succession headed toward the area she knew was the kitchen, Karyn put her car in gear and pulled up to the garage to block the exit.

Thirty minutes later, the garage door finally opened, and Karyn was able to slip inside. As soon as she saw her friend come storming through the door with book bags in hand, Karyn felt a pang of sympathy and guilt all over again.

"Yvette, we need to talk."

Kayrn didn't recognize the sad, broken woman standing before her. Her hair was thrown back in a messy pony tail. She wore a black jogging suit, completely out of character for someone who had always prided herself on being in style—even more than Veronica. The already petite woman appeared to have lost weight since the last time Karyn saw her at the engagement party.

Yvette walked away from the car and toward the driveway, Karyn following on her heels.

"I came over because I'm concerned about you. We haven't seen or heard from you in weeks."

Yvette just gave her an empty, distant stare.

"I know what Sherry did is unforgivable, but you have to believe that she is truly, deeply sorry."

Yvette's stare grazed over the completely full garbage can that needed to be pulled to the curb for pickup, the uncut grass, and the overflowing mailbox before coming to lock on Karyn. "How could she do that to me?"

"We all do stupid things. I'm sure you've done a few as well."

Yvette folded her arms over her ample bosom as the brisk wind whirled around them. "But nothing that would hurt any of you."

"But you have done things to hurt another woman." Karyn held up her hand to ward off Yvette's protests. "I do know that Sherry's completely torn up about this. You two need to talk."

"There's no way in hell I'll be talking to that sneaky bitch about anything anytime soon." Yvette snapped, her pale hand riding up on her jogging suit. "How can you even ask me to do that? I bet she's still going out with Derrick. He's never home anymore."

Karyn clucked her tongue, signaled for the twins to remain in the car. "You know that's bullshit. Derrick played her to get back at you, and she realizes that now." She lifted Yvette's chin and stared into her eyes. "You're our sister and things aren't the same without you. We all love you."

Yvette didn't want to cave, but she also knew how lonely she'd been and how desperately she needed her girlfriends during this difficult time in her life. She turned and walked away. "Come on, let's drop the kids off at school and grab a bite to eat."

Their breakfast lasted for more than an hour and ended with an agreement that Yvette would meet with everyone later that night at Karyn's house.

* * *

Carl was away for the weekend, fishing with his friends and some of his construction crew, so Karyn was able to prepare a quiet dinner for just the girls. After a little trivial chit-chat, an awkward silence filled the air as they dined on a Caesar salad, grilled salmon, twice-baked potatoes and Key Lime pie for desert.

Finally as the night went on, Karyn was unable to take it anymore. They had come to talk things out and she'd be damned if they left with things still unresolved.

"Sometimes, I think we became friends by default," she said, interrupting the women's thoughts that had caused them to drift into their own worlds. "Our mothers spent so much time together doing community service, and with church and all those other activities we would be around each other all the time."

Sherry and Yvette sat on opposite ends of the table, Karyn and Veronica serving as buffers between the two women who would glare at each other at some points, and totally ignore each other the other times.

"Our mothers would force us to go whether we wanted to or not." Veronica picked up the white crystal serving bowl filled with potatoes and passed them to Yvette. "Sometimes we would show up all dressed alike with those colorful barrettes all over our heads. If I had corn rows, you all had corn rows, if I had a ponytail, you all had them, too."

Karyn nodded, looked at the two silent women. "Do you remember that?"

They nodded, but said nothing. Sherry continued to keep her head hung low while enjoying a fork full of the salmon. Yvette appeared not to have much of an appetite as she played with the croutons in her salad.

"It was as if our mothers knew then that we were supposed to be a team whether we liked it or not."

Karyn pointed toward Sherry and Yvette. "When our mothers wanted to go out to the club to get their step on, we would have to watch you two," she said with a grin hoping that would break the ice.

"And that was no fun," Veronica muttered. The aroma from the Key Lime pie's crust baking in the oven filled the air.

"And even though we were older by a few years, we were supposed to keep both of you out of trouble." Karyn's lips lifted into a small smile. "I think you two were actually the ones keeping *us* out of trouble. If we were stuck with you two bad asses, we couldn't hang out with the boys," laughed Karyn.

"No we couldn't," Veronica replied, a knowing smile on her face. "Remember when we would sneak out to the park where all of the guys hung out playing basketball. "Whenever my grandmother caught us, she'd make us come into the house. 'Both of you fast tail ass girls are starting to smell yourself,'" Veronica laughed as she removed the empty dishes from the table and took the pie crust from the oven.

"Don't ask me what that meant, it was some type of southern slang," Karyn said with a little rock of her neck. "Because I thought my shit *didn't* stink."

The other two women didn't respond to Veronica's and Karyn's journey down memory lane, too busy staring angrily at each other from across the table.

So much for Sherry being torn up about it, Karyn mused.

"And you couldn't tell me anything," Karyn said, hoping to make eye contact with at least one of them. "Because just like Yvette, I had a body to die for at the age of sixteen. All the boys loved me."

Sherry stood, grabbed her purse, tossed it over her shoulder. "Excuse me for a moment," she quipped before making her way to the powder room.

Yvette stared down at her plate, playing with the remnants of her food, leaving Karyn and Veronica to share a look and a head shake at the fact that they weren't reaching either of the two women.

Sherry finally came back and sat down, taking another sip of the juice she had insisted on, rather than the wine or whisky which was normally her choice. She shrugged and then went back to looking at Yvette as though nothing had transpired.

Suddenly, Veronica's voice took on a softer tone, "I think we learned a lot from our mothers because they were no joke. They were strong, powerful, dedicated, and financially secure women. Their friendship was true and blue, and there was nothing anyone could do to try to break their bond, not even their significant or insignificant others," she looked pointedly at Yvette, who suddenly took an interest because of Veronica's sarcastic tone.

Tears built up in Karyn's eyes as she continued with, "I remember like it was yesterday, Yvette, you were only eight and your mom had laid out a beautiful yellow and white dress with red strawberries. You always did look like a little Barbie Doll."

Yvette managed a small smile.

"She had asked me to help you dress." Karyn took a long, slow breath. "When I tried to give you a bath, you just started crying..."

Veronica's gaze snapped up from her plate, looking first at Karyn, then at Yvette whose eyes had widened as the memories of that day slammed into her.

Karyn took a sip of wine as though she needed it to go on. "I asked what was wrong. And you said if you told me, he'd hurt you and take you away from your mother." Her voice wavered on that statement. "Then I told you that you could trust me."

Leaning over she grabbed Yvette's hand and stared deep into her eyes. "I felt I needed to protect you from that dreadful man. Your mom was dating him, remember? She trusted Alderman Robertson and he would stay over some nights. She trusted him to the point where he would occasionally watch you when she went to work."

She released Yvette's hand long enough to take another sip of wine. Veronica slid some tissues across the table, then grabbed some tissues and dabbed at her own tears.

"I promised you I would never let anyone hurt you again," Karyn whispered. "Our mothers invited him over for dinner on the pretense of hosting an event to contribute to his political campaign." Veronica shook her head, but Karyn shrugged instead. "They took him downstairs to the basement to…'talk'."

The four girls stood at the top of the stairwell leading to Yvette's mother basement, holding hands and listening in to the argument that ensued. Voices bellowed from the room where the girls normally played as the women confronted the man for what he had done. Soon there was no more talking as each woman pulled out the belts and bats that they had brought along for the occasion. There was no other sound but the whistle of the weapons in the air, mingled with his moaning, saying he was sorry and that he would never hurt another child again. Blood spattered everywhere—on Yvette's doll collection, on the console television, on the books along the wall, and on the industrial white tile.

"We never discussed what we saw that night." Karyn paused to slow her breathing, giving time for the other girls to say something, anything.

"I forgot all about that," Sherry finally responded with a glance first at Karyn, then Veronica whose face was flushed with tears, and finally to Yvette who sat ramrod straight.

"I remember that day." Veronica walked across the room to stand behind Yvette and wrapped her arms around the catatonic woman. "They handled their business that night. They knew how to protect one of their own."

"I thought it was just a horrible nightmare that came at me from time to time," Yvette alleged. "I remember him begging for his life. Begging them to stop."

Karyn looked at her. "Only Veronica's mom reigned them in, reminding them that he wasn't worth going to jail for."

"Some of the women didn't feel that way." Veronica added. "They carried him to the car. We never heard or saw him again,"

Yvette was rocking in Veronica's arms as she said, "They came back and prepared dinner as though nothing out of the ordinary had happened."

"I wonder if they actually killed him?" Sherry asked, as she stared Veronica down for an answer.

"I wouldn't put it past them," Veronica said with a slow grin spreading over her lips. "I've always wanted to choke the life out of bastards who molested children," she said locking a gaze on Sherry. "Any man who rapes a child or a woman deserves to die."

Sherry could only nod to that. She mouthed the words, "Thank you."

Veronica didn't pretend not to know what she meant. "I love you."

Chapter 26

"Your mom was never the same after that day," Karyn said, holding back tears and trying to bring them back to the point at hand. Dessert was long forgotten at this point. All that mattered was getting it all out in the open.

"I believe she always felt responsible for what happened to you," Veronica added.

Yvette was perplexed, sitting stock still while tears fell nonstop down her cheeks. "It's all coming together now. After all these years, I could never explain or understand the nightmares or why my mother took her own life. I couldn't remember where the nightmares had come from or when they started. But I do know that they became worse after that night in the alley…"

Karyn lowered her gaze.

"I remember, I remember," Yvette said breathlessly. "They didn't kill him."

All heads turned in her direction.

"I saw him on television a few months after that night. I felt scared just seeing his face. The camera followed him from the courthouse. He was limping the entire way."

"He probably would walk with a limp. They beat the holy shit out of him," Karyn commented.

"And They never let anything come between them," Sherry chimed in, while finally making eye contact with Yvette. "And now, we must do the same."

"We've kept another, more deadly secret since then, and we've allowed it to destroy something beautiful. We've allowed Mark James to win. He wanted Karyn unhappy. He wanted her to live in fear. We did the damn thing so that wouldn't happen." Veronica looked around at each of the women, then at the hands of the women who were at odds with one another. "We're strong women because our mothers were strong, because of the things we have gone through together. And if you look back, we've been there for each other through *everything*."

Karyn joined the women circle and wrapped her arms around her girls. "I'll forever be indebted to you three. You risked everything to protect my children and me. I don't know what I would've done without you then and I don't want to lose you now because of one asshole." She stared directly at Sherry. "And we certainly can't afford to make the mistake of allowing a man to use us against each other—or allowing a lapse in judgment to hurt one another."

"I love all of you," Veronica said softly. "I've never been close to my own blood sister because of our age differences, but I never felt like I lost out on anything because you all were better than any sister I could've dreamed of." She pulled the girls even closer into the circle for a group hug. "I can't imagine what my life would have been like without you three in it. I know we've had disagreements. And I know we'll have arguments in the future, but I also know that we can get through anything. *Anything!* As God is my witness, I promise you that I will not allow anything to come between us."

Sherry, moved by the women's speech, got up and stood in front of Yvette. "I am so wrong for what I've done. I was weak and stupid. There's no excuse for it and I can say I'm sorry all night long, but it won't change the past. But I'm asking you to please, please forgive me." Tears had formed in Sherry's eyes, and it was obvious she was trying to hold them back so that she could get the words out. "You, Veronica, and Karyn have been in my life for so long I can't remember what it was like before we became friends. I never thought any man could come in and destroy what we have. And I never thought I was the type of woman to fall for a line of bullshit that would make me lay down with my sister's husband. I will keep apologizing and try like hell to prove to all of you that you can trust me. That's all I can do."

Yvette looked away at first, then dropped down into the chair. When she spoke, she wasn't angry, just honest. "I don't know if I can forgive you, Sherry. At least not right now. It hurts too deep. If you were some other woman, some woman I didn't know, then I could just beat your ass and get it over and done with, but—"

"Uh, it wasn't like you didn't try," Sherry shot back.

Yvette opened her mouth to speak, then lifted her chin proudly as she grinned. "I did whip that ass, didn't I?"

Sherry rolled her eyes and smiled.

"Yes, and it's all over my damn carpet," Karyn chimed in, giving them both a sour look. "I'm sending both of you my cleaning bill."

"I understand if you can't forgive me just yet," Sherry replied in the most sincere tone anyone had heard from her yet. She reached out for Yvette's hands.

This time the woman didn't pull away. "You're still sleeping with him?"

"Oh, Hell no!" She shook her head vigorously. "Actually, I guess there's no better time to tell you this but…"

She looked away for a minute, than back at Yvette. "I have so many other family dramas to deal with that I can't bear to lose all of you – you all have been more like a family to me than my own parents – I'd be lost without you."

The foursome joined hands.

"Raynard finally came back into my life."

The gasps that rent the air nearly sucked in all the oxygen around them.

"I know you all might think I'm stupid for giving him another chance, and after everything you all did in his stead, but he's been wonderful to me. He's been helping with KeAnna and Jaynene, who I just found out was raped and that's how she got pregnant."

"Oh, my God!" Karyn shrieked.

Yvette blinked and tried to wrap her mind around that.

Sherry locked gazes with Veronica, whose eyes filled with moisture.

"Raynard has been trying to make up for lost time. He had tried to find me but my parents wouldn't tell him where I was. He hired a private detective to track us down. He's been a godsend for Jaynene. She's recovering from what happened, and I was too ashamed to tell you that I wasn't there to help like I should have been." She looked at her glass of juice. "That's why I'm not touching that stuff again."

Sherry went on to tell them the circumstances that led to the reunion, then Jaynene's story and ended with, "Veronica, thank you for being there for Jaynene. I don't think she could have made it through without her God mommy."

Veronica came to stand next to Sherry, hugging her. "And I might actually have a solution to one of your issues. William and I talked, and if it's okay with you and Jaynene, we would like to adopt her baby." Sherry gasped at that statement, but Veronica just gave her hand a gentle pat. "I've always dreamed of having a child but my biological clock is ticking, and I'm just not sure my body will let me have a baby let alone carry one to term."

She looked out at the group. "Then I thought of Jaynene. I'd love to give her baby a good family, and if William and I raise the baby, she'd still be able to be part of its life and watch it grow into an adult."

Sherry broke down crying, she laid her head on Veronica's shoulder. "I love you so much. You've always been there for me. Always. I don't deserve how good you all have been to me. And for me to…" She shook her head. "Jaynene doesn't want to keep the baby." She paused at the stricken expression on Veronica's face. "To carry the baby nine whole months, then to see it from time to time—it's…it's…she can't do it."

Veronica finally nodded, but the disappointment was still obvious in the slumped set of her shoulders.

Sherry looked Yvette directly in her eyes. "Truly, I hope someday you will forgive me." "To be honest, I was jealous of you. You've always been so pretty and so well put together and you've always gotten what you wanted."

Yvette's subtle smile faltered, torn between the compliment and the insult. "Don't get me wrong, I loved you as my sister but I was jealous of your confidence. All the things I lacked. All of you have it. I never did."

She leaned over Veronica to get her glass and took a calming sip. "I've always tried to be a good person and treat people well and it's always backfired." Her gaze locked on Yvette. "And no, Jackie Shoemocker was the one to fill him in. Lisa Pickett is her niece.

"What!!!"

"Company policy forbid hiring family members so they never

told anyone. But Derrick knew. And he was so upset with you that he wanted more information. First it was asking advice on how to keep your marriage together."

"That's mighty strange," Yvette quipped. "Seeing as you're not married."

"He wanted a woman's point of view."

"And then you just gave him another view."

Those bitter words hung in the air a moment as each woman tensed, waiting for something else to be said.

"It was wrong of me to hurt you in that way," Sherry whispered. "And I promise, from this day forward, I'll never hurt you again. I'm going to work toward being a better person for myself, my children and for all of you, my sisters. Please forgive me. I'll do anything to make it up to you."

Yvette's gaze narrowed on Sherry as she said, "Anything?" Then her lips spread into a vicious smile. "Are you sure about that? Because I know *exactly* what you can do to make things right and settle the score between us."

"Yvette, I know you're not on that trip again!" Karyn snapped.

"Yvette, I'm not taking Derrick's side," Veronica added, ignoring the traumatized look on Sherry's face, "But you really hurt him too. Imagine how he feels. It's not like you were innocent in all this. He didn't start sleeping around until you did. He was a faithful and loving husband and he adores those little girls."

"Maybe, just maybe, we can find a way to persuade Derrick to stay," Karyn commented, with a sigh. "I know Derrick loves you in his own way, but what does he love just as much? His money and his success."

"And Sherry, now that he trusts you," Veronica said softly, "You might be able to find out some things."

Yvette neck snapped around and glared at Sherry. "Trusts her? Trusts you to do what? Suck his dick." Yvette's voice had gone from being pitiful to malicious in record time. "I don't trust you any farther than I can see you. But the *one* thing I need you to do will actually earn back some trust, to *prove* you're as sorry as you say you are," she snarled.

"No more killings," Veronica responded softly. "We're beyond that. There's no way you can even justify this."

Yvette looked Karyn squarely in the eyes. "I can justify it the same way we justified taking Mark out of the picture."

"That was different," Veronica said, glaring at Yvette.

"Personally, I'm afraid that Derrick might know too much already," Karyn added. "If there was ever a valid reason to do what Yvette is asking, that's definitely one."

"So *now* it's okay because we're protecting you?" Yvette shot back. "Once again, we always have to protect Karyn."

"No, that's not it. If one of us goes down, *all* of us goes down," she warned. "Have any of you thought about that?"

Chapter 27

Karyn was experiencing one hell of a day. The one wedding that mattered was the one that was falling apart. The weather forecast predicted rain which predicated a move from an outdoor venue to one totally indoors. She had reserved both the dining room and the solarium for this very reason. Unfortunately, since the management of the place had changed hands, somehow her request was lost in the shuffle. She was scrambling to make things right before the wedding was slated to happen. It was much too late to find some other place. The RSVPs had been returned and counted—air travel and lodging were all secure. Everything was set to go. Now it was all starting to fall apart at the worst possible time. Karyn was close to pulling her hair out by the roots.

"I'm looking at the signed contract right here," Karyn said, holding up a finger to halt Carl's attempt to speak to her the moment he strolled in. "I'm faxing it over again. We requested to have the ceremony on the lawn right outside the solarium, but reserved the solarium itself just in case of inclement weather."

Carl sighed and perched on the corner of her desk in Karyn's home office. She gave him a tired half smile. "No, you have it wrong, the *reception* was slated for the dining room, not the solarium." Karyn paused, listening to the person on the other end. "What do you mean you've already booked it for something else? We were charged for it already! We paid it and I don't remember anyone saying anything about a refund——"

Karyn sent a panicked look in Carl's direction. He only grimaced and pointed to his watch. She nodded, then pointed to the phone, gesturing that the call was important. "Okay, here's the issue," she snapped. "I have a signed contract that states exactly what we've wanted and either you all are going to accommodate us according to that contract, or you're going to refund every cent for things that we paid for and that are suddenly not available. Whoever you all put in the dining room needs to be shifted somewhere else——"

Carl got up and walked out. Karyn closed her eyes, trying to quell the frustration building into a major migrane. She had asked him to come home for lunch because she wanted to talk to him. She had finally found enough courage to tell him what had happened so many years ago. Even though things had been quiet among the group—no flare-ups, everyone doing their part for Veronica's wedding; she still feared that someone was going to slip up. She would rather Carl hear it from her and deal with the consequences, than have it all hit the fan at a time where she couldn't do damage control.

Karyn ended the call, scrambled from the chair aiming to catch up with Carl when the phone rang again. She did a complete one-eighty, went back to her desk and peered at the display. Carl came to stand at the door, chewing on a hero sandwich that was piled high with veggies and turkey as he watched her. She held up her finger and grinned sheepishly. "Baby, I have to take this call she said before snatching the phone up. "Yes," she said to the DJ on the other end. "I received the email with the music list you plan on using and I thought you were joking. I could have sworn the contract said the age group was thirty-five and older. Hip Hop and Rap music isn't going to cut it!"

She sighed, rubbing a hand over the bridge of her nose as she listened to the bullshit coming from the other end. Finally she'd had enough. "Please look at the list I sent you and..." Karyn winced at his reply. "What the hell do you mean you don't have any old folk's music? Why didn't you say that in the beginning? And watch your mouth, I'm one of those 'old folks'. If you can't accommodate us, then I'll hire someone who has something other than the kind of music that'll make my guests fall off their chair!" Karyn slammed down the phone, cursing.

"Busy day, sweetheart?"

She threw a scathing look at Carl, who held up his sandwich and said, "Hey, I'm just stating the obvious." He took another bite and followed it by a sip of orange juice. "What was so important that you wanted me to come home right this minute? I've got a big shipment coming in and since they screwed up last time, I want to be sure we have everything we're supposed to this time."

Carl had just started a new development a few months ago and they were in the final stages of completing Phase II, since all of the houses in Phase I were sold out. His partner was putting on the pressure to get things finished as the economy was shifting to a point where people weren't so reluctant to buy new homes anymore. The foreclosure sweep—people picking up homes due to the misfortune of others—was on a downward spiral. The construction company Carl owned was about to finally cash in on the upswing. She knew this was important to him. Carl was a wonderful architect and developer. Their current house was one of his masterpieces and it was built with Karyn in mind.

Karyn released a weary breath, "The final fitting isn't going to happen in time. The Vera Wang gown will be here, but the bridesmaid's dresses which were supposed to be done by William's designer who lives in California was on short order since the woman didn't make it to Chicago when he had scheduled for her to be here! Now she's saying she can't find the powder blue satin material and she's saying that halter neck dresses aren't her specialty." She tossed another blue sheet of paper onto the desk. "Veronica's niece, who her mother *insisted* had to be in the wedding, has a sore throat. She won't be able to do the wedding songs." Karyn shook her head, exasperated by all of the heat coming down on her now, and this was just the tip of what she'd been dealing with today. "Trying to accommodate everyone's cousin, nephew, best friend's sister, or the family of other distant relatives is driving me up the wall."

"No doubt," he quipped and continued polishing off his meal.

"Carl, I really wanted to—"

The phone rang. Karyn craned her neck to look at the display. She grimaced as she looked back at her husband. Carl shrugged and just looked at her. She soon listened as the makeup artist and hair stylist confirmed their time to arrive. Which would have been wonderful news…if it wasn't for the wrong damn day! "No, get it straight, it's *Saturday* at 7:00 AM." Carl waited patiently as she argued with the woman, who was a friend of Veronica's sister.

Karyn hung up the phone and looked at him, opened her mouth to speak when the ringing echoed in the room. She closed her eyes, then opened them and signaled for Carl to stay put. He looked at his watch again and sighed.

"No, no, no," she said. "We asked for a *Baptist* minister, not a Catholic." She paused to listen, then said, "No we don't want to do mass before the ceremony. We're not Catholic!"

Carl shook his head and left the room. Moments later her heart sank when she heard his truck peel away from the house.

Chapter 28

"We're in the wrong business," Veronica said as she looked over the documents that detailed all the dirt they had managed to gather on Derrick Glover in just a few week's time. Opting to force him to stay with Yvette, instead of committing another murder, which Veronica and Sherry were totally against, they were more than prepared for the confrontation that would take place.

Karyn packed the remainder of the papers in a folder and looked up at the other three women. "I believe he'll be highly impressed with our research."

"Do you think we'll be able to pull this off," Yvette inquired, still unsure if this route would save her marriage.

"It'll be an offer he can't refuse," Veronica said with a mild laugh. "We know that Derrick stole thousands of dollars from his company, which will be especially damaging if we leak that information to the right people. He'd lose *everything!*"

"Well it better work," replied Yvette, sternly. "If not, we're going back to plan A."

No one said a word.

Sherry, who had been rid of Derrick for a few months, was now forced to plan a date for them to meet. She couldn't tell Raynard what they were doing, because she might slip up and tell him more than she had planned—and that would lead to more questions. She couldn't be the weak link this time. And as much as she never wanted to see Derrick again, she had to take one for the team to see this through. Maybe then Yvette would forgive her.

Sherry had baited him by telling him she had information on Yvette that would be beneficial to him in a divorce proceedings. Derrick was more than happy to meet with Sherry since he'd been waiting for the opportune time to file for divorce, specifically, a time when he would have little to lose and much to gain. He wanted the children as it was obvious Yvette had no maternal inclinations whatsoever.

They met the following Saturday night at Sherry's apartment. There would be no distractions or interruptions since the girls were catching a movie with Raynard.

Karyn and Veronica arrived three hours early, parked their cars on the next block and traipsed in all the files they had into the apartment. Once inside, they hid in Sherry's master bedroom. She told them, "He needs to be out of here before Raynard gets home."

"Well, you'd better be good then," Karyn said, pushing her out of the room.

An hour later, Derrick showed up, exactly as planned. His gait was smooth and confident as though Sherry was about to hand him the key to his freedom.

Sherry invited Derrick in, then lead him to take a seat on the sofa.

"Would you like something to drink before we get started?"

Derrick quickly responded, "A glass of wine would be great."

"Sorry, it's juice, water or coffee."

His head cocked to the side as though to say, "What?"

Derrick scanned the apartment, noticing that she had set the mood for romance by dimming the lights and soft music playing in the background.

"It's been awhile, Sherry. I was beginning to think you didn't love me anymore." He removed his jacket and took a seat on the black leather sofa. "What's been going on with you?"

Sherry poured Derrick a glass of juice. He frowned as she offered it to him.

"What's up with the dry house."

"I have children here."

"Never bothered you before."

"It does now," she shot back. Realization hit her. It wasn't uncommon for him to have at least three or four glasses of wine or something stronger before he even kissed her; even more before they went to bed. Whenever he stopped by it was always for just a few hours. And he never, never offered to take her out to dinner, the movies, the theatre—any place outside of the house. Suddenly, everything became clear – he *was* using her just like Veronica and Karyn had said. If she wasn't sure before, she was certainly sure now.

Refocusing, Sherry looked at him over the rim of her glass, "Derrick, baby, once you and Yvette are divorced, we'll get married, right?"

He nearly choked on the juice. "Now, let's not go rushing things," he said smoothly. "First things first. You need to tell me what you have on my wife."

Sherry sat on Derrick's lap, stroked her hand across his face. "Calm down, baby. I'll give you the information, but let's get busy first. I've been missing you. I need some loving."

Derrick shoved Sherry off of his lap. "Look girl, I'm not up for this right now. I'm too stressed for all *this*," he spat as he motioned at the romantic setting and the way Sherry was dressed to kill. "Until I have what I need to get out of this marriage, we can't move forward. If you wanted me, you should've been dropping that information in my hand as soon as I walked through the door!"

"Derrick, are we really going to be together or were you just using me to get back at Yvette?"

Karyn looked over at Veronica, who were perched at the bedroom's threshold, whispering, "She said she was over him but it sounds like she still wants to be with him."

Veronica rolled her eyes, "No she wants to hear the truth from his lips when she already knows it in her heart. We're not here for this! She needs to stick to the plan."

Karyn was fuming, having lost all patience with Sherry. "I'm giving her five minutes to pull this bullshit off. If not I'm going out there."

There was a shocked silence, enough time for Sherry to catch his stunned expression before he covered it with a mild sigh. "Look, Sherry, I like you and all, and I would really love to be with you, but you know as well as I do, that it wouldn't work for us." A coldness that she had never seen had crept into his voice just then. "We would have to start our life someplace other than here and that wouldn't work since I still want to see my children, and your girls are settled here too. It wouldn't make much sense."

Sherry stood over him, stared down at him like he was a child. "So this was all a game to you? And *you* were pissed off because you think Yvette played you, huh? Fucking her friend? Can't get much lower than that, can you, Derrick?" Sherry's face was flushed with anger as her voice started to rise. "Well, let me tell you something, *player*, I'm more like Yvette than you'll ever know."

On cue, Karyn stepped out of the bedroom. "So am I."

Derrick's head whipped around, shock taking over as he jumped to his feet.

Immediately following on Karyn's heels was Veronica offering a solid, "Me too."

Glaring from one woman to the next, he ended on Sherry. "What the hell is going on?" When she just stood there with a smug smile, he stormed toward her, closing the gap between them. "This is between you and me. What are they doing here?"

"Sorry Derrick," she responded sarcastically. "You're sadly mistaken if you actually thought that I was going to let you destroy my girl; just like I was sadly mistaken for actually believing you when you said you would leave Yvette for me."

Derrick lunged at her. "You bitch!"

Jumping in between them, Karyn raised a hand to ward off his fist. "I wouldn't advise you to do that, Derrick," she said with a calm she barely felt. They hadn't taken into consideration that Derrick might get volatile. Neither of them had brought a weapon. Although Sherry might have a bat in her front closet. "You need to sit your ass down and hear what we have to say." She tossed the folder Veronica had been holding toward his chest. He caught it, then thumbed through the pictures and documents, his eyes widening as realization hit. "Where did you get all of this from? What's the meaning of this?"

"It doesn't matter where we got it from, what matters to us is Yvette. And you're done dicking her over. It ends tonight," Veronica said matter–of–factly.

"I don't understand," Derrick replied. He had sat down on the couch with a dazed expression before flipping through the pages. When he finally looked up, Veronica was sitting on the arm of the sofa beside him. Leaning in close, she said, "Here's the thing. You aren't leaving Yvette or your kids."

"What the hell do you mean? I wasn't leaving the kids! I want my girls. Yvette needs to leave." He released a malicious laugh that caused Sherry to cringe. "How are you three whores going to tell me that I have to stay with that bitch?" He tossed the folder back at Veronica, the papers went in all directions. "She destroyed any feelings I might have had for her years ago. She's a lying, cheating tramp, just like this one right here," he said with a nod in Sherry's direction. "It was nothing to get her to spread her legs for me, and it was nothing for her to tell all of your dirty little secrets."

"Well," replied Karyn, cautiously, "If you don't want to be exposed for your own 'dirty secrets' you'll be staying with her whether you like it or not." Karyn still couldn't believe that her friend wanted to force her husband to stay with her, even after all he had done to her. But she wasn't going to argue that point any longer. She knew if Yvette didn't get what she wanted, then her own life would fall apart. "Otherwise, we'll destroy you and make sure you lose *everything*, and we do mean everything. Hell, you might even have to do a stint in the county jail."

"You wouldn't dare!" Derrick said through his teeth.

"Try me," Karyn replied simply. "And you're not just going to stay with her, you're going to honor, and respect her and be the best husband you could ever be." Somehow that came out a bit dry, so she added a little bass in her voice when she said. "You don't want to test us Derrick, trust me. We will fuck up your whole life–you have no idea what we can do." She silently added, or what your wife wants us to do. Karyn tried to sound threatening, she really did, but all she could manage was a half–hearted attempt at putting the screws to him. By all rights, he did have every right to leave. The woman had betrayed him as surely as Sherry had. She didn't see her warming up to Sherry and doing what it took to keep Sherry in her life. Hmph. But Karyn's life on the outside of the prison walls as well as the other women depended on them being successful tonight. Personally, she didn't think it could work.

Veronica peered at Karyn, but said to Derrick. "You have too much to lose at this point in the game."

Derrick slammed a fist into Sherry's wooden table splintering it and causing the skin to break on his right hand. "I can't believe this shit!" He stormed toward the door, opened it, then turned to face the three women before he walked out.

Karyn took advantage of his hesitation. "She's willing to change and do right by you. Honestly, Derrick, Yvette loves you and she doesn't want to lose you. Look at the lengths she'll go in order to keep the marriage. She wants to go to marriage counseling and start attending church regularly as a family. Whatever it takes to bring love and happiness back to the family, she's willing to do it."

Veronica grimaced at that little diatribe. Sherry just stared at her. Karyn was bullshitting, but only she and the two other women knew that. She figured they had enough sense to play along.

Veronica noticed the blood forming on his hand, she grabbed one of the linen napkins and walked over to him. Gently, she took his hand and wiped the blood away. "At one time, you loved Yvette," she whispered. Don't you at least owe it to each other and your children to attempt to rebuild your life together? Both of you all have been on the wrong side of the bed. Suck it up and do the right thing."

After a long silence, Derrick sighed. When he spoke, his voice was filled with pain. "No, I don't want to lose my family. I'm not perfect, and I know I've done some things that I'm not proud of." Derrick took a deep breath, trying to maintain his composure. "It's just, with everything Yvette has done, I'm not sure who she is. I don't know what she's capable of."

"And you don't want to find out either," Sherry muttered causing Karyn to give her the evil eye.

Veronica placed a strong calming hand on Derrick's shoulder. "She had us go through this much to keep you in line," she said pointing to all the documentation they had gathered. "There's no telling what else she might do if she feels she's lost you completely. At least we were the ones who confronted you this time. Next time, it might just be her confronting you, and it might be a bigger threat than what we're throwing in your face."

Karyn, fearing Veronica might have gone too far, cut her gaze in her friend's direction, adding, "Personally, I wouldn't want to be with a man who doesn't want to be with me, but Yvette is different. You know she has her reasons for doing things even though it makes no sense to the rest of us. That's just how it is with her."

Derrick took in her solemn expressions which matched his own. Feeling defeated, he plopped himself back down on the sofa, "What if I just give her the money and walk away?"

Sherry shook her head, lips set in a grim line. She walked over to the sofa and sat beside him. "For some reason, it's all about you. She wants it all—you and the money or nothing at all."

Derrick shook his head. "She can't rebuild the trust we once had. She can't make me love her the way I did in the beginning."

"You've been good at pretending all this time," Sherry said softly, a tear rolling down her cheek as she realized her part in everything. "Why stop now?"

Chapter 29

Yvette woke up to an empty bed yet again. Maybe the women had failed in their mission to get through to Derrick yesterday. She sat by the phone all evening, waiting to hear something, anything from one of them. The phone never rang and she had finally given in to a much-needed rest. Cleaning a ten-bedroom house was no small task. This time the crew refused to come because she had snapped one morning. They had not forgotten.

She reached for the cordless, dialed Karyn's number to find out exactly what had happened last night at Sherry's house. What was Derrick's response to everything they had to say and to the evidence they had against him?

The moment Karyn's voice came in on the line, she whined, "You promised me that this would work. He's still not home!"

Karyn sighed heavily. "Calm down, woman! When we finished talking to him, he was okay with everything. He said he would do whatever it took to save your marriage. Maybe he just needed some time to clear his head."

"If this doesn't work," Yvette said, pulling back the draperies to peer out at the swimming pool. "We're going to have to go back to the original plan. Hell, it worked for you, didn't it?"

"That's a little bit extreme for the circumstances," Karyn said with a calm that Yvette hadn't heard in a long while. "And your threatening me isn't going to help the situation. You can't force a man to stay if he doesn't want to. And we did our part. You need to do yours—and stop pissing him off. And keep your legs closed for a change. He might actually want to sleep with you."

"Fuck you!"

There was a rumble of activity downstairs.

"Shit, he's home!" Yvette hung up without another word to Karyn, scrambled to the bathroom, freshened up as quickly as she could, and came out wearing absolutely nothing.

Derrick strolled into the room, took one look at Yvette, focused on the body parts that mattered and let go of a bored yawn before he asked, "Where are the girls?"

Yvette flinched, a stab of disappointment filled her. "They're with your mother this weekend. I thought we needed to talk about some things." She reached for a robe, slipped it on over her body, then walked over to the bed where he had taken a seat on the outer edge.

"They're always with my mother or somebody's mother. They're never with *their* mother. What's up with that?" he said with a harsh laugh. "All the trouble you went through now you act as if you can't be bothered with them. That's so sad."

* * *

A couple of months following their tryst in New York, Derrick had found more ways to avoid Yvette than a deadbeat dad trying to dodge child support payments. He had even taken to having his assistant do all of his talking for him when it came to discussing anything with Yvette, much to her chagrin. Jackie was too occupied with work to ask what had happened, but she seemed to think something had gone down. She now treated Yvette with a lot more caution than she had on any occasion before that time. The rumors floating around the office was that there was some big fight between Derrick Glover and Lisa Pickett. Jackie put two and two together and had come up with five. Though she didn't share her suspicions with anyone else.

Yvette was on her way to a meeting when the phone rang. Believing Derrick could finally be on the other end, she picked up before it could ring a second time.

Lisa Pickett was crying into the receiver, which only made Yvette sigh with frustration as she snapped, "What do you want?"

"I can't believe you did this to me," she said through choked sobs. "I thought you were my friend."

"Woman, what are you chirping about? Go squeak somewhere else. I've got business to handle. I have to go."

Yvette pulled the phone from her ear, but put it back the moment she heard, "I know everything. I know *exactly* what you did."

Silence, as Yvette put the files down and lowered to her chair.

And now you're pregnant?" Lisa spat. "He's only leaving me because you're carrying his child. If not for that, trust me, I'd still be walking down the aisle with him next Saturday."

Yvette looked at her watch and grimaced. Yes, she was quite aware that everything for Lisa's wedding was all a done deal. Well, that is until Yvette so casually dropped the information that she was carrying Derrick's child only a day after the pregnancy test flashed positive.

He was nowhere near thrilled, but at that point two things could happen, he would marry Lisa and have to try like hell to keep Yvette quiet, which she made sure that he knew was not going to be an easy thing since she wanted the child to grow up knowing both of its parents. Or he could disappoint the woman he loved and do the responsible thing and marry Yvette to save face and his reputation, avoiding any unseemly drama at CNB. He was all set, at least in his mind, to reach president before his thirty-fifth birthday. If it became known that he had slept with another subordinate at the company, that might not happen. CNB was as conservative as a company could get. He had already secretly crossed the line with his relationship with Lisa, but their upcoming nuptials kind of swept all misgivings under the rug. Yvette's pregnancy would signal a lack of personal responsibility on his part.

"I don't have time for this," Yvette snapped, grabbing up the last of her folders. "It's not my fault that you couldn't keep your man in line. He knows what he wants and it's definitely not you."

"It's people like you who give women a bad name," Lisa said softly. "You schemed, sucked up every bit of information from me, all so you could steal my man. Didn't you have any prospects of your own, since you've got it like that?"

The mousy woman had put a little base in her voice? Yvette almost laughed out loud. "Look, Lisa, it's like this, you can't take it personal. Like I told Derrick, you're weak, you couldn't handle a man like him. He's happy now. He loves me."

"You know, people who do the things you do, always think they've gotten over; that they've gotten ahead. But trust me," Lisa countered smoothly. "You'll get what's coming to you. I can only hope that I'll be around to see it."

* * *

"Derrick, please, just listen to me," Yvette pleaded, trying to get a hold of his arms, and hold him still so she could get a word in.

He slipped out of her reach and went to the nightstand. "Oh, I heard you all right." Derrick didn't even bother to get his bags this time, instead he grabbed a picture of the girls. "I could never trust you again. I could never be with you the way you want me to. Everything you've done has come back to haunt me. I'm paying for your mistakes. Just as much as I'm paying for my own."

"What do you mean?" she whispered, crossing the distance between them to place a hand on his shoulder. He had never said anything like that before then.

Derrick shrugged her off. "I didn't get the president's position. I will never rise higher than where I am right now, no matter what I do, no matter what new programs or services I implement. All of my hard work at CNB all these years has been stalled because of your sleazy ass."

"I don't get what you're talking about," she cried, putting a hand on her chest to quell her rapidly beating heart. "I didn't do anything to you, or anything at CNB that would make anyone treat you this kind of way."

"Oh, you did plenty. They won't put it on paper, but several of the board members let me know in no uncertain terms that I've been blackballed because you've slept with Robert Haynes, and Michael Turner and Millicent Linyard and Ernest Bruce and Christine Hardman and Van Southward, and...and let's not forget my boss."

Yvette cringed as her history was laid before her in all its ugly details. And he actually had names this time, not just speculation. What could she say to that?

"And now they can't promote me because the word is out and people will think I landed the position because of what you've done. They believe I asked you to do that to further my career!" He moved, allowing as much space as possible between them. "Now thanks to my *loving* wife, I will never be able to achieve my dream." He flickered a disdainful gaze over at her. "All because I didn't have the presence of mind to realize how treacherous you were. I'll be paying for it for the rest of my life."

He crossed to the window, turned his face to the sun, and laughed. "Lisa Pickett is married to the man that they're promoting to the president position. That's really telling isn't it? She thought that losing me was the worst thing that could ever happen in her life. Now she's happier than ever and I'm as miserable as a bitch in heat," he tossed an angry glare over his shoulder. "I rolled the dice I crapped out the moment you put your mouth on my dick."

Derrick turned back to face her and gave her a smile that chilled her to the bone. "But let me tell you something sweetheart, it'll be a snowball's chance of rolling through hell that I could ever, ever, love you again. I don't even want to be in the same house with you. " He leaned forward and whispered, "And for the record, Sherry sucks my dick a hell of a lot better than you ever did. I'll miss *her* before I would ever miss you." He brushed past her to hit the door. "I'm outta here. See you in court."

Chapter 30

Karyn lifted her hem, tore through the Solarium, unable to enjoy the warm breeze whipping about her, plastering the silk robe to her body. She was grateful that she hadn't put on her real gown just yet. She slowed her steps as she made it to the hallway and aimed toward the dining room, trying to find Jaynene, who was one of the hostesses for Veronica's wedding.

Only three hours before the ceremony and Karyn was overwhelmed with the final details of making sure that the guests would be properly situated. She was quickly adjusting the carefully planned seating arrangement to accommodate the bride and the groom's last minute requests. And that was topped by the fact that once again, she was putting out fires faster than the next one could ignite. Thanks to Carl, her friends, Jaynene and even a more reluctant KeAnna, Karyn had to only be in three places instead of the twenty.

Chicago's historical South Shore Cultural Center was the perfect choice for the ceremony and the reception. The place that held a 1920's elegance was once the epicenter of the South Side's elite events and with recent renovations it had been restored to its former glory. Outside the solarium, chairs with white satin covers had been lined up facing toward the amazing seven foot arch that had been created specifically for the event. Flowers from roses to daises were creatively displayed throughout the entire venue and spilled to the outside area where the ceremony would take place. At the tip of the walkway, the bridal runner was curled, waiting to spiral out and display the fact that the soon–to–be wed couple's shared last name had been engraved in silver.

Karyn made it to the dining room with its cascading chandeliers and cathedral windows giving a panoramic view of the golf course and the lush green areas leading to Lake Michigan. The tablecloths were bright white, and the chairs in this room were covered in white satin, with alternating silver bows tied on the backs of some and blue bows tied on others. A towering vase filled with Calla lilies were the centerpiece for each table. From the door where Karyn stood, she sighed with relief. As a whole, everything looked magnificent.

"Aunt Karyn, here's the new seating chart," Jaynene said, giving her a warm smile as she sauntered through the flower–filled foyer leading to the dining room. Karyn's gaze swept across the page, denoting the major changes, and the fact that the youngster had managed to do in minutes what it would have taken Karyn an hour to do. She was just that frustrated!

"Thanks sweetheart. You've done a fantastic job."

Jaynene beamed at the compliment and the fact that Karyn planted a kiss on her forehead. "Where's your sister?"

"Sampling the food. She said you wanted everything to be perfect."

"Suuuuure. We know what she's really about, don't we."

Jaynene gave her a nod and grin, which warmed Karyn's heart and made her take a deep breath. Everything would be all right. It just had to be. If this young girl could suffer through the things she had, and become the strong, beautiful swan that stood before her today, then certainly Karyn could stop stressing and go with the flow. Jaynene dabbed a napkin to Karyn's forehead.

"Thank you."

"I'll go check on the D.J." Jaynene said strolling toward the tables set with turntables and mixers.

"And make sure he has the correct playlist and the right music."

"Yeah, old folks music," Jaynene said over her shoulder.

"Watch it, young lady."

Jaynene giggled.

Karyn watched her walk away, noting that the dress she wore—the halter top powder blue silk was the spitting image of the dress that Karyn had upstairs. Reminding her that she had to get her hair and makeup done before she got dressed. The guests were due to arrive in four hours, it wouldn't do to have the coordinator/bridesmaid still traipsing around in her silk robe.

Karyn turned, strolled through the foyer, then out to the lobby aiming to make it to the lounge when she crossed paths with the other wedding coordinator on the premises today. The woman, tall, regal and almost model–like, gave Karyn the evil eye. Her wedding had to be shifted to the theatre and it was obvious that she, along with the potty–mouth bride was none too happy. And those two weren't the only people that she had pissed off. At one point she had to call a meeting with the bride, groom, and their respective parents to put an end to her headaches and to make sure there would actually *be* a wedding. They were, at first, concerned when she had to scrap almost all "family" vendors and go with her more reliable sources because things just weren't working out. KeAnna, was the only remaining family member on that score as she would replace the originally slated singer who had mysteriously found her voice, but wanted more money to perform. Finally Karyn told William if they wanted to keep everyone, that was fine, but he would have to pay family and her own vendors as she didn't want anything to fall apart. Family was ditched quicker than a New York minute. Mission accomplished.

Rushing past the ushers, she ran straight into Derrick's broad chest, and nearly fell to the ground. Somehow though, he'd managed to grab her before that could happen. His grip was so tight, it caused her to shriek in pain.

"Let me go!" she shrieked. "You're hurting me."

His gaze, angry and cold, was more unsettling than the pain shooting up in her arms. "All four of you conniving ass witches need to see me in the lounge *before* the wedding."

Karyn stared back at him, disbelief etched in her mind. "Are you serious?" Annoyed, she stepped back, finally dislodging his grip. "I have a wedding to get started. Get out of my way."

Derrick blocked her path, though, unwilling to let her move forward. "It will be in your best interest to gather up your girls for a little discussion," he leveled a deadly glare at her. "or there *won't be* a wedding. Trust me."

She stood there, staring blankly at him which only angered him more.

"This discussion can either happen in private, or I can let loose during the ceremony," he walked away, his gait confident and sure. He glanced briefly back at her over his shoulder. "I'll let you decide. Ten minutes. Be there or else."

Karyn stood frozen, but realizing that time was running out, she scrambled up the stairs to the bride's dressing room where the bridal party was having their makeup applied by professionals. Veronica grinned and winked the moment she saw Karyn, but continued chatting it up with her makeup artist, telling how William had proposed. The Vera Wang wedding dress and veil were hanging on the closet door next to the beautifully tailored bridesmaids dresses. The stout seamstress, who had come through for Karyn, was putting the final touches on the halter top dresses.

Scanning the happy faces in the room, Karyn asked as politely as she could for them to excuse them for a moment. She waited until the room had emptied, closed the door, then relayed what Derrick had said.

Veronica turned to Yvette, bearing down on the smaller woman. "What's this all about? What's been going on with you and Derrick since we had that…little talk?"

"We've been doing well." Yvette lied smoothly, avoiding eye contact with any of them. "Counseling has been a tremendous help. Thanks to you all, I couldn't be happier right now. I truly think we're going to make it." Then gave them a smile, one that didn't quite reach her eyes. "Maybe he wants to surprise me with another honeymoon."

"If things are 'going so well,' as you put it, why would he threaten us before my wedding?" Veronica snapped. "It doesn't make sense. This whole thing with him never made sense! If a man really doesn't want to be with you, you can't force him to."

Karyn nodded. "And the way he looked at me and how he gripped my arms didn't speak to the fact that he's happy." She showed them the bruises that were beginning to form on her upper arms. "We should just take out a few minutes to hear what he has to say."

Sherry's hands, which were holding onto the serving table filled with an array of food, barely held her up as realization dawned. Turning to the other three, she said, "I'm getting an eerie feeling in the pit of my stomach; I think Derrick knows about Mark."

Veronica's eyes went wide, "Why would you say that?"

"Because when I saw him downstairs an hour ago, he looked at me and just shook his head as he gave me this strange look." She made eye contact with each one of her friends. "I thought he was still angry because of what I'd done, but now I feel like it's something else."

"He did the same thing to me when I first got here," Veronica said, her voice wavering as she slumped onto the chair. "I can't believe this is happening on my wedding day. Of all days, it's happening on what should be one of the happiest days of my life. Don't I deserve some happiness?" She gestured to the other three. "Why does all your shit always come raining down on me? I haven't done anything wrong. I didn't even want to help kill Mark. I Kept trying to talk you all out of it."

"Calm down Veronica, please don't get upset," Karyn said, reaching out to rub the back of her shoulder. "It'll be all right."

"You don't even believe that, Karyn!" she spat, whirling to face the woman who was the root cause of this madness. "If you hadn't insisted that we..."—she looked down at Karyn's trembling hands. "Don't you dare try to calm me down when you're shaking in your panties as much as I am!"

Yvette turned to face them hoping to make her lie a little more believable. "Do you think Derrick's only been pretending to be happy with me and was just waiting for the right moment to come back at us?" She looked at each one of them, then said, almost dully, "I told you we should've killed him."

Veronica glared at her then wiped the last of her tears away, smearing her freshly applied make–up. "How can you be so cold? You fucked up and now you want us to clean up your mess. You lied to get him, then slept around on him when you had him." She rolled her eyes in disgust. "Now you want to kill him because he's tired of *your* shit? Give me a fucking break! You don't love him, The only person you love is yourself. Have you ever, ever thought about the fact that you don't need his money. That we," she gestured to the other two, then herself, "have your back? Did you ever think about that?" She glared at Yvette. "We didn't let Karyn down. We didn't let Sherry down. So how the hell would you think that we would let you down, you dumb bitch."

Karyn winced at her vicious tone. Sherry did the same.

Karyn came to stand between the two women. "Let's not think the worst just yet. Remember, we have dirt on him too. If he does know anything," she tossed an angry look at Sherry who cringed under the hard glare, "Then if we go to jail, his ass will be going too."

"Hey, at least then we'll be together!" Yvette threw her head back and let go of a bitter laugh. "All for one…"

Chapter 31

With Sherry, Yvette and Veronica trailing behind her, Karyn found Derrick in the lounge, just where he said he'd be waiting for them.

Approaching him, Karyn tried her best to sound authoritative. "There's too much that needs to happen in this lounge. I found a private room at the end of the hall where we can talk. Let's go."

"Give me a minute," he said with a smirk while taking his time to finish off his drink before popping a couple of hors d'oeuvres in his mouth.

Finally, he followed the women into a room at the far end of the lounge. The women were all seated when Derrick walked in. Karyn's heart sped up when she saw Carl and William stroll in behind him. She took a quick look at Veronica who nearly fell off the chair, but Sherry's arm held her steady, but lost her grip when Raynard sauntered in, taking in all the solemn expressions of the people in the room.

Derrick held up several yellow envelopes in his hand, enough for everyone in the room.

Sherry didn't leave Veronica's side as she asked, "What's going on, boys?"

"I'm as clueless as you are," Carl replied, throwing a look in his wife's direction, taking in the rigid set of her shoulders and the worried expression that had become all too familiar to him lately.

"It'll all make sense to you soon enough," Derrick responded passing the envelopes around as he made a quick sweep of the small room. "Carl, it's a little too late for you," he said with a weary shake of his head as though someone had died. Then he grinned at the groom. "But William, before you walk down the aisle, I would like you to know just what you're getting yourself into. A few months back these bitches –"

Carl moved forward, hands curled into fists. "Hold up, Derrick! You are not going to disrespect them by calling them that." Raynard nodded, flanking Carl's side, ready to take the man down.

Derrick shrugged, slip into the seat next to the door. "Oh, my brother, you may be doing the same once you hear what I have to tell you." He flashed each of the women a grin that made their stomachs lurch with fear. "They're not the sweet little innocent women you may think they are. In fact, they came to me and *threatened* me with information they had gathered about me—"

"Wait one second," Karyn said, getting to her feet. "Today is a special day, Derrick! This is not the time or place to deal with your issues with you and Yvette." Karyn's gaze met Derrick's, begging him with its intensity to keep quiet. "Please don't take away William's and Veronica's memorable moment."

"Oh, it will be memorable," he shot back, grinning. "Not only for them, but for *all* of you as well." He leaned back in the chair, crossing one leg over the other. "As I was saying before I was so *rudely* interrupted, they not only threatened me, but they also tried to force me to stay with my wife."

"Honey, what is this about?" Yvette crossed the room, kneeled in the spot before him. "I thought we were making progress and moving forward. I love you and I've changed, don't you realize that?"

Derrick stood, pushing his wife out of his way. She stumbled until William caught her in a solid grip. "You disgust me," he said with a growl. "I don't like being played, especially by four inexperienced bitches."

Raynard lunged toward Derrick, but William cut him off before the blow landed in the man's face. "You will not continue to speak of my woman like that!" He shouted as he tried to reach around William's muscular frame to get at least one hit in. Carl managed to get through and punch him in the chest, and another to his chin, landing Derrick onto the carpet.

"Man, you need to chill out for a minute." Derrick let loose a little laugh that grated on Veronica's nerves. "You'll be thanking me later, trust me." He stood, turned to the four women with a cocky smile, he said, "Guess what girls? I know enough to take all of you, especially my *loving* wife, out of the game."

That stopped everyone cold.

"Now that I've got your attention, we can really begin. Inside each of your envelopes is a tape." He gazed at Sherry and winked. "And on the tape, my girl Sherry is telling me all about how vicious these four…*women* can be."

Carl glanced first at his wife, then at William before ripping open the manila envelope and pulling out the cassette. He crushed it in his hands.

"Not to worry," Derrick drawled with a wry twist of his lips. "I have an extra copy already lined up for you to hear and maybe the police."

Whipping out a digital recorder, Sherry's slurred voice came across loud and clear, detailing what had happened the night of

Mark's murder.

Karyn fell to her knees, crying out, "Oh no! Oh my God, no!"

"So what is your point, Derrick?" Veronica asked through clenched teeth. "To destroy my life because you've destroyed your own?"

William recovered from the shock of the news relatively quick and went to stand in front of Veronica. "Baby is this true? Did you murder Karyn's husband?"

Carl went to Karyn, his eyes full of pain which quickly transformed to anger.

"I can explain," she whispered, knowing she could do nothing of the kind.

"Yeah, let's see if you can pull yourself out of this one," Derrick taunted with a malicious laugh. "You managed to do everything else so well, even got your girls to do the dirty work. Smooth, real smooth."

"I had no choice!" Karyn cried. "Mark was going to kill me!" She swallowed hard against the memories that flooded her. "I caught him training my son to follow in his footsteps. Mark Junior was only sixteen years old."

"Oh, let's not forget that he sold your ass on the streets," Derrick chimed in. "Heard you were a real good whore for him."

Karyn threw an angry glance at Sherry. "You told him about that, too?"

Carl stormed toward the door. Karyn went after him, grabbing the lapel of his Armani Collezioni blazer. "I tried so many times to run away, but he found me every time. My friends protected me when he threatened to kill me. They did it so that I could live."

Carl shrugged her off. "Why didn't you go to the police?"

"Mark had the police on his payroll. Lots of money can buy you blue friends," she moaned. "There was no one to help me. No one but my friends."

"Is it true?" William said to Veronica, who had gathered the train of her silk robe in her hands, wrinkling it in her grip as she tried not to cry. "I want to hear it from you."

"I didn't pull the trigger, but I'm just as guilty as they are," she whispered softly. "I'd do it again if it meant that I wouldn't have to visit Karyn in a cemetery."

"William, please don't blame her," Yvette said, coming to stand next to Veronica. "She was the only one who tried to talk us out of it. I shot him; I was the one." The admission made Derrick flinch. "And I would do it again, too," she said in a hard tone. Then she took a long breath. "When I was a little girl, a man everyone trusted molested me. I couldn't defend myself but Karyn helped me. I didn't know why I felt that way, but when she needed help, I knew I owed her. Mark was killing her as surely as that man took away my innocence, took away my life." Yvette slowed her breathing, "He was going to kill her. His police friends would've helped him cover it up. I couldn't see my sister go out like that."

Derrick cocked his head in his wife's direction. "Why didn't you tell me?"

"You didn't want to know. All you wanted was to be successful, have a lot of money, and impress people. You never wanted to know the real me, but then again, I didn't show you the real me to begin with." She walked over and stood in front of him, "I only wanted to show you that I was better for you than Lisa. I never took her feelings into consideration. And I never thought that you required anything but a beautiful woman on your arm. That's why you could never love me – not really. You really loved her and I took that away from you. And for that, I'm sorry."

Derrick let the admission swirl around dropped his head and spoke in a soft tone. "It doesn't really matter now. My children matter. I love my children."

While Yvette and Derrick appeared to finally be working things out, in the other corner, things were falling apart, and fast, between Carl and Karyn. Gripping her shoulders as he ground out, "I knew there was something you were holding back! But murder?" He grazed over her as though she had suddenly become a stranger to him. You actually murdered your husband?"

"Well, I wasn't the one who killed him but…"

Sherry sat off in the corner, crying as she realized that with the secret out, she would lose her children, and her friends, possibly forever. Effectively, Mark James, eleven years after the fact, had reached out from the grave to destroy their lives.

"Now that I've heard all of the details," William said with a solemn look at each one of the women. "I must make a confession. I haven't been completely honest with you either, Veronica."

All gazes shifted to the groom.

Chapter 32

Veronica cocked a brow as she moved forward. *What in the hell now?*

William took a deep breath before he began, "I've known you all much longer than you realize."

"What do you mean?" She asked in a voice that was just above a whisper, but carried across the room all the same. "How is that possible that you've known *all* of us? We only connected at the Urban Fashion and Music conferences, and even then, we didn't talk until just last year."

"I used to be with the DEA," he said, leaning against the desk and allowing them a moment to take in what he'd just said. "I'd been on to Mark James and his drug trafficking activities for years." William looked over to Karyn. "He was even worse than you thought. He had so many people killed and he destroyed so many young girls by turning them onto drugs and prostitution." His eyes clouded over. "We were close to taking him down until you all decided you were going to do it yourselves." William moved away from the chair to stand in front of Karyn and Carl. "I didn't know about all the awful things Mark did to you. Unfortunately, I wasn't working on the case during that time. I had taken a leave for a few months when my wife had breast cancer. I apologize for not being there and being able to come to help you. We needed to get him for everything at once, otherwise he'd be right back on the street. I didn't come back on until the night you all tried to take him down."

William turned to face Veronica. "And baby, you, Yvette, and Sherry were three tough ass women to sacrifice everything to do this for your friend. But for the record, you didn't kill Mark."

"What?" Yvette said, with disbelief. "I know I killed Mark. I was there. I saw the blood."

Karyn shook her head, signaling for Yvette to shut up. Hello! The man said he was DEA and the woman was about to admit to every detail. He could be lying to them, wearing a wire or something.

"I saw him go down. I put a bullet in him."

"Right after you shot him, the three of you took off running and never looked back."

Veronica was at a loss of what she should be feeling, torn between relief for finally knowing that they hadn't actually killed anyone, and the shock of finding out her relationship with William was a fraud.

Yvette was surprised and actually disappointed to find out she didn't kill Mark. In some ways it pissed her off. Up until this minute, killing Mark had given her power over her friends—especially Karyn, since the woman now owed her and not the other way around.

Sherry was just confused. How would all of this play out? William had known about all this and never said anything to Veronica? Damn!

"You shot him alright, but it was only a flesh wound. One of Mark's own men finished the job. We couldn't get to Mark in time. He was already dead."

Chapter 33

There was an uncanny silence in the room as everyone took in what they had just been told. Finally, William spoke and doled out the remaining details of what had gone down that night.

Yvette's color returned as she cleared her throat. "William, are you telling me that all these years we've been thinking we killed Mark, and we didn't?" She cut her eyes toward Veronica, "And you were going to marry her today and not tell her?"

Veronica's eyes filled with tears, her back was straight, shoulders tense.

William looked kindly and lovingly at Veronica. "To be honest, I was hoping I'd never have to tell her. I wanted that part of my life to remain in the past. I wanted to start fresh with Veronica, not allow the past to cloud our future. And as an undercover officer," he paused and took a deep breath taking her hands in his. "*retired* undercover officer, I'm sworn to secrecy. It's hard to shake some of those old ways."

Veronica looked at William confused about what all of this meant for her. Had everything been a lie? "You were going to marry me today knowing you haven't been completely honest with me? And your only excuse was "because you didn't want anything to cloud our future?" She shook her head, sighing as she slipped down into the chair. "I can't believe you. How can I marry you now? I don't even know who you are!"

William lowered to his knees, grabbed Veronica's hands in his, "Baby I'm sorry, I know now that would have been a huge mistake. But it wasn't like you were truthful about things, either. So don't point fingers unless you can truly say that you've been completely open with me as well."

"You had been investigating Mark, watching our every move. You knew what he was doing to Karyn. You could've stopped it," she whispered. "Now you're telling me you fell in love with me and came back years later as this big time sales executive to pursue me? Everything has been a lie. You could be lying right now."

William stared deeply into her tear-filled eyes. "That's not completely true. Everything I've told you about me, with the exception of my time with the DEA, has been true. Yes, I fell in love with you during that time. After my wife left, my plans were always to come back for you, if you were available. You were no longer in the country and when I tried to track you down, they put me on another case, and then another. I thought that too much time had passed." He stroked a finger across her cheek. "I've never lied about how I feel about you, I love you. I'm sorry I lied to you, but that doesn't change the fact that I still love you and I still want to marry you today."

"How do we know that the police isn't waiting for us out there," Karyn asked, moving away from a stone-faced Carl. "How do we know that you're not working with Derrick in all this?"

Derrick shrugged. "I just met this dude. Sherry gave me everything I needed."

All eyes turned to the woman who cringed under the hard glares. There was a sudden knock at the door that startled Veronica and

Karyn so much, they practically jumped out of their seats, "Karyn, baby, is everything alright?" Veronica's mother said through the door, trying to open the locked door. "Is my baby alright? I've been looking for y'all."

Karyn cleared her throat. "Yes Mrs. Smith everything's fine."

"Well you need to get a move on it, we have one hour before the wedding and guest are arriving."

"Sure thing. I'll be there in a moment," she said, hoping the woman would stop jiggling the handle and leave them be.

Everyone remained silent until the footsteps faded away to silence.

"Wait," Yvette said crossing the room to Sherry. "How come he's not angry at you?" she said with a nod in Raynard's direction.

"That's because Sherry already told me everything. We weren't going to start our relationship based on lies. We don't have time for it." He pulled up next to Sherry, placed his arms around her waist as he said, "I love this woman. Always have. And we have children to raise and a whole lot of ground to cover. Once the girls are settled, we're going to travel to Paris, Italy, Spain, China, all over!"

Sherry turned to face everyone. "I've been going to AA and Raynard's been with me every step of the way."

Raynard locked an angry gaze with Derrick. "I even know about the night you all tried to corner Derrick. I didn't agree with it, but she was so guilty over what she had done, she felt she had to do it. And I hope, for everyone's sake, that you are all done making her feel low about what she did. Friends don't keep kicking friends while they're down, or keep throwing past mistakes in their face."

Karyn looked at Veronica who focused her gaze on the carpet, then to Yvette who grimaced.

"Know that I'm the last person that can judge anyone, but I'd like to say something here."

There were some nods and murmurs of consent.

"Carl, you might be upset about Karyn, but just think about it. How was she supposed to come out and tell you something so dark? Gee, honey, I had my husband killed. Pass the bacon?"

Carl looked first at his wife, then out toward the window.

"And Yvette and Derrick, it sounds like both of you have done some things against your marriage vows." He went to Derrick, whose scowl showed he did not like the turn of the conversation. "Yes, your wife might have done some devious things to get you to marry her, but it couldn't have happened unless you gave up the good wood."

"But I—"

"Did she smack you upside the head and just take the dick," Raynard said dryly.

"Well, technically, Yeah."

A few chuckles echoed behind that admission as Yvette's face flushed red.

"And you," Raynard continued, "A grown ass man, didn't try to stop her."

Silence.

"Riiiiiiiight. So suck it up."

"Yvette, a relationship built on lies doesn't last. Once trust is gone, the foundation is shaky. Get over the fact that he doesn't love you. Love Yourself." Yvette dropped her head.

"Love goes right out the window the moment trust hits the door." His keen gaze swept to both of them. "Either you all stay together and keep sleeping with everyone but each other, or you go your separate ways and call it a night."

He turned to Veronica, who swallowed hard. "William was there, and he wasn't there for Karyn. How could you expect him to come in and rescue Karyn when she had plenty of opportunities to rescue herself?"

Karyn gasped at the truth of that statement. Carl just glared at her, putting a few inches of distance between them.

"She could have been long gone before things were taken to that level." Raynard looked first to a teary–eyed Karyn, then stone–faced Veronica, and a still flushed faced Yvette, before locking a loving gaze with Sherry. "That's why I've taken the supporter's stance with Sherry. She has to do the work of changing her life. She has to do what it takes to build a bridge to her daughters. She has to accept the responsibility for her mistakes. As her man, I will support her all the way to the end. That's true love, allowing the person to be who they are, and loving them despite their faults."

Raynard kissed Sherry, who nearly swooned at the effect. He turned to face the group and grinned. "Well that's my two cents. I'm going to check on the girls. KeAnna was being a little to chummy with the DJ." He gave Sherry's rear a loving pat and sailed to the door.

Sherry tilted her head to the side, sighing as she gaped at his rear end.

"And quit checking out my ass."

Sherry's giggles echoed down the hallway after him.

"When did he get so smart," Karyn said softly.

"He's always been smart. He's just happy that he's apart of our lives again. That includes all of you, too."

Veronica turned to William. "I'm sorry, William, but I still can't marry you today." She ran to the door and stormed out of the room, only vaguely hearing Sherry say, "I'll go after her."

She couldn't marry William, now that Mark's death was out in the open, that one last skeleton in her closet was creaking in the corner, waiting to tumble out. She couldn't tell him about Simone. She couldn't tell *anyone* about Simone. And as she had just put it to him, honesty was very important. She was still lying through her teeth.

She picked up speed, turned the corner aiming to get to the solarium and tell their guests that there wasn't going to be a wedding today.

Her heart slammed in her chest. Footsteps faltered as a familiar figure came into view.

"Hello Daahhhhling," the thick accented English echoed in the air between them. "Looks like I made it just in time."

Chapter 34

Karyn's stomach churned at how the day had turned out, but at least their past was not hanging over their heads any longer. Unfortunately, losing Carl was a real possibility as his stony expression signaled that there was a lot of ground to cover. She wasn't certain that he would want to broach things at this point.

Carl walked over, and sat down beside her, putting his arm around her shoulders. Karyn placed her head in the nook between his neck and shoulder.

"I'm sorry those horrible things happened to you, Karyn," he said in a sympathetic tone, "I understand why you felt you couldn't tell me. But you must remember, from this day forward, that you are my soul mate, and I promised you that for the rest of our lives, I would protect you and make sure every day of your life was filled with happiness. That can't happen if you feel you can't be honest with me."

"You almost walked out on me when you did find out," she argued.

"That's because I was hearing something as important as that from a stranger, when I should have heard it from you. That's what made me so angry. We could've worked through anything, anything at all, if you would've just talked to me about it first."

"I thought I would lose you."

"Baby, you can never lose me. Till death do us part."

Karyn reached across Carl's chest, squeezing him tightly.

Finally, after so many years of pain, loneliness and seclusion, "It's finally over."

Carl caressed his wife's body until she felt a sense of security. "Baby just remember God's word – "*If My people, who are called by My name, shall humble themselves, pray, seek, crave, and require of necessity My face and turn from their wicked ways, then will I hear from heaven, forgive their sin, and heal their land.*"

* * *

Back in the lounge, Derrick stood looking out of one of the cathedral windows. Dark clouds were forming and drops of rain were beginning to fall.

Yvette came to stand next to him and cautiously placed her hand on his shoulder. "Derrick, I hope you'll be able to forgive me for making a mess of your life."

He didn't turn to look at her. But he didn't shrug off her hand either.

"I punished you for what someone did to me as a little girl, and it's not fair to you because you were one of the good guys. You didn't deserve what I did to you. For what it's worth, I did love you. Actually, I still do. I felt strong when I was with you. I felt like I was somebody…important." She turned him to face her, taking in the frown as he tried to understand what she was saying. "Have the divorce papers drafted, and I'll sign them. Whatever you want is fine. I won't fight you on anything."

Derrick held her hand, but turned back to focus on how dark the sky had became. "I'm sorry for what you've gone through. I don't think I'll ever forget it. As much as I hate the idea of divorce because to me it means failure, there's too much between us to work things out."

Yvette thought back on how she had actually made a career out of making Derrick her own. Not caring who she hurt. Plotting and conniving, taking all of the necessary measures to guarantee he would be hers. But in the end it only brought her pain. Now she realizes that what goes around [Lisa's warning] will certainly come around and most times worst. Yvette nodded, but tightened her hand on his. "It's going to be difficult for me, but I do understand."

He lifted her head and gave her a shy grin. "For the kid's sake, I hope that we can come to some fair agreement."

Yvette grabbed him, wrapped both arms around him. "I wish you the best."

Derrick returned her embrace, pulled away, left the room and with him went everything that she felt was right about her life.

Chapter 35

Karyn grabbed William's hand, "You can't let her go like this. If you love her, go to her."

William paused only a few seconds, looked at everyone in the room, brushed past her and hit the door, Carl and Karyn on his heels as they slid past Derrick who was walking toward the lobby.

Sherry rushed toward them, signaling for everyone to turn around and go back in the other direction.

Veronica and a tall, beautiful, pale faced woman were having what seemed to be a heated conversation.

Sherry stood in front of them, saying, "Let's go back in the lounge. Veronica's talking to an old college friend. Trust me, now is not the time to interrupt."

Karyn moved Sherry to the side, trying to move forward with William right behind her. "Sherry, nothing's more important right now than trying to save their relationship."

Sherry inched forward, blocking their path, sputtering, "But… but…"

"Girl, move," Karyn said sternly, pushing the fleshy woman out of the way.

By now Karyn, Carl, William, Yvette and even Derrick were bearing down on the bride. "Veronica, we need to talk to you," Karyn said, eyeing the woman standing in front of Veronica with suspicion. College friend? Veronica didn't have any *white* friends.

The woman's gaze flickered over the rest of the group before coming to land on Karyn. She extended a hand, saying, "Hi, I'm Simone."

Karyn shook it and released it in one breath. "Hi Simone. Veronica, we need to talk to you now!"

Simone's keen gaze took in William's stature, roaming the muscular body as though she was ready to pounce. "And you must be the groom. William, is it? Nice to finally meet the man who stands between me and…" She trailed a finger across Veronica's panic-stricken face. "My one true love."

Guests were beginning to file out of the solarium. Veronica's mother peered curiously at the group and the white woman standing near her youngest daughter.

"Come on, let's go somewhere else and talk," Veronica said through clenched teeth as she gripped the woman's arm.

Simone didn't move at first as her thin lips lengthened into a sly smile. "Yes, I can see why you would want things to remain… private."

Karyn and Yvette looked at Veronica, then back at Simone but kept their mouths shut as the whole group made their way to the room they had just vacated.

Veronica halted them in front of the lounge door. "I meant alone."

"I would like to think that anything you could say to her, you could say to us," Yvette said with a sly grin that made Veronica glower angrily at her. "I mean, we are your real *friends*, right?"

Simone pulled the light shawl around her shoulders, giving Yvette a warm smile. "Those were my sentiments exactly." She trailed a hand across Veronica's face until it lowered to the cleavage that was exposed in the full beauty. "Certainly you can be *honest* with the man you're going to marry. N'est–ce pas?"

William's gaze locked on Veronica as the woman continued to stand intimately close to the woman he loved. "What's this about," he asked Veronica. He reached out, gripped Simone's hand, halting her movement. "Touch my wife again that way and it's not going to be pretty," he said through his teeth.

"But that is the point, darling," Simone purred, snatching her hand from his. "She is not your wife—yet. And after she tells you about…" she winked at Veronica and shrugged. "She might not be."

Veronica turned, walked into the lounge and nearly cried in frustration when everyone filed in behind her.

Once inside, everyone grabbed a seat and remained silent, waiting to hear what Veronica had to say. She paced the floor nervously before opening her mouth. "Simone is someone I met in France. She helped me in my career."

Sherry leaned over to Karyn whispering, "I told you this wasn't a good time." Karyn nudged her to be quiet.

Everyone looked at Simone who was sitting on the chair with a cold, triumphant smile on her face, waiting for Veronica to actually come up with her version of the truth.

Veronica glanced over at William, whose features were taut with confusion. "Actually, we were lovers, up until I met you. I guess what I'm trying to say is, I haven't been completely honest with you, either. It's amazing how one lie can turn your whole world upside down. Who would have thought ignoring Simone would make her show up here today. I was hoping she would get on with her life."

"Darling, you are my life. You can't just treat people like trash. I thought we had more than that." She flickered a disdainful glance at William. "I could understand your new relationship, and with a man, no less, but what I could not deal with is being brushed aside as though I did not matter to you. As though I never mattered to you."

"I didn't know how to tell you. I'm in love with this man right here and all I've ever wanted is to find my soul mate and have children and…now even that's gone."

"You know, you have a lot of nerve being upset at me," William said to Veronica who parted her lips to protest, but he held up his hand. "This wasn't some little fling, either. No wonder I couldn't find you in Paris! You had plenty of time to tell me about this woman, when I had been open about my relationships. My job required that I keep some things private, but there were no such restrictions on you. What's your excuse?"

She wasn't given a chance to get a word in edgewise as he turned to a smiling Simone, saying, "Thank you for coming today. I think you accomplished some of what you wanted—which was to embarrass Veronica in front of her friends and family. But you have no idea how tight these women are. Real love means knowing what's real and when to let go."

Simone stiffened at the ever so subtle slap in the face.

"But you will not get her back. I'm marrying this woman…today." Veronica's eyes filled with moisture as he took her outstretched hand. "And no amount of bullshit that you have to tell us is going to change that fact." William put his arm around his bride. "She *was* in love with you, might still love you in some ways, but she is not the woman for you any longer. She's mine! Go back to France. Get on with your life, so we can get on with ours."

Epilogue

Karyn, Sherry, and Yvette paced the hospital floor of the maternity ward for hours, excitedly anticipating the arrival of what could only be considered a miracle baby.

One year since the wedding, and God had blessed the newlyweds with their first child. A few minor complications had ensued because it was a high risk pregnancy. The doctor was forced to induce labor a few weeks early, so that things would not become life-threatening for Veronica, as her blood pressure and the onset of gestational diabetes continued to rise to a dangerous level.

As the three women sat in the most uncomfortable leather chairs on the planet, one of Sherry's co-workers approached, gesturing for her to step outside of the waiting room. She put the magazine down in her seat and followed the woman to the nurse's station.

"I know you're not working today," Nurse Blakely whispered. "And you're here with the Butler family, right?"

"Yes, I am," Sherry's gaze narrowed on the younger woman's face, noting the concern etched in her features. "Is everything okay?"

"Oh, yes, everything's fine with Ms. Butler, but..." she looked over her shoulder to make sure no one was coming up on them. "Veronica received the strangest gift." She pointed to the desk not too far behind them. The silver vase filled with black painted roses looked as hideous as the note written on the card attached. The nurse trailed Sherry to the desk and handed the card to her, which said, "Best wishes on your new addition. May you have REST, stay IN love, and always find PEACE."

Sherry flinched at the ominous meaning of the message. Simone was laying a serious threat to Veronica? Or William? Or the baby? Oh, heeeeell no!

"I thought it was strange and wanted to inform the family before having them sent to her room." She waited for Sherry to say something, but when that didn't happen she inquired. "*Should* I send this to her room?"

Sherry found her voice, shook her head. "Absolutely not," Sherry scooped the vase up, went down the hall tossed the flowers, vase, card, water, wrapping paper, and everything that came with it. "If anything else comes like that, let me know. If I'm not on duty, then just have me paged." She jotted down a quick list of names. "Only these people are allowed to come in and see Veronica Butler, okay?"

The nurse nodded, then went to inform the rest of the nurses on duty and noted it in the charts so it was passed on to everyone else.

Sherry returned to the waiting room and slipped into the seat, noticing that Yvette had swiped the magazine she was reading before. "You all are not going to believe this."

"What," Karyn asked with a quick look at Yvette who lowered the magazine so she could actually look at Sherry.

"Do you know that psycho woman sent Veronica black roses?"

Karyn's eyes widened to the size of saucers. "Are you serious?

"You mean, Simone?" Yvette asked as Sherry nodded. "What will it take for that woman to leave Veronica alone?"

"And she left a little note," Sherry said, describing the contents of the card.

"She's taken this thing to a whole new level," Yvette said, with a tinge of admiration in her voice. "That must be some killer pussy Veronica has."

Karyn popped Yvette on the thigh. "That's not funny. Black flowers! That represents death."

"Oh, you know that woman would never kill her…"

Sherry cocked her head at that in a sign of *Are you sure about that?*"

Karyn stood, crossed over to the walkway and began pacing the carpet. "We should give her a call and try to reason with her."

"There's no reasoning with that insane woman," Yvette countered. "A year has gone by, she should be way over it by now." Then her voice became low and deadly. "Maybe we should take a trip to Paris. I've always wanted to go."

Sherry and Karyn looked at each other and in unison replied, "No!"

Yvette gave them a disarming smile.

"No more drama, Yvette," Sherry said, glaring at the woman. "That's what we said, right?" She looked over to Karyn who nodded, then to Yvette who rolled her eyes.

Sherry was happy to be in a better place in her life and was able to make sound decisions. No more impulsive behavior, so threatening and killing someone was out of the question. The best thing to do was to toss them before they got to her room. If Simone shows up again, Veronica and William will figure out how to handle her. Trust me, William isn't letting his good thing go no time soon.

Counseling had changed Sherry's life. She no longer had to dive into a bottle of booze to help her make it through the day. She hadn't touched the stuff since the day Jaynene told about what happened to her. She was working on rebuilding their relationship and gaining her daughter's trust again. The rapist was in jail and it was due to DNA samples gathered when her baby was taken.

Jaynene was doing well, and her relationship with Raynard was tighter than ever. He encouraged her to do whatever was in her little heart and it seemed that every time he said he was proud of her, she tried to do something more to top what she had done to receive such praise. She had made up the difference in her classes in school and had been accepted to three of the top black colleges in the country, with a full scholarship, but since Dr. Washington had amended the child support order on his own and promised to foot the bill, she was now able to attend the school of her choice—Spelman College in Atlanta. He still hadn't reached out to connect with her on a personal level, but there was the fact that now cards, filled with extra money just for her would come on her birthdays, major holidays and for prom and graduation.

Sherry and Raynard were making every effort to reach out to KeAnna hoping she would start attending counseling sessions with them as a family, but that seemed a hopeless cause at times. She moved in with her boyfriend, and they would rarely see her at times. Only mentions of the relationship between Jaynene and Raynard was any seeming indication that she was jealous, but it wasn't enough for her to accept his attempts and mending things between them. She resented Sherry's involvement with him. She resented everything he did for Jaynene. Raynard, much to Sherry's comforting, continued to try and said he always would.

Karyn and Carl had completed a year of counseling and their marriage was finally getting back on the right track. And that was only because Karyn broke down and told him everything. Absolutely everything. Karyn realized that she no longer had to live in fear of every man being like Mark James, and Carl was nothing like that man in the first place, which is probably why she had been attracted to him. Karyn's daughter moved away to California, accepted a teaching position at a private school, married a architect, and was now pregnant with her second child. Mary asked for Karyn to make the trip out to the west coast when the new baby came. She was grateful that Carl agreed to come along.

Mark Jr. was now attending Yale, working on his doctorate since he planned to go into the social sciences and make a career with children who were victims of abuse. This desire sparked something in Karyn who, along with Sherry, created a foundation to support victims of domestic violence and a secondary mission to help women with their experiences with alcohol abuse. Sherry was still attending the required AA meetings and Raynard was there with her every step of the program.

After the nasty divorce settlement, despite promises to the contrary, Derrick was granted custody of the kids and the house and that sent Yvette on an anger binge like no one had ever seen. She still hadn't moved out! She landed a job at a fortune 500 company and was on her way to a top position. Until that same company hired Derrick who became her boss, and summarily put things in place to have her fired. Now he had made it impossible for her to find viable employment in the financial industry again. Yvette was forced to go to work for Karyn until she could land on her feet. She had mentioned more than once that Derrick's days are numbered.

William joined the crew in the waiting area. Smiling as he held up the bundle in his arms and said, "Yvette's doing just fine, but William Jr. wanted to meet his aunts."

The women cooed over the handsome little fellow and looked up at William who was beaming as though he had discovered the rarest gem. Then his brow furrowed as he asked, "Who sent Veronica those strange looking roses? I thought I saw something for her at the nurse's desk."

Yvette shrugged and said, "I think you're mistaken," as William Jr. little finger curled around hers. "I think I'll be taking a trip to Paris next week," she mused out loud then looked up at Karyn and Sherry, who also seemed to be in awe of the new addition to the family.

Sherry pursed her lips to say, absolutely not, but then added, "Raynard always did want to go to Europe. Maybe we could just have a little chat with our friend over there. I'd love to have some French Fries and some French Toast topped off with French Vanilla ice cream."

"That's not French cuisine," Karyn said dryly.

"It will be when we get through," Sherry said in a low and deadly tone that made everyone look her way.

William shifted the baby to Karyn as he peered suspiciously at them. "Ladies, I don't have any pull on international soil."

Karyn shrugged and gave a pointed looked at Sherry, then to Yvette. "But it's just a chat, right?"

"Only a chat," Yvette said with a sly wink.

Sherry kissed the baby's forehead. "Yes, only a…chat."

William could only shake his head as he pinched the bridge of his nose. "I'll book your flights for next week."

To this, the women gave him equally winning smiles.

About the Author

Linda Y. Watson is the author of the controversial debut novel, Necessary Measures. She is a banker at one of the largest corporate banks in the Midwest and has worked in the finance industry for over twenty years. She is also a licensed realtor in the state of Illinois and spends many evenings and weekends helping people to find their dream home.

Linda lives in Indiana with her husband, Elliott, and their two dogs. Between them they have five wonderful children who are all experiencing the joys of adulthood. She enjoys worshipping with her husband and church family. She also loves traveling, reading, writing, dancing and hanging out with her girlfriends.